"You seem to be a popular guy," Jessica said. "Or rather, you have a popular stand given the quality and variety of your flowers."

Too much, too much, Jessica, she chided herself as she turned to walk away.

"Wait," Briggs called out.

She stopped.

"Here. These are for you." He held out a small bouquet of flowers tied with a lavender-colored ribbon. "For all your help with Buddy...and with Will." He glanced over his shoulder. His son and the dog were involved in a bit of good-natured roughhousing.

"My pleasure," she said, examining the bouquet. "Forget-me-nots and violets, right?" She brought them to her nose and inhaled the gentlest of scents. "It's very thoughtful, but not necessary. I was just doing my job."

"I know it's not necessary. That's exactly the point," he said. "Sometimes it's just nice to get something pretty."

Jessica held her breath. It seemed that Briggs was, too.

Dear Reader,

As a longtime Harlequin reader and author, I am pleased to join the Harlequin Heartwarming family of talented writers. Their work conveys the sense of family ties and enduring love that we all value. And since I'm a small-town resident myself, I'm delighted to bring you a story set in the fictional town of Hopewell, Pennsylvania.

Hopewell—my imaginary Hopewell—is located in an actual section of southeastern Pennsylvania called Bucks County. A rural area about an hour north of Philadelphia, Bucks County offers something for everyone: historic towns and villages, beautiful nature and recreational opportunities, unique shopping, and restaurants and cafés to entice the sophisticated foodie or ice cream lover.

I'm composing this letter after having come from the annual block party on my little dead-end street, home to about twenty families. The woods nestle one side of the narrow road, and a brook runs along the other. In between we have residents who range in age from one month to ninety-three years old, from all walks of life and nationalities. Believe me, everyone came to the party to enjoy the conversation and food and drink! And I swear that I have not written any of my neighbors into this story, but my heroine and hero, Jessica and Briggs, might recognize some of their personality traits.

Hope you enjoy this trip to Hopewell.

Tracy Kelleher

HEARTWARMING

Vet to the Rescue

—

Tracy Kelleher

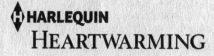

HARLEQUIN®
HEARTWARMING™

ISBN-13: 978-1-335-47569-5

Recycling programs
for this product may
not exist in your area.

Vet to the Rescue

Harlequin Enterprises ULC
22 Adelaide St. West, 41st Floor
Toronto, Ontario M5H 4E3, Canada
www.Harlequin.com

Printed in U.S.A.

Tracy Kelleher has lived on three continents where she's worked, raised a family and multiple dogs, and had a lot of fun. She's worn many hats: medieval historian, advertising executive, and newspaper reporter and editor. When she's not hard at work on her next book, you can find her gardening, riding horses—and having lots of fun!

Books by Tracy Kelleher

Vet to the Rescue

is Tracy Kelleher's debut title for
Harlequin Heartwarming.

Look out for more books from Tracy Kelleher
coming soon.

Visit the Author Profile page
at Harlequin.com.

This book is dedicated to my wonderful family:
Peter and Megan; James and Anne;
and, of course, Lex.

A shout-out to my editor, Kathryn Lye,
who has a sharp intelligence and a sharper wit.

And in loving memory of Bill. You were far from
perfect and could be very naughty, but no dog
ever loved his family more. You taught me a lot.
I always think of you when I eat cheese.

CHAPTER ONE

Lincoln Park, Chicago, Illinois

"YOU'RE SURE FELIX is going to be okay, Doctor? It seems like every week I have to bring him into the office." The exhausted mother sighed. "I guess when they say those little plastic building blocks are for ages five and up, they really mean it."

Dr. Jessica Trombo smiled. "Felix is doing fine. You and he will survive. It's just that puppies are, well, puppies—especially when they're teething." Jessica watched the dog focus on the buttons on her white lab coat. She stepped back, just in case. "Luckily the plastic edges were smooth, and Felix passed the toy with no issues." The same way he'd passed her son's athletic sock three days ago and, the week before, a bra strap. Felix certainly had eclectic tastes and, as proven time and time again, a cast-iron stomach.

"Just make sure your kids put away their toys and never leave dirty clothes—especially socks and underwear—on the floor. Other than that, I think you have an absolutely adorable puppy." Jessica rubbed Felix's belly. The little culprit turned over and splayed his legs in bliss. His tongue lolled to the side. His eye lids fluttered shut. Talk about being in heaven!

There was a knock on the door, and Sarah, one of the office staff, stuck her head in. "Dr. Trombo, you have a call on line two."

Jessica frowned. "Could you ask them to leave a number? I'm still with a patient."

"They said it was an emergency. Something to do with your father." Sarah held on to the door handle.

Her father? Pops never called during working hours. As a fellow vet, he knew how busy she'd be with patients and surgeries. "Ask them to hold, would you? I'll be there in a minute."

Sarah nodded and shut the door.

Jessica looked down at Felix. Her hand had stilled during the brief conversation, but the dog didn't seem to have noticed. In fact, he'd fallen sound asleep on the metal observation table. She couldn't help chuckling. "So, unless you have other questions, I'm satisfied that Felix is in good shape."

Felix's mom scooped up the limp dog. "You'd never know he was hell on wheels, would you?"

Jessica shook her head. "Frankly, you've got to admire his ability to flake out—at a doctor's office, no less. Which reminds me, don't forget to schedule the next appointment for his shots. We've got to take care of our family members." Speaking of which...

Jessica waited for the patient to leave before darting out the back door to the small office reserved for the vets. Line 2 blinked, signaling a call on hold.

She picked up the phone. "Hello. This is Dr. Jessica Trombo."

"Jessica. I'm so glad I could reach you."

She recognized the anxious voice of her father's office manager, Wendy. "Is there a problem with my dad?" She had sudden visions of a car crash or a heart attack. She undid the large clip that held her hair off her face and nervously played with the mechanism. Her auburn tresses splayed across her shoulders.

"He's in the hospital, dear."

"Oh, no." Jessica's worst fear realized. "Is he—is he…"

"No, no, don't worry. Seems he fell. It looks like a concussion and a fracture to his right leg. He blacked out and doesn't remember anything. He's pretty banged up, and they want to keep him in overnight to run some tests and for general observation."

Jessica breathed a sigh of relief—but only just. "Sounds like a pretty bad fall. And you said tests? Are they looking for signs of a stroke?"

"Among other things. But I think he just lost his balance. He was on a ladder at the time."

Jessica groaned. "Don't tell me he was cleaning his gutters. I've told him a million times he should hire someone to do the job."

"You know your dad. No one can convince him that at seventy-one it's time to alter his ways. In fact, he didn't want me to call you, but I insisted." Jessica's father might've been the doctor, but Wendy was in charge.

"You were absolutely right." Jessica glanced down at her watch. "Look, it's four thirty now. I've still got a few patients left this afternoon, but then my plate's clear. I'll ask one of the other vets to cover for me, and with any luck I'll be able to catch a flight out of O'Hare this evening and get into Philly late in the night. Then I'll rent a car and drive up. If it all goes as planned, I'll be at the hospital first thing tomorrow morning."

Jessica's father still lived in the old family home in Hopewell, Pennsylvania, about an hour's drive north of Philadelphia. The quaint town was situated in rural Bucks County—an area of rolling hills long known as horse country, a hangout for artists and the historic location where Washington crossed the Delaware River.

"Oh, I'm so glad you're able to come home, Jess. Your dad would never admit that he needs to take it easy, but it's time we forced him to rest—at least for a little while."

"I know what you mean. But when has Pops ever accepted change?"

Hopewell, Pennsylvania

POSSIBLY NOW.

Jessica's partners at the veterinary practice had immediately agreed to cover for her, and so she'd hightailed it out of Chicago, leaving her studio apartment in River North with clean laundry piled on the bed and the cap off the toothpaste. The plane was thirty-five minutes delayed and the rental car was some anonymous box, but the good news was that she managed to pull into her dad's place just after midnight.

Though, as Jessica unlocked the front door with its colorful art glass, she couldn't help thinking that the Queen Anne–style house was totally her mom's creation. Take the paint colors. The decorative trim on the windows, turrets and wraparound porch had been painted moss green and brick red in contrast to the mustard-yellow clapboards. Those vibrant colors reflected the spirited personality of her late mother, Vivian, an artist who had taught at the local Quaker school and had died much too young a few years back of breast cancer.

Tired as she was, Jessica spent a not-unexpected restless night. She rose to bright sunlight, and after a quick cup of instant coffee—totally yuck but essential under the circumstances—she grabbed the car keys and headed out the door. She gave only a cursory glance to the garden, but it was impossible to miss her mom's iridescent blue irises lining the driveway.

At 8:00 a.m. on the dot, Jessica pulled into the empty visitors' parking lot of Bucks County Hospital. She fumbled with the unfamiliar car lock, tucked her hair behind her ears and settled the straps of her bag on her shoulder. Then she squared her shoulders and headed into the brand-new building. First things first: the information booth, where she was surprised to see the familiar face of Betsy Pulaski-O'Malley. Actually, come to think of it, Jessica wasn't all that surprised. This was tiny Hopewell, after all.

"Betsy—long time no see!" Jessica exclaimed. She and Betsy had played field hockey on the middle school team almost twenty years ago. Jessica immediately assumed the stance of her old center-forward position.

"Gosh, Jessica. It's been a while." Betsy raised her eyebrows, a long-standing trait, especially after scoring a goal.

"It *has* been a while, but you haven't changed a bit," Jessica said. Betsy's mop of curly red hair was only slightly tamer now. Last she'd heard, her former teammate was married, had two kids and was the proud owner of an ornery calico cat named Alfie. News about the husband and children had come via the Hopewell Central High School Facebook page. The cat not so much. Her father was Alfie's long-suffering vet.

"Well, except for the obvious." Betsy rolled back her office chair and patted her bulging stomach.

Jessica craned her neck. "Wow—it looks like congrats are in order." Clearly baby number three was on the way. "When are you due?"

"Any day now, and I feel like a beached whale."

"At least you're still able to work."

"I figure this is as good a place as any if my water breaks."

Jessica agreed. "You know, I'd love to catch up, but I'm kind of in a rush—"

"You're here about your dad, right?"

"Yup. Have you seen him?"

"No, but Wendy is friends with my mom, and Mom called me last night with the news about him tumbling off a ladder. What a mess. You must have been sick with worry. I know if it'd been my dad, I would've had the baby then and there. Luckily my dad doesn't do a thing around the house—not that that makes my mom happy. But anyway, it means he's not about to fall off a ladder."

Jessica was starting to remember that Betsy was a talker—a big talker. "Well, I see word still travels fast around Hopewell. I guess some things never change. But listen, I'd really like to check on my dad…"

Betsy leaned forward and whispered: "Look, it's not officially visiting hours yet, but go ahead." She rattled off the number and directions to Jessica's father's room. Then she scooted her chair back to a more comfortable distance. "And tell your dad that Alfie misses him."

"Thanks, Betsy."

Jessica waved as she walked toward the elevators. The first stop on his floor was the nurses' station. The second was her father's private room.

She knocked. "Hi, Pops. Fancy meeting you here."

Norman Trombo lay propped up in bed. His eyes were shut. His face ashen and unshaved. Wisps of dark gray hair stuck upward from his bald pate. He wore an anonymous blue hospital gown that had been laundered one too many times in an industrial-strength machine. A sheet covered him from the waist down, and a hidden cage raised the material over his half-leg cast.

"Is that you, Jessica?" Norman opened his eyes. "I told them not to call you, that you were busy."

Jessica stepped closer, trying not to show her shock at his weakened state. "So now you're the boss of everybody? Besides, we all know Wendy secretly runs your office. And I'm glad she called me. Why wouldn't I come to help out? That's what daughters do." She pulled an armchair closer to his bed. "I already checked with the nurses on the way in, and the good news is there's no sign of neurological damage from the fall."

"Did they say there's no sign of any brain cells, either?" Her father stretched out his arm to reach the plastic drinking cup on the swivel table by the side of the bed.

Jessica sprang up. "Here—let me." She handed him the cup and pointed the straw in his direction. At least her father's sense of humor was still intact. "They didn't say anything about a loss of gray matter, but I'm sure they were just being charitable. But besides a mild concussion you have a complete oblique fracture of the right tibia. Quite a bid for attention, Pops. I can think of easier ways, you know. How's the pain?"

He shrugged. "I manage."

She ran her hand along the bed railing. "Apparently you're getting discharged later this afternoon. So, when that happens, I'll take you home and stay with you until you're on your feet."

"Tell me you're not doing the cooking."

"I'm afraid so. I'll try not to burn the house down like I almost did when I was twelve."

"I've never looked at a homemade brownie since, I gotta confess."

"Desserts only from the bakery—I promise. But is there anything you want me to pick up at the supermarket?" Last night Jessica had barely managed to scrounge up peanut butter and crackers from the pantry. The fridge had offered a hunk of Swiss cheese that a starving mouse would have rejected. She'd quickly dumped it in the rubbish. What had Pops been living on all this time? she wondered.

He shook his head. "No, I'm not that hungry. But I could really use a good stiff drink. I'm pretty sure there's a bottle of bourbon in the pantry."

"If not, I know that Mom's trusty bottle of Grand Marnier is still kicking around." Jessica, never a big drinker, had had a nip herself last night to calm down after the whirlwind journey back. (Not that it had worked.) She pursed her lips and watched her dad quickly turn away. That had been the wrong thing to say.

Norman sighed and returned her gaze. "I think I'd like to rest up before they come around to teach me how to use those darn crutches. One thing though, if you want to do me a real favor, stop by the office and see if any patients have shown up. Maybe you could handle them before liberating me from this place."

"Good idea." She stood up and slid the chair back against the window. It was obvious her presence wasn't helping matters. If her big brother, Drew, were here, he'd know how to cheer up Pops in a heartbeat, but from what she'd seen on social media he was in someplace like Borneo, or maybe it was Belize. It was hard to keep track of his globe-trotting ways. So, cross off that option.

Instead, she'd help at Pops's practice, a place where Jessica felt confident that she could contribute in a meaningful fashion. "I'll be on my way, then. I'll give the nurses my cell phone number in case anything changes. That way I'll be here in no time to bust you loose."

She kissed him goodbye and headed off to Hopewell Veterinary Medicine, located in a modest brick building next to the volunteer fire station. Across the street was the local theater, and a sandwich board out front advertised an outdoor production of *Kinky Boots* for upcoming weekends in July. Nothing much had changed, except in Jessica's days it would have been something older like *Kiss Me, Kate*.

She parked behind the office and walked in by the side door, hoping for a quiet entrance until she got the lay of the land. She hadn't counted on Alfie.

No sooner had she stepped onto the speckled linoleum tile floor than Gloria Pulaski, Betsy's mom, thrust what was quite possibly the world's ugliest cat into her face. It didn't help that the animal's claws immediately planted themselves deep into Jessica's fleece vest.

"This must be Betsy's Alfie." She winced

and gingerly removed the barbed talons. Alfie still managed to get in a good swipe across the back of her hand. "You know, Mrs. Pulaski, Alfie really needs to be in a travel carrier unless he's in the examining room."

With the help of a good colorist, Gloria Pulaski's hair was as red as her daughter's. She cuddled the feline against her Bucks County Community College sweatshirt. "I know, I know, but I couldn't find it right away. Besides, he hates being pent up."

"Don't we all. I tell you what—we could probably lend you a nice one in the meantime." She walked over to Wendy sitting behind the welcoming counter decorated with an array of photos showing various animal patients—one of the office manager's masterful contributions.

Wendy offered a troubled smile. "I tried to explain to Gloria that we weren't scheduling any new appointments today, but she said it was an emergency." *Sorry*, she mouthed silently.

Jessica waved off her apology. "In that case, let me just get settled, and I'll see what I can do."

"Oh, thanks, Jessica," Mrs. Pulaski gushed. "When Wendy told me about your dad, I was so worried for him *and* Alfie. But now that you're back, I know you'll have everything under control. You were always the serious one."

Jessica wasn't sure whether that was a compliment or not. "In a serious vein, then, why don't you take Alfie to exam room one, and that way we won't need to deal with the carrier. I'll be there shortly."

When the door had swung shut, Jessica eyed Wendy. "Pops owes me big time. Anyway, when I've finished with Alfie, I'll take emergencies or any scheduled appointments that couldn't be changed until around four p.m. After that I need to get ready to collect him from the hospital."

"It won't be easy for you," Wendy said. "All the stairs at home? And aren't the bedrooms on the second floor?"

"Fortunately there's a guest bedroom and a bathroom on the ground floor."

"Sounds like a good solution to me, but I'm not sure how it'll go down with your father. He's not one for change."

Jessica shook her head. "Don't I know it. It's going to take a serious amount of pampering. I thought I'd start with fudge ripple ice cream. Maybe a pint for him and a pint for me."

Wendy laughed. "In the meantime…" She held out Alfie's file.

Jessica sighed. "Tell me the day will only get

better." She grabbed the thick folder and scanned it quickly. "When I'm done with Alfie, we should go over the appointments for the next couple of days and any urgent cases I need to know about."

"Already on it. I printed out the schedule for today and tomorrow—full day Friday, by the way—and a bunch of appointments early Saturday morning. Oh, our tech, Joseph, is in the back, seeing to the two surgical patients in recovery. He can bring you up to speed there."

"Sounds like a plan." Jessica snapped the file shut and prepared for the worst.

Luckily it was better than she'd anticipated. Alfie, the dear, was constipated. She prescribed a stool softener, and he and Betsy's mom were out the door.

But the patients kept coming. Next up, Mr. Mason's cockatoo, Bismol. The bird had a crooked beak that needed trimming. "No problem, Mr. Mason. We'll have Bismol fixed up in a jiffy. Just think of it as the bird version of a mani-pedi," Jessica tried to reassure him.

The elderly Mr. Mason, a longtime bachelor, looked confused.

"You know, having your nails filed and shaped with a colorful nail polish applied at the end?"

Mr. Mason's eyes widened in horror.

"Not to worry," Jessica reassured him. "No

Jungle Red this time." She smiled and reached for the clippers.

The bird took only a minute or two—Mr. Mason longer. But since Mr. Mason was a sweet man, she didn't rush him. As the long-time owner of a gas station in town, he had always let Jessica pay later when she hadn't had enough cash to fill up her rusty old Mazda. Alas, no more favors were in order. It seemed he'd recently sold the place to a new couple in town. "Sweet kids. They want to convert it into a brew pub. Good luck to 'em."

After Mr. Mason, Mrs. Horowitz's Pekingese, Schubert, needed heartworm medication, normally something that Wendy would handle. But Mrs. Horowitz wouldn't leave until she had a chance to say hello to Jessica because Robby Bellona had told her she was back in town. Mrs. Horowitz had given piano lessons to Jessica's brother, Drew, and Drew and Robby had been best friends growing up. Robby had seen her stop at the red light on Main Street.

"Drew was such an entertaining boy. Never on time and hopeless when it came to practicing, but always ready with a pick-me-up or a laugh. He just made my day." Mrs. Horowitz waggled her hand in emphasis.

"That sounds about right." Jessica waited as

Mrs. Horowitz fiddled with a broach of musical notes pinned to her twin set. It was clear she had something on her mind. If Jessica had to make a bet, she'd say it was a not-so-subtle question about her love life.

"So, you have a fella yet?"

Bingo! Jessica gave herself a pat on the back. "Well, I'm kinda seeing someone in Chicago. I probably need to bring him home to pass your sniff test, correct?"

"It's more Schubert's sniff test. I always run people by him first."

Jessica leaned in to give the dog a cuddle and got quite a noseful. She straightened up quickly. "You know, when you get a chance, you might make an appointment with Wendy to get Schubert's teeth cleaned. It's especially important in older animals." Jessica handed the dog a chew stick to help deal with its pungent breath.

And so it went into the afternoon when Jessica was finally ready to take a look at the next day's files.

That was until Wendy poked her head in the tiny office. "I know you don't have a lot of time, but there's one more patient you just have to see."

"Don't tell me it's Dr. Cotton, my old pediatrician? He was always telling me to stand up straight. And I still slouch. I admit it."

"No, this one's new to town. And I don't know who's more nervous—the owner or the dog." Wendy winked.

Jessica rose. She slipped the scrunchie from her wrist and fashioned a neat ponytail. "Then by all means. Examination room number two."

Wendy had been right about the nervousness. A boy who looked to be in his early teens was perched on the far corner of the bench. All gangly legs and scrawny arms, he clutched a rope that was knotted loosely around the neck of an Australian shepherd mix who, in a futile attempt to make itself invisible, had squeezed behind the boy's legs. The boy had beads of sweat on his upper lip. The pup was shedding like crazy.

"Hi, I'm Dr. Trombo, and who do we have here?" Jessica asked in a soft voice. She stayed a few feet away to give them both some space.

"I'm…I'm Will, and this is Buddy—or at least, that's what I call him."

"Do you now?" Jessica crouched down and took a small treat from the pocket of her lab coat. The nervous dog backed into an even smaller space and furrowed its brow. The two brown dots over his eyes jumped to an erratic beat.

A middle-aged man stuck his head in the back door. It was Joseph, the tech Jessica had met earlier in the morning. "Sorry to interrupt, but I just wanted to let you know that Fluffy's now fully awake from her spaying." He surveyed the scene and smiled. "Do you need some help lifting the dog on the table, Dr. Trombo?"

"No, I think we're good, Joseph. Instead, can you ask Wendy to call Fluffy's owners to come pick her up?" The door eased shut, and Jessica inched closer to Buddy. "How long have you had Buddy?"

"Not long at all. I…ah…found him in the parking lot of Hopewell Middle School. There was nobody around to claim him, and he didn't have any dog tags. He looked really lost and scared. I didn't know what to do except maybe bring him here to make sure he's all right. He's really a good dog. You can tell." The boy reached down and fondled the dog's ears. The brown dots eased still. "I hope I did the right thing." He watched as Jessica coaxed Buddy into nibbling on the soft treat.

She took a few more treats out of her pocket and passed them to Will. "Here, why don't you give him some, too. He seems to respond to your touch." And while dog and boy were otherwise engaged, Jessica gently ran her hands along Buddy's flanks and legs. She patted his head, ruffled the thick fur on his back and checked out his ears and teeth. When she was done, she leaned back on her haunches. "Good dog. You were very brave." She gave Buddy another treat for good measure. The dog looked like he could use a few more pounds.

"So, is he okay, then? Not sick, I mean?" the boy asked.

Jessica addressed Will with the same sensitivity she usually reserved for the animals. "Considering that Buddy seems to be a stray, he's in remarkably good health. Judging from his teeth, he's probably around two years old. There's no sign of fleas or obvious problems with his joints or organs."

Will breathed a sigh of relief, but just a little one. "Does that mean I can keep him?" he asked. The tension in his shoulders was still apparent.

"For now, I suppose you can foster him. But you'll need to contact the police about any missing dogs and post flyers to try to find Buddy's owner. You have to brace yourself for the fact that someone out there may be worried about having lost him."

Will nodded. "Of course, of course. I understand there's…there's a chance that someone might claim him. But then there's always a chance that someone might not, right?" Will stumbled up from the bench. His legs intertwined with the dog's. "So, if that's it…"

"Not quite. If no one claims him, I want you to bring him back for a proper checkup, bloodwork and a start on his shot regimen. That's if your family is okay with taking in Buddy. And I would expect you and Buddy to attend the evening dog-training sessions at the office. Wendy, out front, will give you a schedule of the lessons as well as a starter pack of food and healthy treats and some biodegradable poop bags."

"That's so great. Thanks. Umm… One thing I forgot—about paying for this visit? I…I don't have that much cash on me…" The boy stared at his high-top sneakers before braving to make eye contact with Jessica.

"Not to worry. We have a policy of one free meet-and-greet session for all new patients." She saw a look of instant relief unfurrow Will's brow. She straightened up. "One important thing, though. As I said, if—*if*—you're going to keep Buddy for any length of time, you'll need the approval of your family."

"Not to worry on that score. They're cool

with the whole thing." Will bobbed his head up and down. "I guarantee it."

Famous last words. "Well, just in case you— or your family—have any questions, give me a call." She pulled a prescription pad from the pocket of her coat, scribbled down her cell phone number and handed it to Will.

Buddy waggled the two dots above his eyes. Confidence didn't exactly ooze from his expression, and he continued to glue himself to his protector as they stumbled out the door.

"Take care, Will. And you're a lucky dog, Buddy," Jessica called out.

Odds were she'd never see them again, right?

CHAPTER TWO

THE TEACHERS' MEETING at Hopewell Central High School had run late, but after two years on the job, Briggs Longfellow knew that was par for the course. As he waited at the traffic light on Main Street—no matter which way he was driving, the fates decreed that it was always red—he tapped on the steering wheel of his Volvo station wagon. A classic-rock radio station blared Fleetwood Mac, covering up the sound of his noisy exhaust system. He really needed to get that hole in the tailpipe fixed, but now that Mr. Mason had sold his garage, Briggs wasn't quite sure where to go. That was the thing about small towns. You developed loyalty to local people and establishments—unlike living in a big city where ordering online had become the default way of doing business.

That wasn't the only change Briggs had encountered since moving to Hopewell. The transition from practicing law at a large firm in Philadelphia to teaching American history in

a small town hadn't been easy. But as he had
learned from experience, nothing in life came
easily, especially when you were a single parent. His son, Will, was a great kid and he loved
him dearly, but Will was also a fourteen-year-
old. And he had all the hang-ups of a fourteen-
year-old and a few more through no fault of
his own.

Luckily Briggs had the constant support
of his aunt Myrna. Myrna had been there for
Briggs when he'd been orphaned as a teenager,
and she'd stood by him through high school,
college and law school. She'd also been a driving force through all the stages of Will's growing up—from diapers to braces, often backing
up Briggs when the long hours first at school
and then at work had caused him to miss any
number of Little League games and parent/
teacher conferences. Briggs knew firsthand
how hard absences were on a kid, doubly so
for one with a single parent. But Myrna had
given him and Will uncritical love and affec-
tion. Well, uncritical when it came to Will—
maybe not so much to him.

The traffic light finally turned green. Briggs
hung a left up the hill before turning onto a
winding road. In the fifties and sixties, a de-
veloper had neatly paved the first half mile or

so when he'd built a handful of Cape Cods and ranch houses to accommodate the modest postwar boom in the community. Over the years, a succession of owners had enlarged the unpretentious dwellings and put their personal stamps on the kit houses. And now that it was May, gaily colored azaleas and mountain laurels graced many of the front yards. On days like this, Myrna always said it was impossible to be sad, and like so many other things, she was right on this one.

Briggs continued along as the road changed from blacktop to gravel, culminating in his two-story white farmhouse. Black shutters framed the six-over-six paned windows, and flower boxes added a splash of color. Nearby, a red barn gleamed with a fresh coat of paint. Years ago, the buildings had been surrounded by twenty acres of farmland, but as the owners had aged and their children had moved away, the family had sold off much of the land to a nearby horse farm as well as to developers like the one who had built those neat houses on his road, leaving just four acres to the property.

Briggs grabbed his knapsack and entered the house by the kitchen door. The smell of simmering spices guided him to the large pot on the stove. "Ah, chili. Just what I needed after a two-hour meeting on the new state requirements for juniors."

Myrna, a force of nature at barely five feet tall and maybe one hundred ten pounds soaking wet, was sitting at the kitchen table set for dinner. Without lifting her gaze from an e-reader, she inquired in a rueful tone: "Excuse me—where's my hello kiss?"

Briggs lowered the lid. "Sorry. My bad." He gave his aunt a peck on the cheek and glanced at what she was reading.

"Another Agatha Christie," she answered without missing a beat. "And don't bother to point out that I've probably read it a million times already. It's just as good the umpteenth time through."

"Who am I to question your ways when chances are you're right most of the time?"

She looked up, her eyebrows arched. "Most of the time?"

"Okay, all of the time. Meanwhile, let me just check on Will, see how he's doing."

Without waiting for a reply, Briggs left his knapsack with essays to grade on a chair next to the hutch. The country-style storage unit was filled with dishes and cups, family photos and various trinkets that Myrna had picked up at flea markets. He bounded up the steep back steps.

The door to his son's bedroom was closed—not unusual, but hardly the norm. He knocked. "Hey, Will. I'm home. How'd your day go?"

He waited. "Will?"

There was shuffling from the other side of the door, and the boy opened it a crack. "Sorry. I had my headphones on, and…ah…I didn't hear you. I'm kinda busy…ah…studying and stuff. If you don't mind?"

Briggs pursed his lips. Something was up. He could press the matter and probably find out what was going on, but he'd likely get some unpleasant pushback. Or he could bide his time and solicit help from a far more reliable source. Myrna.

Briggs leaned closer to the door and spoke softly. "No problem. I'll call out when dinner's ready. After all, we don't want to get on Aunt Myrna's bad side."

He waited, half hoping. Nothing. It was time to go with Plan B.

Briggs skipped back down the stairs. "What's going on with Will? He's acting a bit weird."

Myrna had abandoned her reading and was standing by the stove, boiling water to make rice to go with the chili. Squares of freshly baked cornbread were already stacked on a serving tray. Briggs went to steal one, and she slapped his hand away. "No snacking before dinner. And give the boy a break. He's doing really well. That's the most important thing."

"Who said I was going to give him a hard time?" Briggs opened the fridge door and grabbed a Rolling Rock. He didn't normally have a beer on a school night, but the meeting had just about done him in.

He closed the door with his shoulder and twisted off the cap before he saw two bowls on the floor. One contained water. "Is there something I should know about?" He raised his arm to toss the cap.

Myrna sent him the evil eye, and Briggs put the metal top into the recycling bin instead of the sink. He set down his beer on the counter and nodded toward the bowls.

"Will brought home a dog," she said.

"What's that? Will got a dog?"

"He didn't exactly *get* a dog," Myrna qualified. "It's more like he's fostering it until the owner is found. The poor thing—Will's named him Buddy, by the way."

Briggs grabbed his beer and took a quick swig before getting serious. "It's never good when they name 'em. So, where's the owner anyway?"

"No one knows. Will found the dog wandering around the middle school parking lot and brought him to the vet, who checked him out and said Will could take Buddy home provided he contacts the police and hangs up flyers. He's already made them, and he plans to put them up around town tomorrow morning before school."

"And what happens when nobody claims the dog?"

Myrna sighed. "Let's cross that bridge when we come to it. Meanwhile, it's costing us nothing—the vet provided the food and bowls and everything else. And Will promised to take care of Buddy—walk him and feed him."

"What about if he's got stuff to do after school? Who's going to walk and feed him then? And what kind of vet volunteers a kid to take care of some stray anyway?"

Myrna reached for the prescription paper tacked to the fridge. "Why don't you ask the vet and not me? Here's the phone number. And keep your voice down, please. He can hear you."

"Will? No way. He's got his earphones on."

"No, I mean Buddy. He's very sweet but very shy. Loud noises scare him."

Briggs rolled his eyes. "Next you'll tell me I need to become a pet expert because of some dog that isn't even ours—yet." He stopped, replaying the words in his mind. "Sorry—that came out a lot crankier than I meant. Blame it on me being tired." He redirected from his half apology. "Truthfully, I really don't need any more responsibilities besides teaching, the nursery *and* taking care of Will."

"Correct me if I'm wrong, but I thought we moved to Hopewell precisely so you'd have more time for the important things in life?"

He shook his head. "Yes, well, I'm still working on that."

Myrna turned to stir the rice. Satisfied it wasn't sticking to the bottom of the pot, she faced Briggs again. "Frankly, I think it'll be good for the boy to have a dog. You should see him with Buddy already. They're like two teenagers in love."

"Which is not necessarily a recommendation for a long-term relationship, as we unfortunately know too well."

Myrna patted his arm. "Don't be so hard on yourself."

"How can I not be? We live with the consequences every day. Not that I would change a thing, mind you." He looked down at the piece of paper in his hand. "Do I have time to make a quick call before dinner?"

She waved him off. "Go, go. I'll just keep the food warm."

Briggs headed to the barn—his sanctuary, his place of solace, especially when the world seemed to be closing in. He slid back one side of the double doors and flicked on the lights. Along one wall was a large workbench with tools neatly arranged on hooks. Bags of potting soil, a small tractor, a rototiller and an assortment of rakes, spades and shovels contributed to the organized chaos. Glass jars lined the open shelves. Hand-marked labels identified the flower seeds that each one contained. And attached to the back of the barn was the pièce de résistance—an elaborate greenhouse, where grow lights warmed seedbeds positioned on tables.

Briggs walked across the concrete floor he'd poured himself two years ago and slid onto an old lab stool in front of the workbench. Bunches of flowers hung upside down from the rafters, and the smell of dirt and dried blossoms lent an earthy comfort to the place. The combination never failed to lower his blood pressure. He pulled out his phone and punched in the number on the sheet of paper. He was careful to exhale before he spoke.

"Dr. Trombo?" he asked when the call went through. The vet's name was printed at the top along with *Hopewell Veterinary Medicine*.

"Yes?" a woman replied.

"I'd like to speak with the veterinarian, a Dr. Trombo."

"This is Jessica Trombo, Dr. Jessica Trombo. And I *am* a veterinarian." Her tone wasn't snippy, more one of resigned edification.

Briggs practically smacked himself on the forehead. This just wasn't his evening for tact. "I apologize. My mistake."

"Actually, you're not all wrong. The usual vet in Hopewell is my dad, Dr. Norman Trombo. I'm here covering for him while he's recuperating from a fall."

"Sorry to hear that—about the fall, I mean, not that you're not capable for stepping in for him." The conversation was going from bad to worse. "I hope your father is getting better," he hastened to add.

"He's on the mend, slowly, thank you. So, can I help you with something?"

After making his introductions, Briggs got right to the point. "You gave your phone number to my son, Will, this afternoon? He brought in a dog that he found?"

"Oh, yes, I remember. Buddy. How's he doing?"

"Let's hold off on the dog for the moment. I'm more concerned about the fact that you gave permission to my son to bring home a stray animal."

"You know, I was half expecting your call. So, why don't I explain the circumstances?"

Surprisingly, she didn't sound at all defensive. Here Briggs had been prepared to tell her what for, and he stewed on that as she continued.

"First off, before agreeing to anything, I examined Buddy to make sure he had no obvious issues and that temperamentally he made a suitable family pet. Other than extreme shyness, probably due to early trauma, he appeared to be an absolutely lovely animal." Her tone was confidently professional. "And to set the record straight, Mr. Longfellow, when I inquired whether your son had permission to care for a pet, Will assured me that his family was fine with him bringing home a dog."

"Will said that, did he? Well, I think he was a little ahead of himself."

There was a chuckle.

Again, her reaction took him off guard. He was expecting her to back up his outrage, not to make light of the fact that his son had lied.

"You know, he wouldn't be the first kid to get ahead of himself when it came to pets. That's why I purposely gave him my number for just the type of conversation that we're having now." There was a pause for what sounded like a long gulp of coffee. (In point of fact, it was an energy drink.) "So, I can understand your hesitation about letting an unknown animal into the house, Mr. Longfellow, but if experience is any guide, it's unlikely to be a long-term commitment. That's why I made sure to tell Will that rescuing a stray dog is usually a temporary state of affairs. But no matter how long Buddy is in his care, he needs to act responsibly, including bringing the dog to training classes. We also provided your son with the proper food and equipment, so everything's set on that score. Now, is there anything I missed that you still feel the need to discuss?"

"Ahh, not that I can think of at the moment." Briggs felt a little overwhelmed as he tried to grasp the situation and formulate his response. As a teacher and a parent, he was usually the one directing traffic.

"There's one other thing I should mention, and it's positive. Studies have shown that pets can provide a highly successful form of therapy for children. In fostering Buddy for however long the duration, your son will experience uncritical bonding. And while he's learning how to care for an animal that is clearly traumatized, the experience will also help him cope with his own insecurities."

Her words were undoubtedly meant to be re-assuring, but they triggered the complete opposite reaction. No one needed to remind Briggs that his son was painfully shy. Briggs regularly blamed himself for the fact that Will lacked confidence, that he felt like he was somehow different, even unworthy.

"Listen," Briggs began. (It was never a good sign to start a response with *Listen*.) "I don't require some stranger telling me what's best for my son or how to deal with his so-called insecurities."

A beat of silence followed as if she were taking it all in. "Let me assure you, Mr. Longfellow, I am in no way claiming to be an expert on raising your son. I am merely attempting to express a professional opinion based on my training as a veterinarian. You, sir, may know what's best for Will. I know what's best for the dog. By the way, have you even met Buddy?"

She had him there. "Well, no. I wanted to discuss the matter with you first."

"Then before you pass judgment, I recommend you meet the canine in question. After that, feel free to call me if you need to talk further. In the meantime, have a good evening."

There was a not-all-together friendly click as she ended the call.

Briggs stared at his phone. It wasn't every day that he was left flummoxed when he'd been convinced that he'd been in the right. Or was he? He took the last mouthful of beer and marched back into the kitchen. "So, where's this Buddy anyway?"

Myrna crossed her arms and gave him a long stare. "Somehow I don't get the feeling the conversation went entirely the way you anticipated. What did he have to say?"

"The he was a she, and she said I should meet the dog." He walked over to the back stairway leading to the bedrooms. "Will? Would you come down?" he called out.

Myrna tsked him. "What did I say about no loud voices?"

Two minutes later, a mess of gawky legs, feet and paws tripped over each other as they descended.

Will and Buddy, the latter now on a proper leash, staggered to a stop at the entry to the kitchen. At the sight of Briggs looming large, Buddy cowered behind Will. The dog held his head and bushy tail limply downward, and the tips of his black ears scraped the wooden floorboards.

Briggs studied his son.

Will's mouth was pursed, his eyes squinting. "This is Buddy, Dad. Don't ya…don't ya think he's great?" His eyes darted between the dog and his father.

Briggs watched Will wrestle with his emotions—emotions that appeared to ricochet between hope and dread. "About the dog—"

"Buddy, Dad, Buddy."

"Right, Buddy. Anyhow, I just got off the phone with the vet, and she said he's in good shape. She also explained that you were fostering him until the real owner comes along."

"But he might not."

Briggs decided to let that one go for now. "In the meantime, why don't we get acquainted?" He took two steps forward.

Buddy scooted backward, stretching the leash taut. His black nose shivered.

Briggs squatted down. "Maybe this'll be better? Here, boy." He reached to pet the dog, but Buddy pulled his head away. Briggs wet his lips and glanced over his shoulder at Myrna. "I didn't know I was so intimidating."

She shrugged. "Baby steps. Take baby steps."

Will stepped closer to Buddy and let the leash fall slack. He fondled the dog's ears. "I was reading that gently rubbing their ears can calm down nervous dogs, especially ones that have had a rough time growing up. Just give him time, Dad. Wait and see. He'll get better. He just needs someone to love him."

And that's when Briggs knew he was sunk. He looked over his shoulder again. "You raised a wise grandnephew, Aunt Myrna. Tell you what. Why don't we have our dinner while Buddy has his? Nothing brings a family together like food."

And love.

CHAPTER THREE

"POPS! IT'S GREEK YOGURT. Who doesn't like Greek yogurt?" Jessica asked, the exasperation in her voice barely concealed as she shifted her eyes between the untouched bowl and her father's grumpy expression. Jessica's father had been home one night, and already they were at an impasse at breakfast the following morning.

Norman uncrossed his arms. "I have nothing against things Greek. Why, I loved that movie where the father keeps using glass cleaner to cure everything."

"My Big Fat Greek Wedding," Jessica prompted.

"They had a diner, didn't they? The family in the movie, I mean."

Jessica saw her chance to go for the win. "That's right. And I bet they sold yogurt there. Seems only right, right?"

Norman waggled his index finger. "Yeah, but I see what you did there."

"So, what's not to like?" She looked pointedly at the bowl and then at her father, who sat with his cast splayed out. A red-and-white-checkerboard cloth covered the surface of the round kitchen table.

He sniffed critically as he worked the spoon through the creamy white mixture. "It's not the Greek part. It's the yogurt. And hey, why don't I see any of the good stuff, like strawberry jam?"

Jessica did her best not to sigh. "You heard what the orthopedist said at the hospital. It's important to lose some weight to take the burden off your joints." She held off mentioning that she'd done all this healthy-food shopping late at night after a full day's work in *his* office, plus bringing him home *and* getting him settled.

Norman didn't bother to address her comments. Instead, he pushed aside the bowl of yogurt and changed the subject. "Did you hear from your brother yet?"

"I let Drew know about the accident yesterday, but what with all the different times zones and his crazy traveling, he doesn't always respond right away. I'm sure he'll touch base as soon as he can." She rubbed one eyebrow, telling herself that her father's dour mood was to be expected after the stress of the fall and his refusal to take any pain medication. And she understood his disappointment in not hearing from Drew. It was just a fact of life that everyone—including her father—thought her brother was the center of the universe and the sole reason the sun rose in the morning and set at night. As a kid she, too, had worshipped Drew. Whereas she was—how had Gloria Pulaski put it?—the "serious one."

Jessica glanced at her watch and decided that she did not have the time to wage a nutritious-food battle. She got up and pulled a box of frozen waffles from the freezer and popped two into the toaster. With her back to the table, she could almost feel her father's glinting sense of triumph. She grabbed a plate from the overhead cupboard and an unopened bottle of maple syrup. She placed them in front of her father without a word.

"Low-cal maple syrup?"

Jessica plunked the silverware down. "Don't go there, Pops. I'm late to go take care of your patients. I'll be back at noon to check on you and get your lunch. In the meantime, I'll inquire about an aide to come in for a couple of hours a day to help you out."

Norman wrestled with the bottle cap before pouring on enough syrup to sink a flotilla of ancient Greek triremes. (Jessica had Greek stuff on the brain, it seemed.) "I don't want some stranger tromping around the house. Besides, why do I need an aide when I have you?" He dug in.

She loved her father dearly despite his foibles, like not putting down the toilet seat and never remembering which day it was to take the garbage out. But this current level of crankiness was a new low. Was it more than the aftereffects of breaking his leg? "You have more faith in my capabilities than I do, Pops. I tell you what, why don't we see how it goes today. But at the same time, I'll ask around—just in case. Anyway, if you need anything, I'm a phone call away. I bought real coffee at the supermarket, and I turned on the machine. I even left you a mug next to it, so you're all set. And there're apples in the bowl on the counter, too. They go well with yogurt, by the way."

He harrumphed.

"And you promised to stay on the one floor, remember?"

He looked at her with raised eyebrows.

Jessica grabbed her shoulder bag and car keys from the side table next to the back door. "You're sure you'll be able to get around on crutches? You don't need any help with…with… your ablutions?"

Her father rested his fork on the side of his plate. "Jessica, I'm a doctor. You don't have to use euphemisms with me for bodily functions."

"You know, Dad, if you're not careful, I'll have Gloria Pulaski bring Alfie around for a visit. He'll keep you in your place."

"That's cruel."

"I know. But it felt really good to say it."

"WENDY, IS IT just me, or is my dad really grouchy?" Jessica piled her bag onto the counter in the waiting room.

"Coffee?" Wendy nodded to the machine that was perpetually on.

"Please. I know that the accident was a shock and he's feeling miserable, but…I don't know. I hate to say it, but it's just he's continually—"

"Irritable? Unreasonable? And this was before his fall. I can't imagine what he's like now. Speaking of which, I'm going to drive over some food that people have dropped off at the office."

Jessica was already at the mini fridge to get milk for her coffee. She lifted the foil off several oven-safe dishes stacked inside. "It looks like there're enough tuna casseroles to last a year. At least they have green beans in them.

You should have seen his reaction when I suggested he needed to eat a healthier diet."

Wendy held out her own coffee mug emblazoned with the words *Vets Get All the Ap-Paws*. "Not to pry, but how often do you make it back to Hopewell?"

Jessica tipped some milk into Wendy's mug. "It's been a while. But in my defense, he and my mom always came out every Christmas to Chicago once I moved there. And well, now he comes out by himself, and we keep up the same traditions—going into the Loop for the day, catching *The Nutcracker* and having dinner on Christmas at his favorite Italian restaurant. All the stuff he and Mom and I used to do—especially with Drew off somewhere remote and all. It's kinda special, you know?"

Wendy sipped slowly. "Did you ever consider not going out?"

Jessica shook her head. "Excuse me, have you tasted my cooking?"

"You've got a point there." Wendy nodded knowingly. "Maybe keep the going-out-to-dinner but nix the other stuff. I don't know—perhaps Christmas dinner here in Hopewell on his turf for a change?"

"You think Chicago's too much? That he's getting too old to run around?"

"We're all getting older. I'm no expert, but maybe he just needs some quiet company. Besides, wasn't it your mom who was the more social one?"

"But the two of them were a team. Team Trombo, Drew used to call them. Vivian and Norman, Norman and Vivian. It was like *bacon and eggs. Salt and pepper.*"

"Laverne and Shirley."

Jessica frowned. "Who?"

Wendy rested her mug on the counter and lifted a stack of charts. "Never mind. I'm betraying my age. Maybe it's just that since your mom died, your dad is reverting to his natural self. Don't get me wrong—I love your dad. We all do. It's just that he can be a bit of a handful."

Jessica thought over Wendy's words. "It may be normal for him to be a handful. But it's not normal for him to be this bad-tempered. When he acts like this, it's impossible for him to be happy." She set her mug down and gave a determined look. "You know what? I'm going to do something about it, and I'm counting on your cooperation."

Wendy saluted her. "Aye, aye, Captain. But first you've got two teeth-cleaning procedures. Joe's already in the back prepping." She handed over the charts.

Jessica wrestled together the folders, her shoulder bag and the coffee mug. She turned to go and noticed something on the pegboard. "What's this?" She peered at the poster. "Whaddya you know? It's a flyer for the stray dog that boy brought in yesterday. I wasn't sure we'd ever hear from him again." She didn't mention the testy phone call she'd had with the boy's father.

Wendy walked over and looked at the printed notice. "Yes, Will and his father came in early this morning just as I was opening up. He's a good-looking guy."

Jessica blinked. "Will? He's a bit young for you, I would have thought."

"I'm talking about the dad, silly. And he's too young for me, too. But, hey, a gal can dream." She put another pushpin in the flyer to make it hang straight. "By the way, he inquired about the dog-training sessions."

"The father?"

Wendy smiled. "No, the boy. But I caught you there, didn't I?"

JESSICA STARTED THE day with teeth and ended with toes, clipping the nails of Sheba, a cantankerous bullmastiff. She had just about decided to anesthetize the one-hundred-twenty-pound dog when Insu Park, the owner and the mayor of Hopewell, announced that Sheba loved show tunes. By the end of the procedure, Sheba was prancing around without a care in the world, and Joseph was hoarse from repeatedly singing every verse of "Oh, What a Beautiful Mornin'." (Joseph was a fan of *Oklahoma!*)

Finally, when six o'clock rolled around, Jessica walked into the waiting room. "Wendy, go home," she declared. "And I can do that," she added when she saw the office manager neatening up the magazines on the coffee table. Wendy gladly obliged, and she left with Joseph, who was still humming on his way out.

Jessica checked that everything was locked up. Since there were no overnight boarding patients, she had one less thing to worry about. At last, she pulled the scrunchie out of her hair. It had been a long day, what with Pops and a full slate of patients. But all in all, she felt pretty satisfied.

"This calls for wine," she announced to no one in particular.

She drove the rental car to the other end of Main Street and parked at the local wine shop, Grape Expectations, formerly called The Foxe and the Hounds. She heard a jingle as she pushed open the door and saw a familiar face.

"Mr. Portobello, a bottle of your finest dry white wine, if you please. Spare no expense."

Mr. Portobello always reminded her of the Genie in *Aladdin* since he had a black goatee with a prominent curl at his chin. She walked over to the counter and immediately spied the donation can for the SPCA. She dug out her wallet and slipped a dollar bill into the container.

"I just happen to have a delightful Verdicchio from Le Marche that would hit the spot for the out-of-town daughter who's come home to nurse her father and the pampered furry members of our town," Mr. Portobello responded.

Jessica didn't bother to ask how he knew. The possibilities were endless.

Mr. Portobello slid silently across the floor in his canvas slip-ons. He wore a blue-and-white-striped boatneck top. The nautical theme was going strong. He reached for the bottle of wine and held it out for inspection. "Will this do?"

Jessica nodded. "I'm not sure who's been more demanding—the pets or my father, but this looks like a wonderful remedy for both."

He rang up the purchase and placed the bottle in a paper bag. "There's an American-history teacher at the high school who has a fondness for this particular wine, too. Perhaps you know him?"

Jessica shook her head. "Can't say that I do. Unless he has a pet who's a patient of my father's."

Mr. Portobello straightened the hem of one sleeve. "You never know." He passed the package to her. "I must say, Jessica, we've missed you—and not just because I've sold you one of my more expensive wines. And that's despite the fact that our history is—how do you say?— a little checkered."

He was clearly referring to her freshman year in high school when, as a committed animal lover, she had led a movement against the fox-hunting connotation of the shop's original name.

"I confess that I was taken aback at first, but you were so earnest and polite, and I always liked a little well-mannered rebellion, you see. Besides, your father has always treated Fernando with the utmost respect." He glanced behind the counter.

Jessica went on tiptoes and spotted the wire cage on the floor behind. Inside, a large white rabbit was munching on a carrot.

"Perhaps you could get your friend Laura to paint him, maybe using the same Botticelli touch she used for the shop's placard?"

In a eureka moment, the teenaged Jessica had brokered a peaceful solution to their "disagreement" by getting her dearest friend to paint a humorous homage to the old and new names, a tableau of the fox and hounds dancing in harmony around an oak barrel overflowing with bunches of grapes. A spray of flowers and a few bottles of wine completed the joyful scene.

"I'll make sure to ask her. Speaking of which, Laura would be the perfect person to share the wine with. Her gallery's still...?"

"Down the street, on the block next to the children's bookshop."

Jessica opened her mouth and closed it. "Doesn't anything ever change in this place?"

"Does it need to?" Mr. Portobello straightened a bottle of rosé from Provence. "Please give your father my best wishes for a speedy recovery."

JESSICA STUCK HER head inside the gallery door. "Hello? Laura?" The overhead lights illuminated several bronze abstract sculptures and turned the hardwood floor a honey gold. On the walls, splashes of color jumped out from bold paintings of turbulent seas and dramatic skylines.

The clip-clop of clogs sounded from the back.

"I'm so sorry. I was on the phone. Is there anything I—" An immediate shriek preceded a bone-crushing hug. Laura Reggio stepped back a moment and then, being Laura, repeated the whole shrieking/hugging EMBRACE (capitals were a must!) all over again.

"Oh, Jess. I can't believe it's you." Laura drew back but held on to Jessica's forearms.

Jessica gulped. "If I can get my breath back, I can confirm it's me—and that it's so good to see you again." She regarded her super, best-ever friend from school.

Laura hadn't really changed, unless you made allowances for the green streaks in her shag haircut. (They used to be hot pink.) Otherwise, her maxi dress and clogs, together with a STACK (again, capitals were definitely necessary) of silver bangles on one forearm pretty much said it all. She was still the counterculture, arty type, once scorned by the in crowd, a reaction that only made her act more outrageously. And Jessica had loved Laura precisely for that reason.

"Let me get a good look at you," Laura implored as she twirled Jessica around. Jessica's bag slipped from her shoulder, and she hugged the wine to keep it from dropping. "You haven't changed a bit. The same long hair and long legs.

Someday you'll trade in your baggy jeans for a cute dress. And don't say it's not your style. But speaking of style, don't you ever gain weight? But then you never really ate that much. I can't believe your mom was such a bad cook. My *nonna* used to fret all the time that you weren't getting enough to eat. I can't count the number of lasagnas she sent home with you, along with strict instructions on reheating them!" Laura laughed at the memory, her dark eyes brimming with glee.

Jessica laughed along with her. She didn't bother mentioning that despite the instructions, she had managed to burn a fair share. No, what was important was that Laura was still Laura. She still talked a mile a minute, embraced life without holding back and, of course, brought up her beloved Italian grandmother, a dynamo in the kitchen and a terror at cards. "I hate to ask, but is Nonna still alive?"

"Are you kidding me? She's indestructible. And I'm going to call her today to let her know you're back. Maybe a few cannoli as a welcome-home present?" Laura dragged Jessica over to the café table and chairs placed in the front window of the gallery and pointed to one chair. "Now, tell me all."

Jessica did as she was told. "Well, as I'm sure

you've already heard, I'm back in town to help my dad."

"Of course I've heard. Nonna plays cards with Mr. Mason."

"Yes, I treated Bismol, his bird, yesterday. But doesn't he cheat? Mr. Morgan, not Bismol, that is."

"Of course, but then so does Nonna. But that's old news. How's your dad? How are you?" She patted Jessica's hand.

"Physically, Pops is banged up pretty good. Psychologically, well, Pops acts like the stubborn sort that he naturally is, only more so." Jessica slumped a little in her seat. "Unfortunately he also seems pretty down, not excited about doing anything."

"It could be the pain."

"Yeah, maybe, but I think it's something more. I hope I can get to the bottom of it and get him out of this funk. I might not be my fun-loving brother, but I'm determined."

Laura made a resolute fist. "That's my Jessica. Ever ready to come to the aid of the needy and the downtrodden, especially if they're furry and have a tail. I'm sure you'll work something out. But what about you? Anything exciting on the horizon?" She waggled her eyebrows, which were dark and fully animated.

Jessica held up her hand. "Before I go there, let me get some glasses and a corkscrew. You still keep them on the shelves in the kitchenette, right?" Before Laura could reply, she took off, returning with the corkscrew and two wine-glasses, along with a tall green bottle of fizzy water from the case in the back.

She placed them on the table and reached into the paper bag. She pulled out the bottle of white wine. "Mr. Portobello was kind enough to select this for me, and I can't think of anyone I'd rather share it with." She opened the bottle and started to pour two glasses.

Laura covered one with her hand. "Just water for me. But you go ahead." She let Jessica finish pouring, and they clinked glasses. "So? What gives?"

Jessica took a sip and closed her eyes. It was the first moment of true bliss since she'd arrived in Hopewell.

"So?"

She opened her eyes and shrugged. "Same old same old. Work is fine, especially if I ignore the overly pampered owners."

"And here I thought it was the overly pampered pets that would be the problem."

"No, the animals are cool. Weird sometimes, but weird is okay. But it's the people who can be too demanding. Just the other day I drew the line at cosmetic surgery to even out a shih tzu's smile."

"Thank goodness there are still some people with common sense around to keep the foolish, rich folks in line. But what about outside of work?"

"Ah, the perennial question. I'm sorta seeing someone. Roger. I met him through work." She held her glass by the stem and circled it around on the table. "He's the firm's accountant." She looked over at her old friend.

Laura pushed out the side of her cheek with the tip of her tongue and nodded. "An accountant's good. Nothing wrong with an accountant, I suppose."

Jessica narrowed her eyes. "I know what you're thinking, but I'm fine with *good*. Some of us don't look for *great*, and don't tell me that I'm settling. That's just who I am."

Laura leaned forward and touched the back of Jessica's hand. "You said it, not me. And if you're sure, I'm happy for you. It's just…just that I want you to have the best. You were always looking out for others, and it's time you looked out for yourself."

"I am," Jessica protested, maybe a little too

vehemently. "But enough about me. What about you?"

Laura squirmed a little on her chair and looked rather pleased with herself. "Well, I've been waiting for you to ask actually." Her eyes were bright. "I just found out that I'm pregnant. I'm over the moon. And you're the first to know."

This time Jessica let out the screech. "No wonder you refused the wine! That's amazing! When are you due?" She looked at her friend's abdomen, but the flouncy cotton dress wasn't exactly formfitting.

"Not for months and months. Tonight I'm going to tell the baby's father. I know he'll be just as happy. I mean, Phil and I weren't planning to get pregnant right away, but what's meant to be is meant to be, especially when you're as much in love as we are." She beamed.

"I'm so happy for you. And for the father, too." Jessica stopped and frowned. "Wait a minute. Did you say Phil? You're not talking about Philippe LaValle?"

"Why, yes. That Phil. After all these years—can you believe it?"

Jessica took a large sip from her glass. "Frankly, no. Phil and you and I might have been best friends as little kids, but in high school Phil was my worst nightmare. He became a member of the cool group, the rich kids' clique." She took another sip.

"I know—I know what you're thinking. But Phil's not like that anymore. It was really all his father's doing. All that stuck-up, snob stuff. The Phil I know and love is the most down-to-earth person. And he loves kids. He even teaches chemistry at the high school."

"If *you* say so, then I'll believe it, of course. It's just that when I think back to high school—which I realize is ancient history—*he* was the one who started the whole 'Prohibition Prude' thing. I went through four years of despair with everyone referring to me as Prudey."

It had all started with the incident with Mr. Portobello and the unfortunate name he'd chosen for the wine shop. Jessica had tried to organize a school-wide boycott of the store, which as Drew had rightly pointed out, hadn't been very effective since all the students were under the drinking age. Jessica could take Drew's good-natured remark, but the taunting of Phil, her so-called friend, had been too much. He'd begun calling her "Jessica the Prohibition Prude," which had soon been shortened to "Prudey" by her classmates. The hurtful moniker had even been enshrined in print in the pages of the high school yearbook.

"You're right. That was terrible. Phil is so sorry for the way he acted. And while I get it's not a valid excuse, he was going through such a hard time at home. His father was always on him to get better grades, win all the riding awards, get into the best colleges, become rich and famous. The pressure must have been terrible."

"Still no excuse for being cruel," Jessica reminded her. "Those years in high school were torture. I felt betrayed."

"I'm sorry you're still upset. And Phil would be the first person to admit you're justified in feeling that way. But people, especially kids, do make mistakes. And the good news is they can learn. They can become better people if they work at it and if they're given the chance. You *will* give him the chance, won't you?" Laura searched Jessica's face.

She glanced out the window. A blue-gray Volvo station wagon was noisily passing by. The model and make were such a Bucks County cliché. The only thing missing was a Labrador retriever with his head stuck out the passenger window. Instead, she thought she saw a bouquet of flowers propped up.

Jessica turned her attention back to Laura. "Okay, because you're my friend and because I believe you implicitly, I'll give him a chance. But just for the record, cruel stuff like that can mess up a kid and play mind games with their self-esteem. Luckily in my case, I had a love of animals to fall back on. Which reminds me— only yesterday I had this young boy come into my office with a stray dog. He was barely a teenager, and I don't know who was more frightened, the dog, Buddy, or the boy, Will. Talk about needing self-confidence."

"Wait a minute, did you say a boy named Will?"

"That's right."

"His dad is Briggs, Briggs Longfellow, Phil's closest friend. Briggs also teaches at the high school, too—American history. He's a great guy—really nice and understanding."

"Well, he might be nice and understanding to some people, but when I talked to him over the phone, he certainly didn't seem so sympathetic about fostering a dog."

"In Briggs's defense, he's a single parent. Taking in a stray dog might be a little much when he's working full time and raising a son who, according to Phil, is really sweet but also super shy."

"Excuse me. I'm prepared to believe that Phil LaValle is a changed man, if you say so, but this Briggs fellow—I don't know."

Laura leaned forward. "Don't be so sure. I haven't told you the best part."

"There's a best part?"

"There's always a best part. Briggs—or 'this Briggs fellow' as you like to call him—"

"I don't like to call him anything."

"Hear me out. Not only did Briggs move to Hopewell to give his son a better life, but he also—now, get this—he also grows flowers on the side."

"Flowers? You mean like daisies?"

"Among other things. Daisies, black-eyed Susans, delphiniums—all sorts of colorful things. He took over the farm on the way to Phil's dad's place. He works a half acre or so and has this greenhouse setup. It's kind of a hobby. How bad can a guy be who grows flowers?"

She suddenly thought of the Volvo that had recently passed by. "Does he make bouquets for delivery?"

"Maybe? Okay, for friends, and I may have asked him to make a delivery to your dad today. I don't think that's a real sideline of his, but he does have a stall at the Saturday farmers' market." Laura raised one of her famously descriptive eyebrows. "And I have it on good authority that he likes Italian whites." She pointed to Jessica's wine.

CHAPTER FOUR

"Pops, YOU CANNOT eat cold tuna casserole standing in front of the open fridge."

"Fine, I'll eat it sitting down." Norman shut the refrigerator door with his backside and hobbled over to the kitchen table. The Pyrex dish hung precariously from one hand as he juggled the crutches.

Jessica dropped her bag and keys and rushed over. "Here—let me." She grabbed the heavy glass container before it, the crutches and her dad went sprawling on the floor. "Couldn't you have waited a few minutes until I got home? I called to let you know that I'd be home late but still in time to fix you dinner." She put the casserole in the microwave and set the timer before hanging up her jacket and retrieving her bag and keys.

The microwave dinged when it was finished, and she spooned a portion onto a plate for Pops and brought it to the table. She pulled out a wooden chair next to him. The seat was painted purple, the spindles gold—another example of her mother's handiwork. "I called Betsy Pulaski-O'Malley at the hospital for the name of a nursing/aide agency and a medical-supply company. But in the middle of the call, Betsy's water broke."

Pops harrumphed. "I already told you—I don't want someone I don't know coming into the house."

Jessica outlined the squares on the tablecloth with her index finger. She found the mindless action surprisingly soothing. "Anyway, Betsy managed to pass on the information before they transported her to the maternity ward. And before you say anything, I held off on hiring an aide, but I checked into getting you a tub chair right away. The woman answering the phone at the medical-supply company promised me one first thing tomorrow morning after I mentioned your name. Apparently you treated their family's elderly cat with diabetes mellitus, and they never forgot it." She willed herself to smile, and as she did so, she noticed for the first time a floral centerpiece in the middle of the table. "That's new." She pointed at the carefree mix of pink, poppy-shaped blossoms and feathery white flowers. The soft colors provided a gentle cheer to counteract the gloom emanating from her dad.

"Yeah, a fellow named something like Walt Whitman—"

"I think you've got the wrong American poet. I have a feeling the guy delivering flowers was named Longfellow, Briggs Longfellow." The irritated voice on the phone appeared to be tracking her in various ways.

"That's the one. Anyway, he dropped them off not too long ago," he said between munches. "Said that Laura had sent them as a get-well gesture. Nice of her."

"Absolutely. And to celebrate—whether you like it or not—tomorrow morning, as soon as that chair arrives, you're getting a shower. Then, after we make you presentable for the outside world, how about you come to the office with me? Check out some patients? Assure Wendy and Joseph that you're fine—back to being your usual grumpy self?"

Pops turned his head away and stared out the window. The sun was slowly setting, and a golden light danced across the checked tablecloth and up the sides of the kitchen cupboard. "I don't think so," he answered. "I'm not up to it yet. The animals' owners would rather see you anyway. They always tell me how much they miss you." He looked back at her, his eyes downcast.

"Me? It's been years since I've been back to Hopewell—on your orders, I might add. Drew and I were always told to go off and fulfill our ambitions."

"That was your mom's dream, really. Anyway, folks are probably tired of dealing with an old fogy like me." He looked down at the tuna casserole and placed his fork on the side.

Jessica patted his arm. "In your current state, I think they may be correct. But enough about work. If you're not going to finish that food, maybe I'll have the rest for dinner."

"I thought you hated tuna casserole."

"I do. But despite my best efforts, I didn't manage to burn it. I might as well take advantage of small miracles. Besides, we have ice cream sandwiches for dessert."

Norman perked up. "Now you're talking."

JESSICA SETTLED HER father into his recliner so he could watch the baseball game on TV. She loaded the few dishes into the dishwasher and let the casserole dish soak in the sink. Finally free of duties, she sat at the kitchen table and rang the founding partner of the Chicago veterinary clinic, Isaac Verner. They exchanged some small talk before Jessica filled him in on her father's progress. "I'm sorry to say, but it looks like my father's recovery will take longer than I anticipated. I was hoping to return to work by Monday, but now I'm not sure," she reported.

"Don't worry about it, Jessica. From the sounds of it, he suffered a pretty bad break. Take all the time you need," Dr. Verner reassured her. "My niece, who just finished her degree, offered to fill in. I know she's got her sights set on going someplace more exciting than working with her uncle, but in the meantime we're lucky to have her."

"I'm glad to hear that. I don't feel quite as guilty about leaving you in a lurch." They ended with some more chitchat before Jessica rang off, relieved—kind of. She didn't want to jeopardize the ability of the practice to take good care of its patients. But at the same time, she liked to think of her professional self as, if not indispensable, at least sorely missed.

She hit the assigned number for her friend, Roger. She had missed an earlier call from him, but now he was the one who didn't pick up. His voice mail directed her to leave a message. Roger had a not unpleasant baritone, much like that of a voice-over announcer in a commercial for car insurance. She glanced at the time and decided she'd just try later, especially since Chicago was an hour earlier than East Coast time. There was a chance he was out to dinner with a client.

She sat there, unsure of what to do next. The television droning from the den provided an innocuous white noise. Pops usually stayed up for the late-night news and one of the talk shows, but for once Jessica figured she could get him to turn in early. She was right. Despite his complaints about sleeping in the ground floor guestroom, she managed to bundle him off to bed once the ball game was done. It proved too much of a battle to get him out of his clothes and into pajamas, so she let him doze off wearing the same T-shirt and sweatpants with one leg cut off that he'd worn all day.

Then she took the stairs two at a time and flopped onto her bed. She glanced around her old room with its decor unchanged since her preteen days. A poster of Justin Timberlake hung over her bed, and Polly Pocket toys lined the shelves. There was a Razor scooter propped against the desk. For a brief moment, she thought of taking it back to Chicago before nixing the idea. She'd probably damage herself on an overly ambitious outing along Lake Michigan. Thinking of Chicago (but not the injuring-herself part) reminded her to call Roger again, but she got the same recorded message. Jessica told herself she'd give it one more shot, but that was before she fell asleep on top of her Snoopy bedspread. (She'd always been a sucker for dogs.)

Thank goodness Pops couldn't make it up the stairs to give her grief first thing the next morning.

SPEAKING OF FIRST thing the next morning…

"Will, I'm late as it is to set up for the farmers' market. If you insist on coming, you've got to get that dog in the car." Briggs held open the kitchen door and shook his car keys. He didn't bother to hide the irritation in his voice.

"Sorry, Dad. It's just…just that I wanted to take Buddy's bowls and some food and water for him. Dr. Trombo gave me all this…this information about how important it was to properly feed and hydrate your dog."

"Dr. Trombo," Briggs muttered under his breath. "In a short time, this woman seems to have taken over the running of this family."

"Excuse me." Myrna narrowed her eyes at Briggs. "As you are definitely aware, there is no mumbling allowed in this household. In addition to which, I'll have you know that *I* run the show." She relaxed a little. "And I'll hear no criticism about that nice Jessica Trombo, either. From what I gather, she's very capable in addition to being courteous."

"A few days ago, you didn't even know who she was. In fact, you thought she was a he."

"That's true, but I've had time to ask around a bit."

Briggs cocked an eyebrow. "That sounds very suspicious."

Myrna waved him off. "Only because you have developed a wary nature. What is important here is that Jessica Trombo treated Will like a responsible adult, and he's acting like one. You should be proud of his response. Most parents would be more than delighted."

"If Will is so perfect, how come he isn't ready to go this morning? He absolutely promised he'd help with the setup. That was our bargain for a raise in his allowance, ostensibly to help pay for this dog thing. And I don't know why Will just can't leave him home, for that matter."

"This dog is named Buddy, and of course Will can't just leave him home. Would you abandon a newborn in the cold?"

Briggs shook his head. "Do I need to point out that it's in the seventies already?"

"No self-respecting mother would abandon her child."

"Will is not the dog's mother."

"A technicality. For all intents and purposes, Will *is* Buddy's mother. I should know." Myrna leveled a stare at Briggs.

He knew when to back off. "Okay, the dog's coming. But we really need to get going."

Will scrambled out the kitchen door, a bag of supplies in one hand, Buddy reluctantly trailing on the leash in the other. The dog buried his head in his neck and let his shoulders curl downward. He looked as if he expected to have to walk the plank.

"Oh, Will, how clever," Myrna complimented the boy. "You found your father's gym bag to carry all of the dog's gear." She smiled a *now what do you have to say?* smile at Briggs.

He growled. "I've got a mind to say something to our Dr. Trombo. And if I happen to see her today, I just might…"

AND SPEAKING OF TODAY…

"I am not going," Norman protested.

It was Saturday afternoon, and Jessica had already seen a raft of patients in the morning. When she'd gotten back to the house, she'd found the tub chair had been delivered as promised. Pops's shower had happened—more or less. More in terms of his personal invectives directed at Jessica while she'd attempted to attach a plastic garbage bag to his leg. Less in terms of the amount of water that had remained in the shower as opposed to dousing the bathroom floor.

"Keep up this bad behavior and there will be consequences," she'd pseudo-threatened. A rabid groundhog would have been more cooperative. And that was merely Planned Activity Number One.

Number Two involved the outing. Hence his current complaints.

"Pops, the farmers' market is going to be hopping. New vendors, too."

"Too crowded—I'll stay home. It wasn't my idea to go to the farmers' market anyway."

"True, but I think we both could use a little excursion." It was the first step in Jessica's campaign to raise her father out of his doldrums. "The weather's perfect, and the first vegetables are sure to be on sale. We can drive to the parking lot, pick up a few things and, who knows, maybe see some people. Plus, check out this transport chair. Look. It folds up nicely. So easy for packing in the car." She made a *voilà* gesture like a hostess on a game show. "Besides,

Betsy Pulaski-O'Malley—you remember Betsy Pulaski-O'Malley, right?"

"Alfie's owner, how could I forget?"

"Right, what was I thinking? Betsy was kind enough to lend us the chair from the hospital's supply. She arranged it even after just having had a baby—another boy, I think. So, we owe her big time."

The farmers' market was held in the parking lot next to Mr. Mason's now defunct gas station and auto-repair shop. Since the brew pub was still in the planning stages, the space offered the perfect central venue.

Her father mumbled something about not wanting to eat any vegetables, but she ignored his complaints. "Look, how about this, I'll put the transport chair in the trunk while you make your way to the car using your crutches. We'll put them in the back seat, so if you feel up to using them instead of sitting in the chair, you have that option." She grabbed her bag and keys and didn't wait for a response. "Just close the door behind you, Pops."

She stashed the transport chair and held open the car door as she waited for him to toddle over.

He lowered himself into the front seat, backside first. "You should turn in this rental car.

It's a waste of money." He shimmied himself around and swatted away Jessica's hand when she went to fasten the seat belt. "My Subaru's seats are a lot more comfortable than this economy car's," he grumbled.

"Good idea." She refused to be deterred.

And in the end, he chose the chair over the crutches. For a man who claimed he didn't need help, he seemed to relish the assistance.

"So, Pops, how about we take a quick tour of all the vendors before we spend too much time at one?" she suggested.

"Fine, but first I want to hit that pastry stand over there to the left." It turned out it belonged to Robby Bellona's wife, Nada. The high school Facebook page had clued Jessica into Robby's marital status. That Nada was so nice and talented indicated Robby was a better person than she'd remembered.

Nada specialized in both sweet and savory baked goods from her native Croatia. Jessica parked her father to the side of the crowded booth and picked up a *borek*, a flaky pastry filled with cheese, and some rugelach for Pops's sweet tooth.

Nada tallied up the order. "Robby told me how you came home to help with your father." She slipped an extra poppy-seed roll into the bag.

"Oh, you don't have to do that."

"It's my pleasure. I'm new to Hopewell. Robby and I met when he was stationed in Germany and I was working there. But I'm eager to get to know more people. I know how hard it is when you live far away."

Jessica thanked her and walked the bag of goodies over to her father, who was talking to Mr. Mason. His garage might've been closed, but Mr. Mason still seemed drawn to the place. "Here, Pops, you can earn your keep and guard the bakery items. And don't touch the rugelach, whatever you do—unless you're going to share it with Mr. Mason."

Mr. Mason blushed. He patted his stomach. "Watching my weight."

"Nonsense," Norman said. "If a stiff breeze came along, it'd blow you over. Why don't you wheel me and this contraption over to the picnic tables, and you can tell me what's new since we last saw each other. Jessica's just going to mosey around the vegetable stands anyway. She's been threatening me with all sorts of green stuff."

"She always was a determined young lady. You never had to worry about her. Now Drew on the other hand…" He began pushing Norman toward the tables. Pops started laughing—

the first outburst that Jessica had heard since she'd been back.

"Jessica, I'm so glad to see you." Gloria Pulaski held her smartphone close to Jessica's nose. "Have you seen the latest photo of Betsy's new baby? He's my third grandchild."

Jessica lowered the phone so she could focus. A squished, red-cheeked baby face poked out from a swaddled Phillies receiving blanket. "Beautiful! What's his name?"

"He's named Arnold, after my husband."

"I thought your husband's name is Perry."

"It is, but Arnold is for Arnold Palmer, Perry's favorite golfer."

"I see." Jessica nodded. She didn't really, but no matter. "Well, give Betsy my best. I was just looking for something to give her as a present—not only for the baby but for helping out with my dad and all." She waved goodbye as quickly and politely as possible and made her way to the various booths with veggies. She bought some salad greens and fresh spinach. And as she wove her way through the crowd, she greeted familiar faces—both two- and four-legged.

And just when she'd almost given up on finding something for Betsy, the sun catchers and the scented soaps not quite hitting the mark, Jessica found the perfect gift—flowers. She made a beeline for the cloth-covered table set with tall metal containers of colorful bouquets and sprays of cherry blossoms and azalea branches. There was a crowd of people, and she edged her way forward to get a better look. Which was when she spotted a familiar set of paws visible under the edge of the tablecloth.

CHAPTER FIVE

"BUDDY," JESSICA COOED. "How're you doing, fella?" She reached inside a front pocket of her jeans and knelt down. Sure enough, she found a dog treat. "I bet you'd like this." She held her open palm under the tablecloth and waited for the dog to inch forward.

Sure enough, a small wet nose peaked out from under the white cloth and twitched at the smell of liver. A pointed pink tongue followed, and finally a black-and-white furry muzzle turned thirty degrees and scarfed up the morsel.

Jessica smiled. She located another treat and held it out, this time a little away from the table. It took slightly longer, but the dog inched one white paw with brown spots and black nails forward. He angled his head, and one dark eye came to light. A quizzical brown spot set against his gleaming black fur wiggled in anticipation. No sooner had he made his brave advance than he pulled back.

"That's a good dog. No need to worry. Remember me?" Jessica lifted the cloth and squatted lower to burrow under the table. She held out the dog treat. Buddy lowered his belly to the ground. He darted his eyes between the treat in Jessica's hand and her face.

"What's up, Buddy? Did you find something?" It was a boy's voice.

Jessica looked over and saw Will bending down to look at what the dog had uncovered.

"Oh, Dr. Trombo, I didn't know you were down there. I thought that maybe Buddy found a bug or something."

"Something better. Liver treats." Jessica winked at the dog. "I see you have a pal, Buddy."

Buddy turned his head and licked Will's nose. The boy laughed. He roughed up Buddy's wrinkled face with his hand. The dog's tail thumped on the pavement. At moments like this, Jessica's heart soared.

"What's Dr. Trombo got for you, Buddy?" Will asked. Buddy warily inspected Jessica's hand before bravely swallowing the treat in one gulp. "That's a good boy. You're so brave. See, everybody loves you," the boy congratulated the dog.

"Will, what's going on there?" A deep male voice came from overhead. "If Buddy's both-

ering someone, you'll have to take him home."
The owner of the voice squatted down to in-
spect.

"There's no problem with Buddy. He's just
saying hello to Dr. Trombo. Right, Doc?"

Jessica registered somewhere in the deep
recesses of her brain that Will had just mentioned her name, but beyond that awareness,
her mental acuity had lodged in neutral. There,
under the draped white cloth, within inches of
her nose, was one of the most gorgeous human
males she'd ever seen. Chocolate-brown deep-
set eyes and high cheekbones that looked as if
Michelangelo had sculpted them. Then there
was his jaw—square and firm—which implied
deeply held principles. Not to forget the irresist-
ible morning stubble conveying just the right
amount of manly neglect. The only thing missing was a lock of his wavy brown hair falling
across his forehead. And as if on cue, he dipped
his chin—my, oh my, he had a perfect cleft—
and a lock dropped forward.

Jessica gathered her wits and held out her
hand to shake. "Jessica Trombo," she identified herself.

"Dr. Trombo?" he asked.

Buddy took that moment to wrinkle his forehead and inch away from the deep baritone. His

nose came in contact with Jessica's hand. He sniffed, looking for another treat.

She laughed. "Just a minute, Bud. I'll get you another one." She lifted her butt to reach for her pocket and dropped her face in the process and was greeted by a wet dog lick on her nose. She laughed again and pulled up. This time the crown of her head bumped into that lantern jaw, and the man's head bopped the bottom of the table. Jessica collapsed onto the ground and, with one eye closed, rubbed her head. "I'm so sorry, whoever you are."

"Briggs Longfellow, Will's dad," he replied. "And no need to be sorry. A simple accident, really." The three of them formed a tight huddle—four counting Buddy, who was squished in the middle, predictably petrified.

"Mr. Longfellow, hello," Jessica managed. "I'm afraid I got Buddy a little excited by bribing him with treats. I was just so happy to see him here with Will. You never know when someone brings in a stray if it'll work out. And it's nice to meet you in person, too, by the way." She reached forward to shake his hand but realized hers was dripping with dog slobber. "Let me just wipe this off." She used the denim of her jeans and tried again.

Briggs went to reach out, but there was no

room in their little huddle. "Maybe it would be better if we stood up and made the introductions above the table?" he suggested.

"Good idea." She nodded.

When Buddy sensed all three were getting up, he bounded up as well. So, of course, everyone's heads, including the dog's, hit the underside of the table. The sound of shaking flowerpots penetrated below.

"Oh, no," Jessica moaned. "Your flowers."

Briggs made it up first, followed by Will, Buddy and then Jessica. "Any lasting damage?" she asked.

Briggs righted a few tall buckets and rearranged the flowers that had slipped out. A wet patch puddled on the white tablecloth, but otherwise the damage appeared minimal. "Nothing lasting," he announced. "But maybe you could help untangle Will and Buddy?" He nodded toward the trapped bundle of boy and dog.

"No problem." Jessica unknotted the dog's lead from the table leg. "Sit, Buddy," she commanded, reinforcing her words with the proper hand motion. Buddy did as he was told while Will used the free end of the lead to unravel his legs before reattaching it to the table.

Briggs looked in amazement. "How did you do that?"

Jessica glanced over. "What? Oh, you mean Buddy. *Sit* is the easiest command for a dog to learn. And Buddy seems very food responsive, so I think he will be a good candidate for training—with a lot of reinforcement, of course."

"Of course." Briggs still nodded in wonder. Then he looked around. "Will? Maybe you could fill up the watering can over there from the tap in the garage. We lost a bunch of water in the tussle."

"Sure, Dad." Will went to the back of the tent to get the can, and Buddy tried to follow. He stretched the lead tight, and it threatened to topple the table all over again. Will looked up, unsure what to do next.

"I'll stay close to Buddy, Will," Jessica volunteered. "I've got a few treats left in my pocket. That should keep him content while you get the water."

The boy nodded. "If you're sure?"

She winked. "No problem." And before Buddy could try to lurch away yet again, she pulled out another liver snack.

"You seem to have an endless supply," Briggs observed.

"Occupational hazard, I'm afraid. Some women wear expensive perfume. I, on the other hand, am covered in 'eau de liver treats.' What can I say? I'm a magnet for dogs." As if to prove her point, Buddy nudged his mouth toward her pants. "No, no," she reprimanded him. Buddy's ears wrapped tightly to the sides of his face. "Sit first, then treats." Jessica brought her closed fist to her chest. "Sit, Buddy. Sit."

The dog immediately obeyed.

"Good boy, but that's my last one," she warned in a soft voice.

"That's amazing the way he responds to you. I mean, he's afraid to get within three feet of me," Briggs said.

"Trust me, bribery works every time."

"I'll remember that." He stared at her with this dreamy smile that had Jessica grinning back in a way she was sure looked absolutely silly. Luckily he saved her from further embarrassment when he spoke up: "I've been meaning to say that I'm sorry about the phone call the other evening." (How quickly his irritation appeared to have vanished!)

She waved him off. "I wasn't exactly Ms. Congeniality." (How suddenly she managed to drop her initial scorn!)

"It's not a good excuse—I'd had a long day, and Buddy was the unexpected bonus that tipped me over the edge. Myrna told me to give the dog a chance—"

"Myrna's your wife?" Jessica didn't mean to be too obvious, but...

"No, my aunt. She lives with Buddy and me. Will's mom's not in the picture."

"Oh." An explanation but a mystery at the same time.

"Anyway, Will posted flyers and checked with the police concerning Buddy as you instructed."

"And no word about a missing dog?"

"Here's the water, Dad." Will came back, spilling water out of the watering can and down the side of one leg.

"Oh, thanks, son." Briggs filled the tall metal cans. "I was just telling Dr. Trombo how you put up notices but hadn't heard anything about a lost dog."

Will nodded and reached for Buddy's lead. The dog welcomed him back by dancing on his hind legs. "Yeah, so I'm going to bring him to obedience class Monday evening like you said to do. I saw from the website he's supposed to get his first shots before the class, so Aunt Myrna made an appointment for that morning."

Ah, the mysterious Aunt Myrna.

"That's great news. I look forward to seeing

you then." She smiled at Will before she went back to staring at Briggs.

He tipped the watering can to top off a bucket but kept his eyes focused on her. Only when the water started dribbling over the sides did he seem to realize he'd filled up the container. "Oops. I guess I got a little enthusiastic." His mouth stayed open, and then he blurted out, "Is there anything I can help you with, by the way?"

Jessica looked around, aware that a larger crowd had gathered around the booth, including Mrs. Horowitz—naturally, Mrs. Horowitz. She held several large branches of pink dogwoods, but her interest seemed to zero in on the conversation between Jessica and Briggs.

"Well, I was hoping to get some flowers for Betsy Pulaski-O'Malley," Jessica explained— for everyone's benefit. "She's just had a baby. Even so, she's been helping me out with stuff for my dad. But I can wait if you've got other customers first."

Mrs. Horowitz held up one hand, which held a killer of a purse—capable of coldcocking several pickpockets with one blow—and blocked anyone else from getting too close. "No, you go right ahead, Jessica. We can all wait." She gave a large wink, which had Jessica worried.

Briggs helped her choose a mixed bouquet of cherry blossoms, Russian sage and fiddlehead ferns. (She only learned the names because he informed her.)

"Let me know what Betsy thinks," he said as he rang up the purchase. He held out the bouquet. Jessica leaned forward, and the edge of the tissue paper surrounding the bundle kissed her cheek. "I'm always interested in feedback," he added.

A sigh arose behind her. Jessica turned. Mrs. Horowitz had her frosted nails pressed to her bottom lip. "Aren't we all," she murmured.

"Thanks," Jessica mumbled, completely embarrassed. "And…ah…well, I'll leave you to it. You seem to be a popular guy. Or rather, what I meant to say is that you have a popular stand—completely understandable given the quality and variety of your flowers." *Too much, too much, Jessica*, she chided herself as she turned to walk away.

"Wait," he called out.

She stopped.

"Here. These are for you." He held out a small bouquet of flowers tied with a lavender-colored ribbon. "For all your help with Buddy… and with Will." He glanced over his shoulder.

His son and the dog were involved in a bit of good-natured roughhousing.

"My pleasure," she said. Because it was. Truly. She examined the bouquet. "Forget-me-nots and violets, right?" She brought them to her nose and inhaled the gentlest of scents. "It's very thoughtful, but not necessary. I was just doing my job."

"I know it's not necessary. That's exactly the point," he said. "Sometimes it's just nice to get something pretty."

Jessica held her breath. It seemed that Briggs did, too.

And then Mrs. Horowitz clapped.

CHAPTER SIX

LATER THAT DAY, Laura held open the door to her gallery while Jessica mounted the steps with two takeout coffees in hand. "Dare I say you're the talk of the town?" she quipped.

Jessica wiped her feet on the cotton rug (hand-woven in Namibia) and took what she now considered to be "her" chair at the café table by the front picture window. After she'd dropped Pops at home for an afternoon nap, she'd decided to check in on Laura. "One decaf latte for you, and a double espresso for me." She set the cardboard cups on the table. "And I don't know what you're talking about. All I did was rattle a display table and spill some water from flowerpots."

"Is that what you call it?" Laura eyed her suspiciously over the rim of her cup. "Everybody and his little brother—"

"Meaning Mrs. Horowitz and Gloria Pulaski."

Laura nodded. "Among others. I won't name names, but they went into minute detail, gushing about the looks you two shared." Her eyebrows played a major role in the retelling.

"Looks? I don't know what you mean." Jessica pretended to be ignorant as she tried to dislodge the lid from her cup. She had never managed to drink through the little hole in takeaway lids without dribbling down her chin and on whatever light-colored outfit she happened to be wearing. Even after removing the lid, the coffee droplets around the edge of the cup found their way to her jean jacket. At least it was dark. "If you're talking about the fact that I happened to run into Briggs Longfellow... well, yes, I did meet him. But I spent more time interacting with his son, Will, and Buddy, their new dog—a patient by the way. So, really it was all very professional." She took a generous sip to keep herself from prattling further about such nonsense. The liquid scalded her tongue. That would teach her!

"I've never heard of flowers being part of a professional relationship." Laura leaned forward. She was not easily put off. She was worse than a bloodhound—but much cuter.

"If you're talking about the flowers I bought, they're for Betsy Pulaski-O'Malley—try saying that name three times fast, why don't you? Anyway, they're to congratulate her on the baby and say thanks for all her help with Pops—getting the transport chair and the name of an agency."

"Does that mean you found someone to help out?"

"Did I locate aides, yes. Was I successful? No. Pops is dead set against having help come to the house. Thank goodness Serafina, who's been cleaning my parents' house for years, is tolerant of his moods. So, at least the place isn't a total wreck."

"I'm sorry to hear about your dad, but you're getting off track here. I'm talking about *the* flowers."

"*The* flowers?"

"Please, playing dumb was never one of your strong suits. You know what flowers."

"Oh, you mean the flowers that Briggs gave me—the velvety violets and the most delicate forget-me-nots? They're positively charming… almost innocent, one might say."

"Might one?"

Jessica's gaze shifted to a mid-distance never land, and she barely managed to hold back a sigh. Briggs's bouquet of flowers made the long-stem bloodred roses that Roger had ordered online for her last birthday an insult. Then she snapped back to reality. "By the way, Briggs apologized about our initial phone con-

versation, which, as I told you before, was not
exactly sweetness and light. I mean, when was
the last time a guy actually apologized?"

"You're right." Laura nodded. "Except for
Phil, of course."

"Of course." Jessica wasn't yet sold on Phil.
She'd have to wait and see.

"And I'm sure Roger would have done the
same, correct?"

"Of course." Actually, Jessica couldn't remember the last time Roger had apologized, let
alone any time. But then Roger was not the sort
of guy who needed to apologize. He was such a
gentleman. He never blurted out anything inap-
propriate. But rather than praise Roger's com-
mendable traits, she found herself exclaiming:
"Why didn't you tell me that Briggs Longfellow
was such a hunk? Jeez, I practically drooled."

Laura bowed closer. "Incredible, right?" she
replied almost imperceptibly.

Jessica looked around the empty gallery.
"Why are we whispering?"

Laura sat back and sipped her coffee. "Good
question."

"So how come no one's managed to snap him
up? It's not like eligible bachelors are a dime a
dozen in Hopewell."

"From what I gather, he doesn't seem to have

been looking around for company—of any sort. And nobody's quite sure about his personal situation, or what the story is regarding the nonexistent mother of his kid. Is she an ex or something else? Did he say?"

"Give me a break! I only just met the man. We didn't share our professional profiles on LinkedIn, let alone deeply personal secrets. Besides, you're the one who's known him longer. And isn't Phil—*your* Phil—his good friend?"

"It's true. But Phil is useless when it comes to getting any gossip. Somehow it's this big secret, and for the life of me…"

"Well, it's going to stay a mystery. The most contact that we're likely to have is him dropping off and picking up Will from beginner dog-obedience classes. Hardly occasions to pry into what isn't my business to begin with. Look, I'm headed back to Chicago as soon as Pops is on his feet and functioning." She put up her hands in mock prayer. "Please, Pops, make an effort, for my sake."

"Okay, I know that Hopewell isn't your idea of heaven, but you can't leave just yet. Or at least, if you go, you have to promise to come back." Eyes wide, Laura stared at Jessica without blinking. She nodded vigorously, a blatant hint if ever there was one.

Jessica shrieked. (The second time in a few days, and more than she'd done in all her time in Chicago.) "Phil proposed, didn't he?"

Laura squealed back and shook her hands in the air in hallelujah fashion. Wisely, she had already placed her coffee on the table.

At that very moment, Mr. Mason walked by and appeared perplexed by all the commotion on the other side of the window. *Is everything all right?* he mouthed.

Laura got up and ran to the door. "Not to worry, Mr. Mason. We're just talking like girlfriends do."

"If you say so," Jessica heard him answer. She grinned. She wondered what kind of conversations he had with his bird, Bismol. Very serious ones, she was sure.

Laura rushed back and started talking a mile a minute—even faster than usual. "So, I told Phil about the baby the other night. Needless to say, he was over the moon and proposed then and there. He wants to look for a ring together, but on a teacher's salary I said that's the last thing we need to bother with. But then he called and said he found the perfect one. He's bringing it over soon."

Jessica took the last gulp of her now lukewarm coffee and stood up. "In which case, I should go. Leave you two to have your special moment."

"Absolutely not," Laura insisted. She shooed Jessica to sit again. "When I told Phil you were dropping by, he was so glad. He really wants to talk to you."

Jessica smiled tightly. Anything for her friend, but still.

And then, like something out of a French farce, the bell over the front door rang. No, it wasn't Phil but a couple from New York City who were on a weekend trip to Bucks County and had heard from friends how wonderful Laura's gallery was. They especially liked that she carried abstracts by contemporary female artists, not the usual bucolic landscapes of lambs gamboling among wildflowers and bumblebees. Or aged rock stars on velvet.

Laura took them in hand. "I can't tell you how excited I am to hear you say that. I have three women showcased in the current exhibit, but I also have some works on paper that are a preview of a show to come in a few weeks. I really shouldn't display them yet, but I'm happy to give you a sneak peek since you've come so far."

Jessica watched Laura guide the visitors around the space, impressed by her passion for the art and ability to convey that fervor to potential customers. Her business acumen was also apparent when she pivoted to works with a lower price point more in line with the clients' range.

"She's amazing at what she does, isn't she?" A male voice came from the vicinity of the door.

Jessica turned around to see who spoke. It'd been almost fifteen years since she'd seen him, but it was hard to forget Phil LaValle. For a start, the scar across his right cheek was a dead giveaway. He closed the door and stepped closer to Jessica. He still had the vestiges of a limp. Both it and the scar were byproducts of an accident in a jumping competition when he'd been fourteen. The pony had clipped a hay bale, somersaulted and landed on Phil. He had been the lucky one. The horse had needed to be euthanized.

"Laura told me you were in town." He offered his hand. "If you're okay with shaking, that is."

Jessica was surprised at his tentativeness. This Phil was different. And it wasn't just the extra twenty pounds and the shaved head. This Phil didn't act like the whole world owed him something.

"Jessica?" he asked again.

"Phil," she acknowledged as they shook. "I'm surprised you didn't call me Prudey, like in high school." That was unnecessary, but she was entitled to a childish moment or two.

He winced. "Ouch—not one of my finer moments. I can only say that I'm truly sorry, and I take full responsibility for my awful behavior. And I hope that I've learned a thing or two since then. I swear, I never meant it to get out of hand like it did."

"But when it did, how come you didn't come to my rescue?"

He shook his head. "I was a coward, I admit it. I wasn't brave like you, Jessica."

"I never considered myself brave. If anything, I always considered myself a poor also-ran to my superhero brother. That whole Prudey episode just made me sink further into myself."

"But you always acted like you didn't care."

"Precisely because I cared so much."

Phil nodded. "And you think you know someone…" He sighed. "Well, we can at least agree that neither of us understood each other as teenagers and that I treated you badly. I'm extremely sorry. It's taken me this long to try to get my head screwed on right. For that I can thank years of therapy and the love of a good woman—speaking of which, here she comes."

Laura was seeing the black-clad couple out the door. "Come back anytime. I'm glad you found a piece that you liked." She looked over at Jessica and Phil. "Oh, and before you leave, you might like to meet the artist's daughter. She's here with my fiancé." Laura led them to the café table.

"Jessica, I'd like you to meet Cecile and Jonathon. They just bought a work of your mother's."

Jessica held out her hand. "Nice to meet you."

"You must be so proud of your mother. What a master of color!" the woman gushed. "And to think she was cut down in her prime. We can't wait to hang this work in our apartment in Brooklyn." They chatted a few more minutes before leaving.

Jessica looked at Laura. "What was that? You sold a work by my mother?"

She pulled over a third chair but not before bending down to give Phil a kiss.

"Right, a watercolor. A view of the garden in your family's backyard. With the giant tree with the treehouse."

"Yeah, I remember the treehouse. It was our special gathering place."

"Before I ruined things," Phil qualified.

"Lots of things killed our treehouse days—puberty, family stuff, riding accidents," Laura argued.

"Don't soft peddle it, Laura." Phil reached for her hand. "I've already apologized to Jessica, not that she has any reason to accept it."

"Wait a minute." Jessica held up her hand. "Before there's any more true-confession time, I need to back up a moment. What's all this about you selling my mom's art? I never knew you represented her."

"I didn't."

"You mean that Pops let you have some pieces?"

"No, your brother, Drew. He sent me a portfolio of stuff he said your mom had given him. I think he's interested in putting together a scholarship in your mom's name at the Quaker school where she taught. He thought mounting a show of her work would be a way to raise money."

Jessica shook her head. "He's never said anything to me, and I'm pretty sure he hasn't brought up the matter with our dad. Have you seen the family house? It's practically a shrine to my mom."

"Weird family stuff never seems to stop," Laura said. "Not to change the subject—but to change the subject—I was really hoping you and my beloved could meet and let bygones be bygones."

Phil placed a light kiss onto his fiancée's cheek. "Jessica hasn't known me in years."

"Which means she doesn't know that you nursed me back to health after my appendix burst—"

"You did happen to collapse in front of me while I was jogging on the tow path."

"That you tutor underprivileged kids in the summer to help them get into college—"

"I'm not the only teacher. It's a program, and who wouldn't want to participate?"

"And you help support this little enterprise of mine." She waved her hands around.

"What do you mean? You just made a sale. And besides, I want you to be able to spend more time on your own art instead of selling other people's. I think of it as an investment—part of my own plan to retire early."

Jessica placed a circled thumb and forefinger in her mouth and whistled. The shrill noise stopped the ricocheting back and forth. "Listen, you two, I get the picture. You love him," she said to Laura. She shifted her gaze. "And you love her. And through whatever mysteries of fate—"

"Including a ruptured appendix," Laura reminded her.

"*Excuse me*. It's my turn to speak. Through whatever quirk of destiny, you have found each other again in adulthood and now appear to be a match made in heaven." She turned her full attention to Phil. "It's clear to me from our brief encounter that you are no longer my youthful treehouse gang member nor my teenage nemesis who, perhaps unwittingly, made my high school years a time of misery. But by all accounts, you've become someone of estimable character."

"You sound like you're giving a eulogy at a funeral," Laura commented, but she had a smile on her lips.

Jessica narrowed her eyes in mock disdain. "If I keep getting interrupted, enough time will pass that it might well be that occasion." She pointed a warning finger. "So, to get back to the present, I just want to say, who am I to hold a grudge? It all happened a long time ago, and I'm too tired taking care of my dad to try to remember why I shouldn't like you, Phil."

They both stared at her.

"That's the most I've ever heard you talk at one time," Laura said in amazement.

"Probably because that's the longest you ever

let anyone else talk without interrupting," Phil pointed out.

Laura punched him good-naturedly. He grabbed her fist and kissed her fingers. Putting her other hand to her heart, she pretended to swoon.

Jessica stuck out her lower lip and blew a puff of air. "Enough of this amorous silliness. And, Phil, just for the record, I accept your apology, okay?"

"See, I told you." Laura nodded in approval. "And now that that's settled." She grabbed Jessica's hand. She was a big hand-grabber, as was evident. "Tell me this means you'll help me with planning the wedding. *Ple-ease*. I can't think of anyone I'd rather have."

"What about your mom? Surely she wants to be involved."

"She and Dad moved to a fifty-five-plus community in Hilton Head two years ago. She's over the moon about everything, but frankly, I think she'd be relieved if I told her I was taking charge of the arrangements—along with your sensible input and excellent sense of organization." Laura flashed a toothy grin. "Pretty please with gumdrops on top?"

Jessica rolled her eyes. "Okay, enough. I'll

help you as long as I'm here, but I can't guarantee for how long."

Laura sat up straight and ran her hand along her floor-length cotton skirt. "I knew you'd come around. And I promise it won't be much work."

Famous last words, Jessica thought, but the newlyweds-to-be were already back to billing and cooing.

CHAPTER SEVEN

"BUDDY, WHAT A pleasure to see you again! And look, you've made another good friend," Jessica said when she entered the examining room. It was Monday morning, and Buddy was her first appointment. He was in for a general exam and to get a number of shots, just as Will had mentioned at the farmers' market. Jessica would have been lying if she hadn't hoped that Briggs could have taken the day off from work and brought in Buddy himself. A girl could only dream!

"Hello, Dr. Trombo, I'm Myrna Longfellow," the woman in the examination room spoke up. "I believe you already met my grand-nephew, Will, and his father, Briggs, my nephew."

"Yes, Ms. Longfellow—"

"Please, call me Myrna. Otherwise I feel like I'm here for a job application, and I'm way beyond convincing someone that I'm the perfect person to fetch coffee and tea for half the salary of a man."

Jessica laughed, but not too loudly. She didn't want to startle Buddy. He was crouched behind Myrna but had gained enough confidence to stick his head around one leg of her warm-up pants. Definitely an improvement. "Frankly, Myrna—and, please, call me Jessica—I'd say you seem more than capable of fulfilling the CEO's job at full pay plus a signing bonus." She watched Myrna dig into a little plastic bag and give Buddy a small morsel. The dog thumped his tail softly. "And Buddy seems to think so, too, which is high praise."

Myrna scratched the dog between the ears. "I'm old enough to know that bribery works. The whole house smells of me cooking chicken livers, but I figure it's worth it."

Jessica knelt down. "Absolutely. I saw Buddy on Saturday at the farmers' market, and he seems to be gradually adapting."

"He adores Will. Who wouldn't? But then I'm biased. Buddy still needs to get used to Briggs, but at least he doesn't cower in the corner every time Briggs comes into the room."

"Dogs, especially shelter or abandoned dogs, frequently have issues with men." Jessica took one of her own treats from her lab coat pocket. "I know it's not as tasty as your aunt Myrna's, but maybe this will do?" She offered it to Buddy on an outstretched open palm. He braved one, then two steps forward before taking the treat ever so gently. The glancing pressure was like a whisper. "Have you gotten any inquiries about lost dogs?"

Myrna shook her head. "So far, radio silence. But rather than continue to wait, we decided to begin the training classes."

"Yes, Will mentioned that. And it's good that you brought him in for a checkup and the usual inoculations."

"Obviously I don't know what, if any, he's had, and I thought I'd let you be the guide."

Jessica eyeballed the dog. His chart indicated that he'd already gained a pound, and it was evident. His coat was also shiny and brushed. "Good idea. We'll start him on a series of puppy shots today, and we'll give you a printout for your records. By the way, it looks like you gave him a bath. How did that go?"

Myrna chuckled. "I don't know who was wetter in the end—Briggs, Will or Buddy. Briggs insisted on filling the old horse trough by the side of the barn, but Buddy didn't want any part of it. In the end, Briggs stripped down to an undershirt and cargo shorts and carried the dog into the trough. Will soaped him down while Briggs held Buddy, and, let me tell you, his clothes were absolutely plastered to his body by the time they were done. I just wish I'd thought to take some photos." Myrna's eyes were bright with laughter.

Jessica could just imagine. She cleared her throat.

"As soon as Briggs let go, Buddy jumped out and shook off, spraying everyone within a mile. I couldn't stop howling. But then I had Buddy's bed waiting for him in the kitchen. I'd put treats on it, so he was more than happy to let me give him a good drying off with some bath towels. But wouldn't you know it? I forgot that they were Briggs's."

Jessica gave Buddy a belly rub. "I bet that didn't go down too well."

"That was the weird thing. I expected Briggs to object, but he seemed to take it in stride. Buddy's his first dog, and he's learning as well."

"Sounds like everybody got in on the experience. It kind of reminds me of helping my father take a shower the other day. Not only was he wearing swim trunks, but he was impossible about keeping the plastic garbage bag on his cast. You'd think I was torturing him."

"Oh, dear. I heard about your father's accident when I was at the wine shop."

"Mr. Portobello's?"

"Of course. But speaking of your father, couldn't you get an aide to help out?"

"You'd think, wouldn't you? I love my father to pieces, but he's as stubborn as they come. Even before I came in today, he told me yet again not to contact the healthcare agency."

Myrna shook her head. "It's difficult being incapacitated, especially for someone like your father who prides himself on his ability to do things for himself. It's a very common trait among older people, you know."

"You sound as if you speak from personal experience." Jessica wondered if she'd met Pops.

"I was a nurse, specializing in geriatric care." Myrna's reply was strictly professional.

"Then you must be a saint, that's all I can say. I'm ready to tear my hair out, and you'd think as a vet I'd have more patience with those in need. All I can say is it's a lot easier dealing with cantankerous four-legged beings than a grumpy old man."

Jessica stood up. "Speaking of which—not that anyone would ever call you cantankerous, Buddy. You're such a sweetie—let's get started on a more thorough exam, followed by a first course of shots. And if Buddy's still with you a few months from now, it'll be time for the next round. Meanwhile, I'll just get Joseph, our tech-

nician, to help out. Buddy may be a little sleepy
later today from the shots, but if there's a more
severe reaction, just give us a buzz. We're always happy to see patients like Buddy." And
because she could, she gave him an extra treat.
"So, you got everybody wet, right, fella? I like
that image."

Myrna smiled and didn't say anything.

JESSICA WAS DOING the attendance for the beginner dog-training class that evening and
had checked off boxer puppy Earl, bullmastiff Sheba and two dachshunds, Peanut Butter (with the yellow collar) and Jelly (with the
purple collar). Next up was Schnitzel, Robby
Bellona's miniature schnauzer. Robby offered
a hello and a foil-wrapped double portion of
stuffed cabbage from Nada.

They had made it this far without an incident.
True, Peanut Butter had taken an intense interest in Earl, but nothing that couldn't be fixed by
seating the owners farther apart in the clinic's
waiting room.

"And just to reassure everyone, Sheba is a
large dog, but she means well," Jessica informed
the humans.

Denise, the hair salon owner and Earl's "pet
parent," didn't seem entirely convinced. It was,

apparently, one thing to have Peanut Butter sniff enthusiastically at her dog's rear end and quite another to have Sheba tower over him.

"Maybe Mayor Park, Insu, you could keep Sheba by the water cooler for now until we all start our drills?" Jessica suggested. "And if Sheba gets a little excited, would you just sing? Anything will do. Nursery rhyme. Show tune. Christmas carol. That will calm her down right away. In fact, I'm sure we'd all be happy to join in. Certainly, the harness I've lent you should keep her from lurching."

She looked to the front door and checked her watch. "I thought we'd have another member joining us this evening, but I don't want to hold up the class any longer. So why don't we just begin."

Which was, of course, when the door opened.

"Will, good to see you could make it," Jessica announced as the boy stuck in his head.

"H-hi." He held on to the door and waited for Buddy to reluctantly follow him in. The dog had assumed his *I'm going to get as low to the ground as possible so nobody will notice me* posture.

"This is Buddy, everyone," Jessica said, making the introductions. "Buddy's a little shy, so we'll give him time before we attempt any people or dog hellos. Will, you can sit over in the chair next to Schnitzel." She pointed to the empty chair.

Robby waved his hand. "I'm Robby, Schnitzel's owner."

There was the sound of the door opening again. "Sorry we're late. I'm afraid it's my fault," came the voice behind her.

Jessica hesitated before turning back. "Mr. Longfellow—Briggs, I didn't realize that you were coming as well."

"I thought for the first class it'd be good to get an idea, even though Will's in charge," he explained. "Will, you can take the seat. I'll just stand in the back."

"Nonsense," Jessica responded. "There's room for everyone. Why don't you take my chair since I'll be up and about most of the time?" She picked her papers off the seat and started to move the folding chair.

Briggs hustled over. "Here, let me." He put his hand on the back next to hers.

"Really, it's no big deal." She fumbled. "I've already got it."

He looked at her. She looked at him. His hand didn't move. Neither did hers.

There was a cough from the class. Jessica glanced over and saw Robby looking amused.

She backed off. "Please, go ahead," she said to Briggs. "I don't think it takes two people to move a folding chair. This way I can distribute the handouts, and we'll all save time."

Robby sucked in his cheeks. "If you say so."

Jessica was definitely going to make him pay.

"So," she said when everyone had settled. "Welcome, beginner dogs and pet parents. I'm so glad you could join us. I'm Dr. Jessica Trombo. Please call me Jessica. Normally, my father, Dr. Norman Trombo, gives this class, but I'm substituting until he gets back on his feet."

"Nada says the stuffed cabbage is for Norman, by the way," Robby volunteered.

"That's very kind." She nodded. "The purpose of this class is to help you and your dog live happily together, and by learning certain trained behaviors you should be able to achieve this goal. Just remember that some dogs and some owners learn faster than others. It's not a competition. And as you can see from the handout, you and your dog will learn several important skills—the heeling position, a basic *sit-stay*, a right turn. And then the more advanced—leaving your dog, telling him to stay and finally come."

"I'm not sure if I can master all those, let alone Schnitzel," Robby joked.

"There're no winners and losers, Robby." She was being charitable. "Our goal is to assure happy coexistence." She swiveled back to the center of the group. "And just as important as the instruction itself is the motivation. Your dog must feel that interacting with you is fun. Dog training is about rewarding good behavior, not punishing bad behavior. A reward can be treats—lots of dogs are very food oriented. Right, Will?"

The boy, suddenly singled out, blushed. He nodded nervously. Briggs gave him a reassuring smile.

"Additional rewards can be pats or cuddles, especially around the ears. Still other dogs thrive on cooing voice interactions. I bet you coo at Earl, don't you, Denise?"

She agreed. "Especially after he's done his business, if you know what I mean."

Jessica noticed Briggs bite back a grin as she did the same. "I think we all do," she said. "But we have to be careful. Because dogs, like humans, sometimes do things because they want attention—and that attention can be good, like getting treats, or bad, such as yelling. I'm sure this never happens to any of your pets, but how do you think I should react if a dog happens to pee in the office?"

"You mean like the puddle over there?" Mayor Park pointed to a generous wet spot by the corner of the counter.

"Exactly. It's no big deal—accidents happen, and we don't want to call attention to whoever did it. Speaking of which, I'll just get some paper towels and disinfectant." She went behind the counter and reached for a roll of towels and one of the many bottles of spray cleaner.

Briggs rose. "I'll be happy to take care of it. I had plenty of experience when Will was a baby." His son instantly looked mortified and began nervously patting Buddy.

Jessica's gaze went from the father to the son to the dog before going back to the father. "You're sure?"

He took the paper towels. "I've got this, Jessica."

She nodded and went back to the class.

"So, the last thing I want to emphasize is that whatever lessons you take from this class, you really need to reinforce them at home—you *and* your dog. Learned behavior involves practice, practice, practice. I know you can all follow these directions—even you, Robby, despite the fact you and my brother never listened to me when I begged you to give me a ride home in high school."

Everyone laughed.

"Okay, let's start with the simplest learned behavior—*sit*. Any volunteers?" Jessica looked around. She saw Briggs look up from spraying the floor. "I tell you what. Will, why don't you and Buddy come to the middle of the group, and I'll use you two as guinea pigs. Then we'll all get to try. Sound good?"

She watched Will look over at his dad. Briggs winked and nodded at his son.

Jessica put her arm around the boy's slender shoulders. "I'll walk you and Buddy through the whole thing. And don't worry—you'll be great."

She took the leash from Will's limp fingers and guided the two of them to the middle of the circle. "Okay, Buddy, let's show your fellow classmates how it's done. Most important," she announced to everyone, "the treat!" She took a soft chew out of her pocket and held it up like a trophy.

Then she focused on Buddy. "What a good dog." She waved the treat in front of his nose. Buddy was forced to tear his nervous gaze from the floor tiles, and he stared at Jessica's hand. Now that she had his attention, she smiled and looked straight at him. "Buddy, sit." She bent her elbow and brought her hand with the treat to her chest.

Just like that, he sat. The class clapped.

"Good job, Buddy." She immediately rewarded him for obeying but also to distract him from the noise. She could see the dog starting to shake. "Now, Will, it's your turn." She handed him another treat. "Just get Buddy's attention with the treat. Then give the command firmly while you bring your hand to your chest. This way he'll have a visual cue in addition to your words."

"You're...you're sure?" he asked. "I don't know..."

"Never doubt the power of liver treats—especially with Buddy. We've got his number thanks to your aunt Myrna's tutelage." She passed the leash to Will and nodded.

The boy wet his lips. For a minute, Jessica wasn't sure he would do it. But then Will repeated the instructions just as she had demonstrated, and Buddy, good dog and liver-addicted hound that he was, obeyed at once.

Jessica exhaled. She hadn't realized that she'd been holding her breath the whole time. "What a good dog. Don't forget to praise Buddy and give him the treat. That was a lot to ask of him, and he rose to the occasion."

The class clapped and congratulated Will. His grin was enormous, his eyes shining with relief and pride.

Jessica glanced at Briggs. His expression was more excited than Will's. He shifted his gaze and caught Jessica's. *Thank you*, he said silently.

She nodded, followed by the sudden need to look away. "So, now that Will and Buddy have shown you how it's done, let's everyone have a go. Stand up, and I'll distribute the treats. If you'd like," she said to the dachshunds' owner, Alice, "I'll take Jelly while you work with Peanut Butter. And then we'll trade off."

Organized chaos ensued, with Jessica seemingly in multiple places at once.

That's great, Denise. But don't give Earl the treat until he sits.

Robby, you want to retrieve Schnitzel from the behind the counter?

Insu, Mayor Park, I think Sheba's getting a little anxious with all the commotion. That's why she's growling. Now's probably a good time to sing her a show tune like we discussed.

"I know the lyrics to all the songs from *The Lion King*," Denise volunteered. She was no competition for Joseph, but Sheba was soon sitting like a pro.

By the end of the hour, not only had the dogs had a workout but their owners were chatting and exchanging information and admiring each other's pets.

"Next class, I'll bring snacks," Denise offered, and everyone agreed they'd take turns.

Robby got Will's phone number in case he needed a dog sitter after he'd seen how the boy had retrieved Schnitzel when she'd run behind a desk and later crawled into a closet.

And Jessica couldn't help noticing that Alice Cane, who owned the local photocopying and printing store, had glued herself to Briggs, yakking away while interspersing coquettish grins and pats to his arm. She'd even done the classic gesture of repeatedly tucking her hair behind one ear. Talk about obvious.

Although Jessica couldn't help noticing that Briggs hadn't seemed to be objecting.

"MAYBE YOU AND Will would like to stop by the house this evening." Alice leaned into Briggs's shoulder. "You could meet my daughter, Candy— Candy Cane—cute, no? I think she must be about Will's age."

Briggs pulled back and smiled. "I'd love to, but it's a school night and we're both tied up—

Will with homework and me with grading papers. Maybe another time?"

"Oh, that would be wonderful. Why don't you give me your contact information, and I'll coordinate something." Denise rested her hand on his upper arm.

Briggs was barely listening. Instead, he watched Jessica as she gathered up her things. Robby was helping her fold the chairs and put them into the closet. He moved closer to her and said something that must have been amusing because she was laughing.

"Here, let me help," Briggs offered and joined them before Alice Cane could corral him further. There was something about the woman that rubbed him the wrong away, particularly how she insisted on grabbing him. He wasn't against touching per se, just unsolicited touching—jeez, this was a dog-training class and not a singles' pickup joint.

Jessica handed Briggs two of the chairs. "Oh, thanks—they go in the coat closet by the side door."

He hustled back after handing them off to Robby. "Anything else I can help with?" Briggs asked. The others in the class had already started to trickle out. Will was waiting outside with Buddy to see if he had any business to do before the car ride.

Jessica gathered up her folders and looked around. "I think that about does it. I just need to grab my bag from the office, turn out the lights and set the alarm."

"Why don't I wait for you?"

She blinked. "That's not necessary, but thanks. It's a little late by Hopewell standards."

Robby gave Briggs a knowing look and said his goodbyes. Briggs ignored him and waited for Jessica to close up shop. The parking lot was busy as other members of the class pulled out.

"Well, this is me," Jessica announced. She unlocked a Subaru wagon with the key fob. "And thanks for walking me to the car. I'm pretty sure I know my way home, so I can take it from here. If I'm not mistaken, Will's waiting to go, too."

Briggs glanced over. "Yeah, I see. By the way, I wanted to thank you for how you handled Will tonight."

She shrugged. "It was no big deal. Sometimes how to get over our fears is to just jump in and not give ourselves a chance to back out."

"That's true. But your tactic of getting him to participate was really supportive."

"I'm glad you think so. I don't know about

Will, but I'm afraid of failing all the time. Talking in front of a group of people is not one of my strengths. Put me in the middle of a pack of wild dogs, and I can confidently hold my own. But in front of a bunch of students? I hope I wasn't sweating bullets too obviously."

Briggs grinned. She looked genuinely anxious about doing a good job. "Not to worry. You had them eating out of your hand. If you wanted to see fear—you should have seen me when I first started teaching at the high school. I was a wreck. I kept having these dreams that I'd show up for class without my clothes on."

She was staring at him in a curious way. Then she cleared her throat. "That's a pretty typical anxiety dream, all right, but thanks for the kind words." She opened the driver's-side door and reached over to put her stuff on the passenger seat.

He held the door until she was seated.

She looked up.

"And sorry about being late tonight. I had to drop off my aunt first."

"Oh, yes, Myrna. I met her today when she brought in Buddy for his appointment. She seems like quite a person."

"Yeah, we're lucky to have her." He closed her door and watched her put on her seat belt.

She lowered her window. "Thanks again."

"No problem. I'll be seeing you soon then."

She gave him a tentative smile. "Sure, I'd like that." She started the engine, and Briggs watched her taillights until she took a right turn.

"You ready to go, then, Dad? I think Buddy is kind of tired after his big day and class and all. Didn't he do great? I couldn't believe what a super job he did. I can't wait to tell Aunt Myrna."

Briggs let his son prattle on as he unlocked their station wagon. Will was so excited about the evening, and Briggs didn't want to put a damper on his enthusiasm. But the truth of the matter was he couldn't stop replaying the conversation he'd just shared with Jessica.

"Are we going home, Dad?" Will interrupted his dad's reverie.

"Uh?" Briggs looked over. "Sure thing, Will— right after we pick up Aunt Myrna. And you guys did great this evening, by the way. I would have frozen on the spot if Dr. Trombo had asked me to go first." He started up the engine, put on the lights and took a right out of the lot.

"Jessica, Dad, *Jessica*. She told everybody to call her Jessica, not Dr. Trombo. Isn't that cool? Maybe she'd let me volunteer at the veterinary clinic. It might help with the science project I'm working on."

"Sure, that sounds like a good idea. But I'm not sure how long she's here for. You could always ask her dad when he gets better." He headed up the hill.

"I suppose so. But she's so easy to talk to, don't you think?"

Not for me, Briggs thought. He leaned forward to check the house numbers to make sure he didn't miss the driveway.

"There's the house where we dropped off Aunt Myrna, Dad. Just on the left." Will pointed.

"You're right, Will. Thanks for being my navigator." He pulled up the steep driveway and parked behind a car. "I'll just be a minute. Why don't you switch to the back seat with Buddy? That way your aunt can sit in the front."

"Sure thing." Will slipped out and opened the door to the back. "Aw, look—Buddy's sound asleep. He's all tired from his first day of school. I'll just give him a hug to let him know how great a job he did."

"Another good idea." Briggs watched the two snuggle close together. He walked to the front porch. He hadn't mounted the steps, let alone rung the doorbell, when footsteps reached him from behind.

Jessica stood there. Her keys were fisted in her hand. "Are you following me?"

"Yes, no—well, yes, in a way. I thought you knew."

"Knew what?"

"That I came to pick up my aunt Myrna."

"Your aunt Myrna?"

"Like I told you—we were late getting to class because I had to drop her off here first."

"Your aunt Myrna knows Pops?"

Jessica unlocked the front door. The sound of laughter drowned out the sound of a television.

She turned back to address Briggs. "It would appear so."

CHAPTER EIGHT

"Pops?" Jessica marched into the den.

"Aunt Myrna?" Briggs was close behind.

They both stood there, staring wide-eyed at their elders. Neither of them blinked. Jessica didn't bother to take off her jacket. Briggs hooked his thumbs into the waistband of his jeans and drummed his fingers on the denim.

"You kinda surprised me here, Pops."

"You think you could have informed Jessica about your visit beforehand, Aunt Myrna?"

Jessica and Briggs glanced at each other, silently sharing a series of emotions: confusion, amusement and finally the uncomfortable awkwardness that the younger generation had for its elders when they did something a little too personal.

Norman was sitting in his leather recliner. The chevron-patterned afghan, which Vivian Trombo had crocheted from remnants of psychedelic sweaters from the Swinging Sixties, was draped over his elevated legs. Myrna was stretched out on the couch, surrounded by a pile of faux-fur pillows. Vivian had acquired them at a yard sale.

Norman held a tumbler of dark liquid in one hand. Myrna's glass sat on a coaster on the coffee table. A plate of ball-shaped cookies sat in the center.

"I don't know why you're so upset, Briggs," Myrna remarked, all sweetness and light. "When you said you were going with Will to the training session, I had this sudden inspiration that it would be the perfect opportunity to stop by and see how Norman was doing. We were just watching *Some Like It Hot* on TV. We've both seen it a million times, but it is an absolutely fabulous movie. I haven't laughed so hard in a long time."

Briggs eyed her glass. "Not to be too prying, but it looks like you shared more than a movie."

She chuckled. "Somehow, I find your concern touching. And not that it's any of your business, but I happened to make bourbon balls today. It was only natural to bring some with me. And a little liquid accompaniment seemed appropriate. There're more cookies if you would like one." She waved her hand to the coffee table.

"No, thank you."

"I'm driving."

Each of their rejections had a veneer of politeness.

"So, you're old acquaintances, then, Pops?" Jessica asked.

"We first met at the town council meeting about widening Canal Road," he explained. "I didn't really know anything about Myrna, and she didn't realize I was a vet."

"Naturally, we were both against widening the road. Quality-of-life issue," Myrna added.

Norman looked at her. "And since then, I guess we've seen each other a couple of times at the supermarket."

Myrna nodded. "You're right. Senior Citizen Discount Day on Tuesdays. And it's only after your fall and this whole Buddy thing that I found out your last name, Norman. I mean, I had no idea Jessica was your daughter when she gave her number to Will that first day. How funny is that?" She sounded so innocent.

"Oh, you have to try those bourbon balls that Myrna made," Norman urged. "They're terrific. It's something to have real baked goods around the house."

"I'll take that as a statement of fact, Pops, and not criticism of my skills—which, I admit, would be justified," Jessica said, peering more closely at the sweets. "I gotta say they look pretty good."

"And while you were tied up tonight, Myrna was helping me with using the crutches. We even did a few stairs. She was a nurse, you know."

"Yes, she told me," Jessica said. "And I think it's great you have someone knowledgeable to help you. Maybe with all this progress, then, you'll be up to coming to the office soon?"

Norman folded back into his chair. "Not quite yet. I'm not ready to handle the animals—or their owners."

"Speaking of which, how did the class go?" Myrna asked.

"Pretty well for the first time," Jessica said.

"Jessica's being too modest," Briggs added. "She was fantastic. Everyone was totally engaged, and not only did we all learn something, we also had a good time. What more could you ask for?"

Norman and Myrna looked knowingly at each other. "What indeed?" replied Myrna.

There was a knock on the front door. Jessica went to answer and returned with Will.

"I got worried when you didn't come back to the car right away. It's…it's all right that I knocked?" Will asked.

Briggs strode over to his son. "Will, I'm so sorry. We got caught up talking to Aunt Myrna and Jessica's father. I should have let you know. By the way, Norman, this is my son, Will. Will, say hello to Dr. Trombo."

Will raised his hand haltingly. "Ni-ice to meet you, Dr. Trombo."

"And where's this dog of yours that Myrna was telling me about? Buddy?"

"He's…he's in the car sleeping. It was a long day for him. That was okay to leave him, right? I left the window down a little to make sure he had enough air but couldn't jump out."

"You did the right thing, son," Norman answered. "I can tell you're a natural with dogs. I bet Jessica could use your help around the office."

"Gee, that would be amazing! I was just saying to my dad about maybe helping out. You see, I've got this science project that I wanted to ask Jessica about."

"Of course! I'd be happy to assist if I can," she said. "And after I've gone back to Chicago, Pops can show you the ropes. He taught me everything about being a vet."

Briggs held up a hand. "You're more than generous in making the offer. But right now,

I think it's time to get Buddy home before he wakes up."

"Fair enough." Jessica picked up the ceramic plate that held the cookies. The dish had been a gift from one of her mother's students. "I'll just gather up the rest of the goodies. The container's in the kitchen, I presume?" She gave Briggs a knowing glance and cocked her head for him to follow.

"Please, leave some for yourself. And keep the plastic box if you want," Myrna offered.

"No need. We've got plenty." Jessica smiled and pushed Briggs in the direction of the kitchen. When they'd crossed the threshold, she turned around and whispered, "Can you believe the two of them in there? How come I never heard anything about these Senior Citizen Discount Day hookups?"

"I know what you mean. And bourbon balls? Myrna usually only makes them for the holidays."

Jessica removed a couple of cookies from the plate…and then took a few more just for good measure. *Real baked goods in the house*, Pops had said. Not exactly diplomatic, but who was she to pass up some excellent-looking sweets?

"You don't think something's going on between the two of them, do you?" Briggs asked.

"I don't even want to know. I've been determined to get my dad out of his current funk, and if this little get-together helps, maybe I shouldn't complain. But still. Really?" She made a face.

"Shh—keep it down. He might hear you."

"I doubt it. With the TV going and them cross-examining Will, I'm pretty sure they can't hear a thing."

"Oh, Jessica," her father called out, "I forgot to tell you, someone named Roger called. From Chicago. He said your cell was turned off so he called the home phone instead. I told him he could call later after the class."

Jessica secured the lid onto Myrna's container and pushed it at Briggs. She waved at him to follow her into the lounge. "Thanks, Pops, for taking the call. I'll get back to him. I'm sure there's no emergency."

"Oh, I didn't know. Something about work, perhaps?"

Jessica shook her head. "Nothing to do with work, but it's no big deal."

"In any case, I think that's our cue to leave," Briggs said.

Myrna hoisted herself from the couch. "I might have to join Buddy and make an early night of it." She arranged the cushions neatly across the back. "Norman, don't bother to get up. Jessica can see us out—can't you, dear?"

"Nonsense. Good manners are meant to be used," he replied. And with unexpected speed, he flipped the leg rest down, grabbed his crutches and hopped to a standing position. "See—I couldn't have done that without all your help."

Myrna grinned. There was a hint of a blush to her cheeks. "It was my pleasure."

Briggs and Jessica eyed each other suspiciously. Will looked around at everyone. "I'll take the cookies," he volunteered.

THEY SAID THEIR GOODBYES, and Briggs loaded everyone into the car.

"Hey, Aunt Myrna, can I have these cookies? They look delicious," Will said looking ever hopeful.

"No, Will," Briggs replied as he backed down the driveway. "They've got alcohol in them."

"Nonsense—the cooking burns off all the alcohol. It's just the flavor that's left," Myrna noted authoritatively.

"He doesn't need to develop a taste," Briggs retorted.

His aunt eyed him. "You seem a little tired. Must be the long day and evening." She paused.

"I just hope Jessica doesn't have to wait up too long for that phone call." She left the statement hanging.

He grunted and drove home in silence.

THE NEXT MORNING Jessica came down to the kitchen prepared to outwit Pops. She had decided that instant oatmeal was an acceptable compromise between his craving for Danish pastry and her desire to feed him granola with 2-percent milk.

But when she reached the kitchen table, she found him already digging a spoon into a bowl. She peered over, pulled back and then peered again. "Is that yogurt? Greek yogurt?"

He nodded and dug in. He made a face but not as bad as Jessica had anticipated. "And don't make any smart-alecky remarks, young lady," he said after swallowing. He plunged his spoon in again.

Jessica felt his forehead. "Strange—you don't appear to have a fever. So why are you voluntarily eating unsweetened Greek yogurt?" She went over to the counter and flicked on the switch to the coffee maker. Before she'd gone to bed, she had filled it with water and put in the ground beans. Would there ever come a time when she wasn't organized?

Norman smacked his lips. "I've had better, but I'll survive—especially since Myrna told me that putting a tablespoon of honey in it wasn't going to kill me."

Jessica started to reach for a mug and paused. "You talked to Myrna about breakfast?" She pulled down an oversize striped purple-and-orange one. She definitely needed the extra hit of caffeine.

He nodded. "Of course. She was a nurse. Who better to ask?"

Well, I'm a doctor—for animals it's true, but there's still a medical correlation, she wanted to say but didn't. It sounded whiney even to her ears.

"Anyway, she agreed with you that the yogurt was the healthier way to go."

Jessica poured herself a generous cup of coffee. "Thank you, Myrna," she said before bringing it over to the table. "I thought I might try calling the agency for an aide to come today since I'll be at the office again."

"That won't be necessary." He scraped the last of the yogurt from the bowl. "I don't mean to make you get up again, but could you pour me a cup?"

Jessica smiled and got him coffee. She didn't bother saying anything when he dumped in two heaping spoonfuls of sugar. "Maybe you'll actually like the person the agency will send?" She took her first sip, grateful for the jolt. To say last night had been a fitful sleep was putting it lightly. "You know, I really don't like the idea of leaving you by yourself for so long."

"I won't be alone—at least not for a couple of hours during the day. Myrna was nice enough to offer to stop by after she's finished doing errands. And she's happy to pick up groceries from time to time. You see, we're all set then. You'll have help for me at home, which will free you to look after the clinic. And who knows? Maybe Drew'll make an appearance. That would be a real treat."

He seemed to notice her colorful coffee mug for the first time. (Who could ignore it?) "Your mother's, right?" His smile faded.

Jessica nodded. "One of her favorites."

"Well, I guess you can't have everything."

She studied her father. He still looked like the Pops she'd always known—disheveled, balding hair, the same plaid pajamas and maroon flannel bathrobe with his initials on one lapel—a Christmas present from years ago. But this sadness was different. It hung on him like a weight around his neck—not a good look.

But it was more than a temporary sadness. Clearly he was lonely—bone-deep, soul-wrenchingly lonely. She was here with him now, but that wasn't the point. Ever the good girl, he could count on her to come when trouble called. But day-to-day she wasn't there. Neither was Drew. The fall and the pain and emotional stress of breaking his leg were good reasons for Pops to be low, but they were merely contributing factors, not the cause. Mom had died more than two years ago, but did grief function on a set timeline?

Jessica wasn't an expert on grieving, but she was pretty sure that no amount of tuna casseroles and well wishes from neighbors could heal the pain—the emotional pain—that he was feeling. Then again, maybe whatever was going on with Myrna could help. Jessica had made it her mission to get Pops out of his funk, but she had been thinking along the lines of getting him to take a pottery class at the local arts council or having morning coffee with "the boys." The last thing she had figured on was him having a relationship with Myrna. But was she jumping to conclusions that they were up to something?

Jessica needed to call Briggs and pick his brain on this matter. After all, it affected his life and his family as much as it had an impact on hers.

"Okay, Pops, I'll hold off on hiring Nurse Ratched for now, but let's keep an eye on your progress. And I say that as your daughter and a medical professional—even if you don't have a furry tail and bark. Well, come to think of it—you do bark now and then."

CHAPTER NINE

"So, Briggs, I've been meaning to ask you something." Phil LaValle caught up with Briggs in the teachers' room at Hopewell Central High School. The main brick building had been built in the 1940s and designed along classical architectural lines typical of WPA projects. Unfortunately, the expansion in the 1950s had lacked any flair whatsoever, although the boys' and girls' bathrooms were definitely bigger.

More recently, two additional wings had joined the mother ship. One wing was devoted to the performing arts, and the other, with bigger windows and better air-conditioning, housed science labs and a gymnasium.

Briggs was just about to make himself a single espresso. The fancy barista machine was a much-appreciated luxury that the PTA had sprung for after the school had achieved improved test scores for three years running. (A priority of a high school in rural suburbia.) He decided to change the request to a double and hit the start button again. To say he'd had a miserable night's sleep was putting it mildly. He passed on the sugar and instead took one of the shortbread cookies from the communal stash.

"What's up, Phil?" he responded. "And please don't tell me you've decided to run away to Hawaii and become a professional surfer. Because if that's your plan, I'm going to have a lot of explaining to do to Laura when she's stood up at the altar."

Phil shook his head. "Not a chance. If Laura ever found out I was even considering such a plan, she'd be on the first plane out of here and would break my hypothetical surfboard into teeny, tiny pieces. Then she'd probably set fire to the whole thing for good measure. Besides, we have a baby on the way, and I'm psyched. I suppose you heard?"

Briggs sipped his coffee and nodded. "Believe me, the whole town knows. Mr. Portobello was delivering a new-baby present of a bottle of wine to Betsy Pulaski-O'Malley and got all the news. Congratulations, by the way." They moved over to a small couch by the bulletin board.

"Thanks." Phil paused. "Let me just come out with it then." He was clearly nervousness. "I was hoping that you'd agree to be my best man. I don't have any brothers, let alone sisters, and you're the best friend I have."

Briggs slapped his friend's back with a good-natured swipe. "I'd be honored. That's amazing, seeing as I'm fairly new in town. Just let me know what you'd like me to do about wedding preparations and stuff like that—although I'm no expert."

"That's fantastic. Thank you so much." Phil breathed more easily. "We'd like to have the wedding in about four weeks, after school graduation. And, as you'd expect, Laura's running the show. So, I'm just here to take orders. But if I find myself having a mental meltdown in the middle of the night, I guess I know who to call. That's the job of a best man, right?"

Briggs held up a hand. "I really wouldn't know, never having been a best man—or a groom, for that matter." That last part just came out. Briggs rarely talked about his past, and the personal stuff—never.

Phil seemed taken aback. "Gee. I didn't realize... Not that you had to have been married... I mean, families come in all shapes and sizes."

Briggs drank the rest of his coffee in one gulp. "I guess there's still a secret remaining in Hopewell. But let's keep it that way, for my sake."

"Sure, sure. No problem." Phil waited a beat. "Anyway, Laura is meeting with Jessica today. You've met Jessica, I gather?"

"I presume Laura told you."

"Who else? So, Laura's going to ask Jessica to be her maid of honor, which will be great, seeing as they've been best friends since forever. And thank goodness Jessica has decided to forgive me for my mortal sins as a disgruntled teen."

"Now that's something I haven't heard about. Sounds like potential fodder for a best man's speech."

"Please, no. The less said about that matter the better. But just to bring you up to speed, when we were kids, the three of us—Laura, Jessica and me—were sworn buddies." He went briefly into the background. "Then high school happened—and not in a good way."

"It's sometimes the case. I'm not looking forward to Will entering that stage."

"Well, I know I've told you about the bad riding accident I had my freshman year." He made a vague gesture to the scar on his face.

Briggs nodded.

"That whole thing basically put a kybosh on my riding career, something my father could never deal with. I was convinced I was a total failure. I lashed out at the world in any way I could—including making life miserable for my friend Jessica."

"We've all done things we're not proud of," Briggs said. He knew the situation only too well.

"I know, but this was bad. So, was it any surprise then that she buried herself at her dad's vet clinic?" He shook his head. "But to make a long story short, she went off to Cornell for undergrad and vet school, only visiting from time to time. Once her mother died, she really cut ties with Hopewell. Even Laura got only the occasional email or text."

Briggs looked down at his coffee cup. There was a lot to digest in what Phil had just told him. It presented as many questions as it did answers. He looked at his friend. "But I'm sure you're going to make it up to her now."

"I'm going to try. We've already had a good talk, with me offering an enormous mea culpa. And being Jess, she accepted my apology. She's great." Phil seemed to perk up. "Anyway, with Jessica on the scene, the wedding plans should progress totally smoothly. For every pie-in-the-sky idea that Laura proposes—a big reason why I love her, by the way—Jessica will talk her down and make a spreadsheet of practical solutions."

"I would have thought that Jessica already has a lot to do, what with helping out at her dad's business and taking care of him. You sure she doesn't need more help?"

Phil shook his head. "She'll handle it fine. Even as a kid, Jessica was the one who kept her family together. But I'll let Laura know just in case."

Despite Phil's denials, Briggs thought Phil and Laura were asking a lot from their old friend, but he didn't say anything more. He figured he could always discreetly ask Jessica after a dog-obedience class. Somehow he'd started to assume that the classes would become part of his regular schedule.

Briggs felt his phone vibrate in his pocket. "Sorry. This could be Will."

Phil stood up. "Not to worry—take the call. I need to prepare for my AP Chem class anyway."

Briggs waved goodbye. He was already looking at the caller ID on his cell phone.

It was an unknown number.

"Hello?" he answered.

"Hi, Briggs. This is Jessica Trombo. I got your number off the registration sheet for the dog-training class—I hope you don't mind. And I'm sorry to bother you during the day, but do you have a minute to talk?"

He stood and looked out the bank of windows. The view wasn't anything spectacular—the teachers' parking lot and the playing fields beyond, but it was pleasantly familiar. "Is something wrong? Something to do with Will?"

"Will's doing fine with Buddy. He texted me earlier that he's going to stop by the office later this week, which is all great. No, it's another matter entirely. I'm calling about my dad and your aunt."

He switched his cell to the other hand. A group of students was just leaving the field, which meant the period was about to end. "My free period is about up, and I have to go teach my next class. But if it's something urgent…"

"Not urgent, really. It's just…I don't know… strange." She hesitated a moment. "Pops told me this morning that Myrna was planning on coming regularly to help him out. It's a very generous offer, especially because apparently she's adamant about not taking any money."

Briggs frowned. "I guess she's taken an interest, just trying to help."

"You think so? I mean, you don't think something else is going on? I don't know, like they're developing some kind of a relationship?"

"Relationship?"

"The thing is my father's been lonely ever since my mom died. He took her death badly, you see."

Briggs noticed Jessica hadn't said that it had been hard for the whole family.

"Now that he's met your aunt, I think he may be starting to come out of his doldrums. But I'm still worried, worried that he may be...I don't know...viewing Myrna's offer to help as something more than it is. I just don't want him to get hurt—he's pretty vulnerable, especially after his recent fall."

Briggs rubbed his forehead with an index finger. "I also don't want my aunt to get into something *she*'s not prepared for."

"So, what do you think we should do?"

"Do?"

"Do you think we should talk to them, either separately or together?"

"Whoa. They're both adults. Unless Myrna or your father asks for advice, I think this is something for them to work out on their own. Saying anything at this point would just be overreacting. And besides, I would find it extremely awkward to ask my aunt about her love life. I mean, is this a topic you'd bring up with your father?"

"Heavens, no. I'm just trying to do the right thing by my father—and your aunt."

"Are you sure? Maybe this is more of an issue for you than for them."

"Excuse me, I don't think any issues, which I may or may not have, have anything to do with this discussion." She didn't bother to conceal her indignation.

Briggs tried to explain. "Look, I don't like to butt into other people's affairs. Just like I haven't asked you about the phone call you got the other night—from Roger in Chicago? I figure that's none of my business." He winced. Where had that come from?

"You're right. It's not." She sounded offended. "But for the record, Roger is someone I'm fond of, possibly more than fond of. We just haven't managed to connect these days—one thing or another, what with the time difference and various obligations. But I'm sure we'll figure something out. And if we're on the subject of working something out, you'll notice that I haven't inquired if Alice Cane made any plans for the two of you to get together. She was putting some pretty obvious moves on you in class. Not that I'm being nosy."

The buzzer rang, signaling the end of the period. Briggs couldn't believe he was having this exchange. Just like high school! "I'm sorry, but I have to go and teach now. But I'll let you know if Myrna says anything to me about your father—which, frankly, I don't think she will." He rang off while she was saying goodbye.

And he realized as he raced out the door, he had never answered her about Alice Cane.

CHAPTER TEN

"So, I've made this file that I've called 'Laura's Wedding,'" Jessica announced as she opened her laptop. She and Laura had gathered that evening in Laura's apartment above the gallery.

Years ago, Laura's father had invested a modest amount of cash in the then dilapidated building. Since then, real estate prices in town had skyrocketed as the area had become desirable to young married professionals. Luckily, most families from the old days owned their properties, so they could still afford to live in Hopewell. For their children or grandchildren only time would tell.

The good news for Laura was that her parents showed no urge to sell. They charged her a reasonable rent that had risen only modestly despite the changing marketplace. Laura called the arrangement "Family Rent Control." She'd moved in after finishing art school and opened the gallery to supplement the meager income from her own art. Despite her seeming lack of business acumen, the place had thrived as she rode the wave of the new-moneyed inhabitants. Not that she lived a glamorous lifestyle, mind you. Her furniture still consisted of thrift-store finds and discount furniture. (Did absolutely everyone own a particle board bookcase?)

As if to prove the point, she and Jessica were sharing a lumpy, tumbledown couch covered with a faded Indian spread. A haphazard display of her art covered the walls, and a jumble of sports equipment (soccer balls, tennis rackets and skis) was clearly Phil's contribution to the decor. From the look of things, Jessica figured he had semi-moved in. But at that particular moment, he was nowhere in sight.

"Should we wait for Phil?" she asked. "It'd be good to get his input seeing as he's also a star player—not as much as the bride, of course, but still vital."

Laura chuckled and shook her head. She'd fashioned multiple hair clips and barrettes in her chin-length bob. Somehow on her it looked appropriately charming. "No, he's at school giving a review session for the AP Chemistry test coming up next weekend. Apparently the kids are panicking, but he'll calm them down. He's a good calmer. I can testify to that. Phil's a rock." She grabbed a handful of popcorn from the bowl on the coffee table and munched loudly. "Don't worry. I'll fill him in later, but just to be sensitive to his part in the proceedings, I think you should rename the file 'Laura and Phil's Wedding.'" She pointed emphatically at the screen.

Jessica corrected the title. "Good point, 'Laura and Phil's Wedding.' And you'll see that I've started to make a list of things that need to be addressed, starting with the obvious—" she pointed out the headings "—the date, time, place, how many people you want to attend as well as those participating in the wedding."

"Naturally, I want you to be my maid of honor. And Phil asked Briggs earlier today to be the best man. So at least two things are set. You will do it, right?"

"Of course," Jessica reassured her. "Even if I'm back in Chicago, I promise I'll be here for the wedding."

"What a relief." She fanned herself. "Then there's food, music and the officiant." Laura ticked off the topics with her fingers.

"Those are all fine—" Jessica typed away "—but before we get to those items, let's decide on the stuff I mentioned first."

Laura grabbed another handful of popcorn.

"Okay, from the top. The wedding is the first Saturday after school closing."

Jessica paused her tapping on the keyboard. "But that's only four weeks away."

"I know. Won't it be great? June—the start of summer but still cool enough. And the best news is Phil will be finished with grading exams and not yet involved in teaching summer school."

Jessica whistled. "All right. A little tight, but let's do it. We've got the when—now for the rest."

Laura quickly settled on the back garden behind the gallery, with overflow into the gallery, which could also serve as a backup in case of rain. Since it would only be a small affair—roughly forty people—the space should work perfectly.

She started to state the names of people she wanted to attend. "And by all means, include Roger."

"I'll be sure to let him know," Jessica said. If she and he ever connected, that is. Their ongoing game of telephone tag was becoming a bit of a joke.

Laura rattled on with the names of potential guests without bothering to take a breath, and Jessica entered the information as fast as she could. "Hold on, hold on. I think I've got everyone, but I may have missed one or two. Tell you what. Why don't I email you the list? You and Phil can go over it later and send me the final version. That way we can issue the invitations as soon as possible. You'll design them, I presume?"

"You betcha, I'll design them. Who better understands my aesthetic than me, right?"

Jessica nodded. "And the printer?"

Laura put a finger to her mouth. "That's right. A printer."

"How about Alice Cane? She's a student in my dog-training class, and I know she owns the print shop in town." Jessica congratulated herself. She could be an adult and not let her petty jealousy get in the way. It was that, wasn't it?

"Perfect. Why didn't I think of her?"

Jessica filled in that column. "Now, food."

"Easy. I've already got that one under control. My *nonna* absolutely insists on catering the wedding. I'll settle on the menu with her, but even she agrees that Nada Bellona should make the cake. You've bought her baked goods at the farmers' market, haven't you?"

Jessica looked up from the laptop. "Nada'll do a great job. And Nonna is a must. Just please tell her someone special would dearly love lasagna." She batted her eyelashes.

"Even if it's only a portion for one, I promise you'll get it."

They ran through more items—Denise (Earl the boxer's owner) and her staff at the salon would do hair and makeup. Jessica would talk to Wendy, the vet clinic's office manager, about her husband, Carl. He was the facilities manager at a local pharmaceutical company, and *organization* was practically his middle name. He would know about renting chairs, tables, linens, lighting and candles.

"I've used him for setting up show openings here at the gallery. He's reasonably priced and has excellent taste," Laura agreed. She reached for more popcorn. "Hey, how come I'm the only one eating?" She held up the bowl.

"It's hard to type and eat at the same time," Jessica protested, but she took a handful and placed it on the coffee table. "And as for music, what about Joseph from the vet clinic? He has a solid baritone."

Laura clapped. "Perfect! I know that he's also a member of the Hopewell Gay Men's Choir. And for a little instrumental accompaniment for the procession and recession..." Laura seemed stumped.

"Please, I have the answer, the only answer. Mrs. Horowitz! Hopewell's piano teacher extraordinaire!" Jessica ate some popcorn in triumph.

They both squealed. Which of course called for more popcorn.

"Okay, let's not forget. Who's officiating?" Jessica asked.

"Oh, that's easy. I asked the mayor."

Jessica nodded in approval. "Very classy. Insu Park, who, by the way, is the owner of Sheba, a really large bullmastiff." She held her arms out to show how large.

Laura studied her gesture. "He should probably leave Sheba at home."

"You're right. After all the dog-training sessions, Sheba could be the star of the show. But no one's stealing your thunder on my watch." She looked down at the list. "So, if I'm not mistaken, I think we've got a plan. I'm sure there'll be more to add, but for now, a little celebratory glass of wine for me and fizzy water for you?"

Laura stood up and stretched her legs. "Speaking of more to add, let's put down Mr. Portobello for the drinks—alcoholic and non."

Jessica reopened the laptop. "But of course," she said in a very bad French accent. "For tonight, though, I just happened to bring along a personal supply." She reached in her bag and brought out a bottle of sparkling water and another of sauvignon blanc. "Glasses?"

"No problem." Laura found two wineglasses. She was just handing them to Jessica when she stopped. "Hold on. We forgot a crucial detail."

Jessica scanned the spreadsheet. "Nothing comes to mind..."

"Flowers—don't forget the flowers. I'll have the rest of the decorations under control, but there's got to be flowers. Lots of flowers, lots of colors. And I know just who'd be perfect."

Jessica raised her eyebrows.

"Briggs. Have you seen his greenhouse and garden? They're amazing, just the look and feel that I want. And you're the one to ask him, seeing as you've bonded over dog training and stuff like that."

Jessica rested her fingers on the keyboard. "Actually, I may not be the best person to ask Briggs to supply the flowers."

Laura put up her hand. "Whoa, Nelly! What's going on? The whole town already has you two tying the knot—which, frankly, is taking away some of the deserved attention from *moi*!"

Jessica rubbed her mouth. "Well, if you really must know..."

"I must, I must."

"I called him earlier today about Pops and his aunt Myrna. They seemed to have developed some kind of relationship without letting either of us in on it. I mean, it's wonderful to have someone else to help out, but I just don't want to see Pops get hurt. He's still grieving from Mom's death, and I'd hate it if he got burned."

Laura curled up on the sofa. "And what did Briggs say?"

"He implied that it was none of our business. He also had the nerve to say that my concerns about Pops and Myrna might have more to do with my own issues."

"Not to take sides in the matter, but do you think that maybe he has a teeny, tiny point?" She turned her voice into a squeak for the last words.

"It's not like I don't want Pops to have company after Mom's death. I don't want him to be lonely—really, I don't."

"Are you sure?"

"What do you mean?"

Laura shimmied closer. "Think about it. You mom always seemed to be the social director of the family. Your father—well, he was supportive in his own way. After all, he did hire the carpenter to build the treehouse, which we all enjoyed. But given his druthers, you've gotta admit he always preferred being at the office treating animals rather than coming to our recitals or sporting events." Laura set down the glasses and unscrewed the wine bottle and the sparkling water, pouring a serving of each.

Jessica took her glass as Laura handed it over. "You're right, of course. Mom planned all the family get-togethers and holiday celebrations. Without her, things just kind of fell apart. There really wasn't any reason to come home—except in emergencies."

"All the more reason for you to be happy that your dad has someone who gets him doing things."

"I'm all in favor of him doing things. But I had imagined him joining a club or playing in a bocce league in the park."

"Aha! You *say* you want your dad 'out there'—" she made air quotation marks "—but what you're talking about is group activities, mostly with men. A clear sign that you, my dear, are afraid your dad will replace your mother with someone else and forget her. And if we're going down that path, the logical extension is that *you'll* forget her as well." Laura brought the glass of water to her lips and waited.

Jessica shook her head vehemently. "No, no,

no. This isn't about me. Please remember—I'm the responsible family member who's always supposed to be there for everyone else. My dad has a fall, and I rush home. My mom was diagnosed with breast cancer and had surgery and follow-up treatments. Who was the person who visited her in the hospital and helped her when she came home? Me, and I was only a freshman in high school. And when she died? I was the one who made the funeral arrangements 'cause Pops was so out of it. I was even there for Drew, the wunderkind of the family. Who drove my big brother around on his vacations from college when his license was suspended for too many speeding violations? Not Mom—she was teaching. Not Pops, either. He was seeing patients."

Laura put down her glass and reached to hold her friend's hand. "It's all right. I see where you're coming from. So, you're the one who takes care of everyone else. But maybe it's time you started to take care of yourself? Just a thought."

Jessica let her eyes wander as she pondered her friend's words. She took in Laura's art on the walls—the pointillist landscapes of the hills and trails around Hopewell, the intimate studies of the apartment that said as much about Laura as about her decorating skills and the generous but insightful portraits of the ones she loved— Phil, her mom and dad and even one of Jessica from high school. Wow, she was good. Jessica felt Laura had captured everyone's essence.

"Phil's right, Laura," she conceded. "You need to spend more time on your own art— not just promote other people's."

Laura wet her lips. "Okay, change the subject, why don't you. Still, don't think this is the last time we have this discussion. But as far as my art, thanks. I love owning a gallery and discovering new talent and fostering it. But I agree I need to get back to my own stuff. It's just that after all these years—years of rejection from dealers and getting shut out of contests—it's a scary thought."

"Which is why you shouldn't put it off. The longer you wait, the scarier it gets."

"You're right. And maybe I'm right, too. Do what's important for you. Talk to Briggs. Please. Because, in the end, what matters most?" Laura batted her eyes.

Jessica sighed. "I know. Your wedding. Okay. I'll talk to Briggs and ask him about doing the flowers. In fact, I know just how to approach him."

CHAPTER ELEVEN

STARTING ABOUT 3:30 P.M. on Friday, Jessica found herself repeatedly glancing at the large clock that ticked away in the back office of the veterinary clinic. Its round dial with Roman numerals and large black hands was like something out of a British murder mystery. She could imagine some mustachioed English constable watching the time as he waited for the local vicar to confess to killing the housekeeper or stealing money from the donation box—or whatever constables did in those types of books.

Jessica had never been a murder-mystery fan, either as a child or now as an adult. For birthdays, relatives had usually given her something like *Black Beauty* because of her love of animals. And while she'd had nothing against animal stories, she'd much preferred to escape the loneliness of her teenage years with the aid of swashbuckling novels—things like *The Count of Monte Cristo* or *The Three Musketeers*. When she'd read those stories, she'd felt completely transported from pokey Hopewell. And while she didn't live in Italy or France, she had made it to Chicago, not a bad alternative. It was a big city. It was different. But was it really what she was looking for? Coming back home had raised some interesting questions.

One thing Jessica was sure about, though, was the annoying *tick, tick, tick* of that clock. She pushed back her chair and scrambled onto the desk, determined to stop the darn thing.

There was a quiet knock on the door.

She looked over her shoulder to see Wendy enter with Will. She could've been mistaken, but it looked like he'd grown another few inches in the span of one week. And how was it possible for the boy to be looming and crouching behind the office manager at the same time?

"Will Longfellow is here, Jessica, about his project." Wendy looked up. "Something troubling you?"

"The noise from this thing is driving me crazy." She held the rounded sides of the clock and tried to peer behind it. "Unfortunately it seems to be hardwired." She hopped down and patted her hands. "Will, good to see you."

"I could...uh...come back later. If...if that's better for you." He rubbed the side of his forehead.

"Nonsense. Wendy, maybe you could call Robby Bellona? I know he's technically a plumber, but maybe he could help out or find someone who could deactivate this thing?"

"No problem. Enjoy." Wendy winked as she closed the door behind her.

"Will, why don't you have a seat and tell me about your project." Jessica indicated the office chair, and she perched on the edge of the desk. She balanced her hands on either side.

He looked at the seat and grimaced. "Are you sure you don't want the chair?"

She leaned over and patted the Naugahyde cushion. "Honestly, I'm tired of sitting. Better if I stand up."

Will lowered himself down. His hips were so narrow, he could have fit two of himself and then some.

"So?" she prompted again.

"So—" he looked at the linoleum floor tiles "—my science project is about nonverbal communication between humans and animals."

"Cool. What made you think of that topic?"

He slowly raised his gaze. "Well, in case you haven't noticed, I'm…uh…not a big talker."

Jessica waved off his apprehensions. "It's an overrated skill. Trust me, most people have nothing to say anyway. Better to say fewer, wiser words."

Will nodded, seemingly a little more at ease. At least he was now making eye contact. "I've already collected all this research—read articles and stuff online. But I was thinking it'd be good if I could do some actual research myself."

"What a good idea! Much more convincing. Are you going to focus on certain species and how they interact with humans?"

The boy considered her question. "Since I've gotten Buddy, I'm really interested in dogs and humans."

"Makes complete sense. How is Buddy, by the way? Are you still practicing *sit* and basic heeling, *forward* and *halt*?"

He nodded enthusiastically. "You should see how well he's doing. He even does *about turn* without too much prompting. But I think I need to vary it up. Otherwise, he starts anticipating that we're always going to turn in one direction and not the other."

Jessica jumped off the table and clapped. "There you have it. Even though Buddy can't talk, he's telling you that if you keep doing one thing, that's what he anticipates. When you communicate clearly and decisively, he'll know exactly what to do."

Jessica turned back to the desk and started searching through the drawers. "Here." She handed him a spiral notebook. "I want you to keep a proper log. Every time you interact with Buddy, whether it's with a formal training lesson or just playing around, see how you and he communicate. Write it down, noting the date and time and what the actions and responses are. And it might help to think about actions and reactions as an accumulation of steps, a kind of dance. Do you or he get the responses you desire immediately or after a while? What's the learning process like?"

She waggled her fingers. "Do you have a pen? Never mind—here's one." She pulled the ballpoint out of her twisted bun. Let loose, her long locks spilled against her shoulders while she paced. "And why not expand beyond how you interact with Buddy? You can also observe how other owners interact with their pets. Just make sure to get permission from the owners if you want to use their names." She stopped and pointed to the notebook. "Better write that down so you don't forget."

Will flipped open the pad and began scribbling. "I guess I could observe the class, too, right?" He was picking up on her enthusiasm.

"Exactly. You've got a range of dogs there, all with different personalities. So, that gives you a good sample size."

"I could even observe how Aunt Myrna and Dad communicate with Buddy." Will looked for approval. His pen was poised.

"Perfect. I can imagine that your aunt and Buddy have already developed some form of routine."

He nodded. "Aunt Myrna puts his treats in this pottery jar that sits on the hutch, and you should see the way Buddy lies in front of it. As soon as she turns around and sees him there, he sits up and wags his tail."

"I love it." Jessica laughed.

"Even Dad and Buddy have their routines."

"Really? I didn't think your dad was such a big fan of dogs."

"He claims he isn't, but that's not the case at all. It's just different between the two of them. You see, Buddy's more afraid of Dad—like the way he pulls back if Dad suddenly raises his hand, even if he's going to do something else."

Jessica shook her head. "Oh, dear. Someone— a man, probably—must have hurt him in the past."

"Yeah, that's what I figured. But I think they really want to be best friends. In the evening, after dinner, Buddy has learned that when my dad's finished grading papers or preparing a lesson that he usually goes to his greenhouse in the barn. Buddy can be fast asleep, but as soon as he hears Dad go to the kitchen door to put on his shoes, he comes and stands with his head pointed right at the door."

Jessica did her best not to smile at his running monologue.

"And Dad says something like, 'Aw, c'mon, it's time for *my* me time,'" Will continued, "but Buddy just stands there without moving. My dad makes a show of reluctantly getting the dog leash, and the two of them go out together. Buddy's so happy, he's wagging his tail, and when they walk, you should see the way the tips of his ears flap up and down. Look, I'll show you a video I took of them." He stood up and reached into his pocket, pulling out his cell phone.

Jessica watched the short clip. "That's so cute." And so unexpected. Especially the way Briggs pretended to be irritated before going on their companionable trot. "So, I guess Buddy comes back in after your father's settled in the barn?"

"No, that's the really weird part—Buddy stays with him in the barn the whole time. He sleeps there while my dad putters around. Dad even got Buddy what he calls 'Buddy's barn bed.' Then when it's time to leave, Dad just whistles and Buddy wakes up, and they come back inside."

Jessica was amazed. Shy dogs like Buddy usually took weeks, even months to open up. That he'd already bonded with Briggs showed there was something special about the dog— and the man. "I guess Buddy's truly part of the family."

Will put his phone away. "That's what Aunt Myrna says. She claims she'll fight anyone who tries to take him from us. Aunt Myrna can be very possessive."

Jessica knew who not to cross. "Listen, I think you've got a good idea of how to do some primary research. Why don't we talk about what you've put together after the second training session next week? I want to see notes, lots of notes—a real lab-results log."

She walked over to the office door and took the lab coat off the hook. "But in the meantime, I've got another idea. You mentioned wanting to help out. Fridays are when a volunteer from the high school usually comes to help Joseph by cleaning out cages, walking the dogs and socializing with the animals that are here after procedures. Maybe you can start pitching in, too? I've got appointments with patients now, but when you're done, I can drive you home. I know you said your dad is busy after school on Fridays—getting ready for the farmers' market. So, it might work out for all of us." She opened the door. "C'mon. I'll introduce you."

Will clicked the pen furiously. "I don't know. Someone from the high school? I'm…I'm sure they'll think I'm just…just in the way." He hung back, his shoulders stooped.

"Nonsense. We all have to start somewhere. And she's really nice, and I think only one year older than you."

Will visibly gulped. "She?"

"Yeah, Candy. Her name's Candy Cane."

JESSICA MADE THE introductions and left Will in Candy's capable hands.

"I know, isn't my name pathetic?" Candy rolled her eyes. "It was my mom's idea when I was born. She thought it sounded cute. Cute?" Candy was definitely not "cute." She had dyed purple hair shaved close to her skull on one side. She favored flannel shirts and loose jeans.

Candy opened a large cage and hooked a leash to the dog's collar. "This is Daisy. We need to get a stool sample as part of the tests before her hernia surgery tomorrow morning." Daisy was an overweight corgi whose stomach barely cleared the floor.

Will watched the dog reluctantly waddle after Candy as she led the way to the back door. "She doesn't look very happy. And…and…I don't think your name's so weird."

"Well, you're the only one, then. You wouldn't believe how people tease me. Everyone says that's what high school is all about—getting used to people being mean." Candy handed Will a metal pooper scooper. They walked down the sidewalk toward the little park with its Victorian bandstand.

"That's middle school, too," Will mumbled, "especially if you're a new kid."

"Yeah, we moved here just before I started middle school, after my parents got divorced. Now I live with my mom in a town house outside of town." She let Daisy sniff the daffodils. "Your dad teaches at the high school, right?"

Will nodded. "Yeah, it'll be kinda weird when I…uh…go there next year."

Candy shook her head. "Nah, it'll be cool. Everyone likes your dad. Don't get me wrong— he's tough but fair. And he respects students' opinions, doesn't try to indoctrinate you. You know what I mean?"

Will didn't, but he nodded anyway. He'd never heard other people talk about his dad, let alone praise him. It made him proud.

Daisy finally did her business, and Candy handed Will the lead. "Here, hold this, please." She used a scooper to pick up the poop. "We'll take this back to test."

Will was in awe of the way she was so matter-of-fact. Out of nowhere he blurted out, "I don't have a mom."

Candy stopped. Daisy panted and took the moment to sit down. "What do you mean? Are your parents divorced? Or did she die? I'm so sorry if that's the case. I didn't mean to be insensitive. It's just that, well...you know how people are curious. They especially like to gossip about their teachers."

Will rubbed the tip of his nose. "I just don't have one. She left us." He had never discussed this with anyone outside the family, but somehow it seemed okay now.

"Well, that sucks big time. Do you know who she is?"

Will shook his head. "It happened right before she and my dad graduated from high school.

They agreed to keep her identity a secret until I got older."

Candy mulled over the information. "I don't know what to say except that she was pretty young when she got pregnant. Not much older than me. I mean, if it had been me, I'd have been scared stiff."

Will had never thought of it that way. He studied Candy and couldn't imagine her being a mom.

"We should head back now," she said. "Just jiggle Daisy's leash. She'll get up and walk. She may look like a slug, but she's pretty well trained."

Will did as Candy suggested. Daisy angled her head as if to ask *Really?* but responded to the command. Will needed to add this to his notebook.

They followed the path out of the park. "Anyway, I bet if your mom had a chance to meet you now, she'd be really impressed," Candy assured him. "You're smart. You love animals, and Dr. Trombo—Jessica—thinks you're cool. What more do you want? Besides, moms aren't all they're cracked up to be. Take my mom. She's such a pain, always on the lookout for a man. It makes her seem kinda desperate. She even told me how great it was to meet your dad at the first dog-training session. I guess you were there, too, weren't you?"

"She was at the class?" Will squinted and tried to picture the other students. "Does she have a boxer or two dachshunds?"

"Dachshunds—Peanut Butter and Jelly. I named them—lame, I know—but I chose them 'cause they go together."

"I think the names totally fit."

"Really?" For the first time, Candy didn't seem so sure of herself.

They crossed the street and circled around to the back of the clinic. She opened the door.

"I'm never going to be like that," Candy declared.

"Like what?" Will looked her in the eye. Candy was so determined. And the same height as he was.

"I'm never going to be like my mom— worried about growing old alone. I'm going to go to grad school and do research on gorillas, like Dian Fossey. Then I'm going to live in the jungle and study how they interact with each other and the environment."

"You're going to be all by yourself?"

"Mostly. Some other scientists will probably

come and go, and there'll be guards to look out
for poachers."

"Wow, you're brave."

Will was in love. No doubt about it.

CHAPTER TWELVE

"AUNT MYRNA! Aunt Myrna, I'm home," Will announced as he rushed into the kitchen. He dumped his backpack onto the floor and slipped off his hoody. He missed the hook on the wall, and it fell on the ground.

Myrna was standing at the counter near the electric tea kettle. "Good to see you, too, Will. But excuse me—your jacket and backpack." She pointed in the direction of the boy's mess. The kettle whistled.

Will looked over his shoulder. "Oh, right. Sorry." He made a show of placing the backpack on the wooden side chair and hung up the hoody somewhat more carefully. The cuff of one sleeve dangled dangerously close to the floor. "Where's Buddy? I want to tell him I'm home. I bet he missed me, seeing as I was gone all day." He hollered and clapped his hands.

"He's with your father in the barn. I'm surprised he didn't hear the tea kettle. Usually that's his cue to come running for a treat."

"I'll go find him and let him know." Without bothering with his jacket, he raced back outside.

"Door!" Myrna called out, but it was too late. She walked around to shut it. Which was when she saw that not only had Will forgotten to close the door, he'd neglected to mention there was also someone else standing there now. "Why, Dr. Trombo, Jessica, come in, please. I was just making myself a cup of tea, and I'd be happy to make one for you, too."

Jessica stepped inside. "No, thanks. I'll be heading home to check on Pops. I only followed Will to the house after dropping him off because Laura asked me to talk to Briggs about doing the flowers for her wedding. Also, I should have said something earlier, but I wanted to thank you for helping out with my father. I really appreciate it. It hasn't been easy for him." Being grateful didn't make Jessica feel any better toward Myrna.

"Or easy for you, I bet." Myrna ran one hand down the side of her denim skirt. She didn't look any less awkward than Jessica felt.

"Well, family is family. You do what you have to do."

Myrna nodded. "You know, don't you, that

I'm only trying to help. Your father's a lovely man. I'm simply aiming to be a good neighbor."

"As long as he understands that's what you're offering." Jessica thought about saying something else, but she bit her tongue. "In any case, I won't keep you. The greenhouse—I presume it's nearby?"

Myrna offered a half smile. "Yes, it's attached to the red barn at the side of the driveway. And before I forget, thank you so much for all you're doing for Will, and I don't just mean helping him learn how to take care of Buddy."

"It's a pleasure. Will's great."

"Not everyone recognizes that because he's terribly shy."

"Not unusual for teenagers."

"No, he's always been that way. We've done everything we could—seeing therapists and trying to get him involved with different things. But it's hard. I know it troubles Briggs terribly. He just wishes he could make all of Will's problems go away."

"As any parent would, I'm sure."

"Yes, I suppose you're right. But it's a little more complicated. Briggs's parents died in a car crash when he was just about Will's age, and I never had kids of my own—except for taking care of Briggs. So, the two of us learned on the fly, so to speak."

Jessica hadn't expected this admission of vulnerability. Not from Myrna, someone who emanated confidence.

But that moment quickly passed when Myrna changed the subject. "As to Buddy, the effect he's had on Will and on all of us is remarkable."

"That kind of bond is always special. That's why I became a vet. Any animal, especially an abused one, needs patience, discipline and love—so much love."

Myrna nodded. "Funny, that bit about love— that's just what Will told us the first night Buddy was with us. The poor thing was hiding behind doors and under the table. He was reluctant even to come out to eat, and if we offered him a treat, he would run to a corner of the house and hide it, like a secret hoard. It was so sad. But now he eats with us and takes treats. He even tries not to wince when I go to pet him. You can see him working so hard to overcome his baked-in fears and learn to trust us. It makes you wonder why people do such cruel things to animals."

"Like Will said, animals demand love, and some people aren't capable of giving it," Jessica said.

They stood in thoughtful silence until she pointed to the kettle. "I should let you make your tea. It shouldn't be hard to spot a red barn."

IT WASN'T. BESIDES, she could have found it from the ruckus.

Jessica knocked on the double doors, not expecting anyone to hear given the noisy laughter. She grabbed the handle and shoved aside one door. She could only stare.

If someone had told her that after so short a time, she'd see a stray dog who'd been afraid of human contact, a shy boy who could barely get out a word let alone a full sentence and a grown man who found it an imposition to grunt on the phone—that all three of them would be holding hands (though, granted, in the case of the dog, it was front paws), dancing a jig and squealing (there was no other way to describe the sound), well…she would have said, *Not a chance*.

But there they were. Buddy was hopping and skipping on his back legs. His tongue was hanging out, and his eyes were bright. Will, barely able to keep from tripping over his untied shoelaces, had a wide grin on his face and was calling out, "Good boy, Buddy. That's a great happy dance." And Briggs. Yes, Briggs was there, gliding along, chuckling and sighing all at once. His gaze darted between the boy's ebullient face and the dog's merry leaps. The whole scene was a picture of what? Joy? Freedom?

Love, thought Jessica. Definitely love.

The spell was only broken when Will stumbled over his own feet and brought the three of them crashing down. He landed on his butt, and Buddy sprang to the side before bouncing back to lick him. The dog must have thought the tumble was all part of the game.

And meanwhile, Briggs wobbled to his feet. "You guys have tuckered me out." He bent over, his hands on his knees.

Then he looked up and saw Jessica. He stood up straight.

She tamped down her own laughter. "Don't let me stop you," she said.

Will gave her a low wave. "Hi, Jessica. Buddy was just demonstrating his new trick, the Buddy Dance. It was the first time we showed it to Dad." The boy's face was red with exertion, his T-shirt sweaty in that ripe, teenage-boy way. He beamed at the dog. "You were awesome, Buddy. Sit." Will brought his fist to his chest as he gave the command.

Buddy sat down immediately and thumped his tail on the concrete floor.

"Look at you, Buddy, look how far you've come," Jessica praised the dog.

Will checked his pockets. "Oh, no, I don't have a treat for him."

"Not to worry. I've got some." Jessica burrowed in a pocket and produced a liver snack. She knelt down and held her palm out. "Here, Buddy—this is for you." The dog couldn't resist.

"You've got the knack," Briggs said.

Jessica looked up. "I've had lots of practice. And my treats are first class." She and Briggs stared into each other's eyes for a moment. More than a moment.

Briggs clapped his hands. "Okay, fun time's over. Why don't you take Buddy in the house, Will? Aunt Myrna will be wondering what's going on, and you know she needs to be kept abreast of everything."

"E-v-verything," the boy echoed.

"And I need to get my flowers in order for tomorrow's market, or the stall will be empty. And if that happens, I'll get this urgent phone call from Gloria Pulaski wondering where I am."

Jessica raised an eyebrow as she stood. "Gloria?"

"Yeah, she runs the market," Briggs responded.

Will took the dog leash from the table and clipped it to Buddy's collar. "C'mon, boy. It's

Aunt Myrna's turn to make a fuss over you. You want to see Aunt Myrna?"

At the sound of her name, Buddy tugged Will to the door.

Jessica watched them head outside and shook her head. "We'll have to work on loose-leash walking at the next class, I see." She turned back to Briggs. "It's like he's already part of the family—Buddy, I mean."

Briggs nodded and waited for Will to slide the door shut. "Don't tell him, but I let the police know that unless some sweet old lady calls saying she's lost a dog, we've decided to keep Buddy. And even then, I'm willing to arm wrestle her into submission."

"Quite a change."

"In Buddy? For sure."

"Not just Buddy."

There was another silence while the two of them avoided looking at each other.

"I actually wanted to talk to you about something else," Jessica announced. She took a few steps forward and glanced around the neatly organized tools, the spacious workbench and jars of seeds lining the shelves. She inhaled the earthy smells of compost and potting soil. Toward the far end she saw the opening to the greenhouse with rows of tables, seedlings and overhanging grow lights. "This is quite a setup you've got," she said.

"Yup, this is my folly." He guided her through the different areas. "Obviously, here's where I work on planting and potting as well as storing things from previous seasons." He pointed to the seeds and bunches of flowers hanging from the rafters.

"You sell dried flowers, too?"

"Sometimes, or sometimes I mix them with fresh ones. I like to combine the textures. It's not like I have any real training other than reading gardening manuals and scouring the internet. And over here—" he guided her to the greenhouse "—is where I start the annuals and tender perennials from seed or corms, the bulblike tubers. When the temperature and timing is right, I transplant them outside. Of course, the perennials stay outside all year."

"Of course." His explanations far exceeded Jessica's gardening knowledge. Oh, her mother had roped her into weeding and planting bulbs, but Jessica simply hadn't been born with a green thumb.

She peered through the glass of the greenhouse. Outside to the left, there were stands of flowering trees, including dogwoods, rhododendrons and cherry trees. She thought she spotted flowering quince, but she couldn't be sure. Straight back was a hedge of hydrangeas and azaleas. The shrubs outlined multiple furrowed rows. Some of the rows had blooming flowers, and Jessica recognized the muted hues of columbines and Lenten roses. Other rows were covered by plastic tunnels that sheltered burgeoning plants.

Jessica pivoted back to the barn. "Gee, that's quite an operation. Were you always into farming?"

Briggs shook his head. "Not at all. I'm born and bred in Philly. Growing things was this fantasy I had of what it'd be like moving to the country." He waved off her anticipated response. "I know, I know, the clichéd dream of a city boy. And I quickly learned there's no such thing as a part-time farmer, so I cut back my ambitions to mere gardening—my kind of gardening, which means growing flowers and flowering trees. I don't know what it is, but I found there's something special about producing things that don't serve any purpose except to add beauty to life and relieve the daily drudgery."

She shook her head. "I didn't expect such a romantic view."

"It's not all romance, trust me. But the analytical part has a real appeal, too. You get into planning—like buying the equipment, the seeds and the stock. Then there's the whole problem of blooming cycles and how to extend them over as long a time as possible. You learn a lot because the plants teach you so much."

"That last part I can understand. It's one of the reasons being around animals is so rewarding. In middle school and high school, I had this German shepherd. I named her Zebra because she had this stripe down her forehead." Jessica mimicked the placement on her own face. "Zebra was the best company ever. She let me hug her all the time. I loved the feel of her fur, especially on her ears, and the smell of the pads of her feet—this strangely comforting aroma of dust and something like Corn Flakes. It was the best. Made me forget all the stupidness of teenage years."

Briggs straightened a shovel. "Not that I was prying, but Phil happened to mention that he'd made your life miserable back in those days. He said that he wasn't sure you'd ever forgive him for the way he acted, and he's felt terrible about it ever since."

She was surprised that Phil had confided to Briggs. Or was she? Jessica was beginning to think of Briggs as the type of person you—

meaning *she*—could confide in. "We both should have gotten over it a long time ago." She dismissed what had once seemed such a traumatic event with a shake of her hand. "When he spoke to me about that, and when I saw his love for Laura, I knew it was time to let bygones be bygones. Not that it was easy. What he did was harsh, but he was a kid, a troubled kid. I like to think that I did the right thing now."

Then she laughed. "You know, it's funny. I have no trouble forgiving animals for behaving badly, but I needed to learn how to forgive humans. I know it's not exactly the same, but when Zebra was a puppy, she used to take my slippers to sleep with. I'd retrieve them, and they'd be all slobbery, totally icky. A real pain. But I forgave her because I knew she loved me because she only took *my* slippers, nobody else's."

"So, do you think Phil picked on you in high school because deep down he actually respected you? He thought you were strong enough for it not to bother you?" Briggs asked.

"That's a theory, but I'm certainly no psychologist. In any case, it did hurt me. But not anymore. We all move on. Even Zebra." Jessica smiled in thought. "By the time she grew up, she'd stopped stealing my slippers, but sometimes I'd still put one next to her while she was sleeping for old times' sake. I knew she liked the smell. I could watch her like that for hours. It was better than TV. And that's the kind of memory I prefer to keep."

"I know exactly what you mean about finding contentment in the weirdest things," Briggs said with genuine enthusiasm. "I can walk around the greenhouse every morning before work and get completely mesmerized. I know it's silly, but there're times it almost breaks my heart to cut the flowers to sell them. I want them to stay like that forever even though I know they'll just die."

A kindred spirit, Jessica understood. "It's not silly. You want what you love to last forever, even though you know that it can't, like my Zebra." She blew out a slow breath. "In the end, when she wasn't able to get up on her own, I knew it was my turn to show her how much I loved her, too. So, I hugged her, as tightly as ever, and let Pops put her down." Jessica rubbed away tears that were more than a remembrance.

"I'm sorry you had to do that," he said softly.

"Me, too. But you do the right thing for the ones you love." She hadn't confided that story to anyone. Not even Laura. But she wasn't sorry she'd done so with him.

She sniffed. Time to change the subject. "So, when did you decide to sell flowers at the Saturday market?"

"Oh, I can't claim any credit for that. It got so I was growing more than Myrna had vases for. After that, I started giving away bunches to friends and people at work."

Jessica smiled. She was coming to realize that stern Briggs Longfellow was a softy at heart.

"Then one day I was bringing flowers to a fellow teacher who'd landed in the hospital. Gall bladder surgery, I think it was. And the woman at the front desk—"

"Betsy Pulaski-O'Malley."

"Exactly! Anyway, she asked me where I got the flowers, and I told her I grew them. Then she said her mom—"

"Gloria."

He pointed at Jessica. "Bingo! She said her mom, Gloria Pulaski, ran the farmers' market and she was sure she would love to have a flower stand. Before you know it, Gloria called me, and I reluctantly said yes."

"As far as I know, no one has ever said no to Gloria," Jessica consoled him.

"I had no idea what I was getting into— stuff like obtaining a Tax ID Number and insurance, making a display and signs, getting a tent and benches, all the pricing, labeling, arranging bouquets, loading up everything and transporting it. I'm sure I've forgotten half of what's involved. It turns out the Fridays before are actually more work than the market itself." He exhaled. "Luckily, I knew my customer base, having lived in Hopewell for a year already. I had a good idea which varieties to grow and sell, though I like to mix things up now and then and surprise people—and myself. Sometimes it works, sometimes, well… not so much. You learn pretty quickly, let me tell you." He laughed.

Jessica stood next to the large worktable. Tall metal flower cans were lined up in rows. Some held masses of flowers. Others just water. Various sizes of scissors and secateurs were strewn about. A large roll of brown paper was affixed to the end of the table. A staple gun was at the ready.

"Well, I can see you're busy, so I won't keep you long. And it's time I got to the real purpose of my visit," she said. "You see, Laura wants me to ask you if you would be willing to do the flowers for her and Phil's wedding. I know it's a lot to ask and all."

"And she sent you instead of asking herself?

194 VET TO THE RESCUE

That doesn't sound like Laura." He tipped his head and arched his eyebrows.

"I know what you mean. But she somehow thinks we may be closer, or I don't know what. That was until I told her I kind of lost it over the phone with you the other day. About which I am truly sorry."

He waved her off. "Not to worry. You asked my opinion, and I gave it. We don't have to agree."

"Well, Laura gave me her opinion, too. And she seems to be in your camp that the problem is more *my* issue than Pops and Myrna's." She waved her hands willy-nilly in a gesture of frustration.

"I think we all have issues, one way or another. I guess it's a question of how we deal with them. Sometimes I feel really good about how I'm handling life, totally in control. I tell myself what a great job I'm doing—though I think Myrna might disagree." He rolled his eyes. "And there're other days when I question just about every decision I've made and wonder why I seem to be screwing things up for me or Will or Myrna."

Jessica couldn't imagine Briggs doing anything that would consciously jeopardize his family. "Don't worry. Buddy will keep you on the straight and narrow. He has his priorities—you're put on Earth to take care of him first."

"And don't forget the liver snacks."

"See, he's already trained you. But now I've really gotta get going. I promised Pops I'd order pizza, and he doesn't like to have to wait for his pepperoni and mushrooms. I try to tell Conte's Pizzeria to load up on the mushrooms and go easy on the pepperoni," she said, referring to the local pizza joint. "I'm trying to keep his cholesterol down, you see. But somehow Pops must have a direct pipeline to the chef because they never seem to get my message."

"Wouldn't it be easier to cook for him?" He joined in her laughter.

"Not if you knew my cooking." Jessica reached out to the sliding door.

"Here, let me," Briggs offered. "It can stick sometimes."

Their hands reached for the handle at the same moment. Hers touched on cold steel. His found the back of hers, and she felt the warmth of his calloused fingers. Her breath caught. They stood like that for a count of one, two beats. And then they both nervously withdrew.

"I'll do it." Briggs grabbed the handle and slid the door open. It screeched along the metal runner. "That really needs oiling."

He stared at the track and pursed his lips before raising his face. "Let me think about it—the flowers for Laura, that is. I'm flattered, of course, but I'm not sure that I can do her justice with the type of part-time operation I've got going."

Jessica sidestepped out the door. "No problem. Just let me know. In the meantime, I'll be seeing you at the training classes, I guess." She walked along the gravel driveway.

"Jessica?" he called out.

She turned. "Yes?"

"Will you be at the farmers' market tomorrow? Myrna said something about how she was going to bring your dad."

Again, news to her.

"I've got a surgery first thing in the morning. But I'll try to stop by afterward. Why?"

"Because by then I'll have the answer."

The issue was, to what question?

Just then, her phone vibrated, and she checked the caller ID—Roger. *Later*, Jessica told herself. *I'll see to the call later.*

CHAPTER THIRTEEN

THE NEXT MORNING Daisy the corgi was still groggy after her hernia surgery, but the procedure had gone without a hitch. After monitoring her vitals and administering IV fluids and pain medicine, Joseph put her in a spacious cage with a cozy warm blanket.

"You can leave her with me now if you want," he offered Jessica.

"That'd be great. I was hoping to make a quick trip to the farmers' market, but I'll stop back later in the afternoon to check on her. If everything continues to go well, she should be able to go home tomorrow, possibly tonight. But if it is tomorrow, I don't mind coming in even though it's a Sunday. I know her owners would love to have her home as quickly as possible. In any case, I'll just give them a buzz and relay the good news."

Normally, her dad's practice was closed on Sunday, and back in Chicago at her larger clinic, a Sunday pickup would have meant a surcharge to the customer. Jessica understood having such a policy compensated for paying overtime. But here in Hopewell, where Pops's practice catered to a small community, it didn't seem such a big deal to accommodate, especially when it reassured both the pet and the owner. It actually made her feel good that she could do so. Who would have thought that practicing veterinary medicine in dinky little Hopewell would have advantages over the state-of-the-art facilities in Chicago?

Looked like there were a number of things about Hopewell that were surprising.

"HEY, I DIDN'T expect to see you here."

Will turned around. He gave a nervous little wave. "Oh, hi, Candy. I'm…ah…I'm helping my dad with his flower stall."

Will had come early to the farmers' market to set up the tent. Briggs had squeezed him and Buddy into the station wagon along with all the stand's paraphernalia. Aunt Myrna and Norman Trombo planned to come later in his aunt's car.

Candy hopped off her mountain bike and walked closer to where Will was holding one tent pole.

"That's the last one, and the sandbag ought to keep the tent from moving if there's any wind,"

Briggs announced after placing the weight on the base of the pole. "You can let go now." He glanced up and spotted Candy. "Oh, hello there. I'm Will's dad, Briggs Longfellow." He held out his hand.

She reached over and gave him a firm handshake. "Candy. Candy Cane. We haven't met, but I know who you are because I'm a freshman at the high school. And I think you met my mom and our dogs at the training class— Peanut Butter and Jelly?"

"Right, the dachshunds. Nice dogs." Briggs didn't mention her mother. "I didn't know you two kids knew each other." He raised his eyebrows at his son.

"It's not like we really know each other." Will's face had turned red.

"I help out at the vet's office. Will and I met there the other day," Candy informed him.

"We walked Daisy," Will offered, "but you don't know her. She's a dog, a corgi."

"Oh." Briggs nodded like he understood completely. "Did Will tell you about his dog? Buddy?"

At the sound of his name, Buddy sprang up. His leash was tied to one table leg. The table lurched.

"It's okay, pal." Will rushed to the dog's side

and undid the loop. "This is Buddy," he announced proudly.

Buddy dipped his head and gave Candy a perplexed look. His dots raised and lowered in an off-tempo jitterbug. Then he turned his head away and attempted to hide behind Will's leg in a *you can't see me* maneuver.

Will reached back and rubbed Buddy's forehead. "He's a little shy. It takes him a while to warm up, but he's really great once you get to know him."

Candy didn't seem to take offense. "No worries, Buddy. I know I can be kind of scary. My mother tells me that all the time. I should carry dog treats around with me like Jessica always does."

"Jessica's amazing like that, isn't she?" Briggs agreed.

Will and Candy looked at him, then looked at each other.

Briggs cleared his throat. "I tell you what. Buddy's been stuck here for a while. Why don't you both take him for a walk? Let him stretch his legs. You could also do me a big favor and stop at the Bean World Coffee Shop booth. Pick me up a large iced coffee, black. And get some lemonade or something else for yourselves."

He slipped his wallet from the back pocket of his jeans.

"That'd be great!" Candy exclaimed. "I biked all the way from our town house, and I'm really thirsty."

Briggs nodded toward the bike. "You can leave it here if you want. One less thing to deal with." He handed some money to Will.

THE TWO TEENS took off with Buddy. Even though only a few people had gathered at this early hour, the dog was a bundle of nerves. He tugged sideways on his leash, making a beeline to one side and then the other.

"Do you mind if I stop and make him heel?" Will asked Candy. "I want him not to get into bad habits."

"Of course. I wish my mom would be as good about working with Peanut Butter and Jelly. I love them, but they're totally out of control. She got them because she said that she needed lots of love."

"Grown-ups are weird," Will agreed, then looked down at his dog. "Tuck in and sit," he commanded. When he got Buddy to sit next to his left side, he gave a brief tug to his leash. "Heel, Buddy."

They started off again and had to start and

stop numerous times before Buddy achieved the hang of it. It worked until the dog picked up the scent of the organic-dog-biscuit vendor.

Will checked the price. "Jeez, they're expensive." He looked down at Buddy who appeared mesmerized. "Okay, one treat," he declared, "otherwise we'll never get out of here."

He bought a poodle-shaped dry treat, broke off the pom-pom from the tail and fed it to Buddy who gobbled it down. They started to walk again.

"Speaking of weird, did you see how your dad reacted when I mentioned Jessica?" Candy glimpsed sideways at Will. They waited while Buddy inspected a baby's sock-clad foot poking forward from a carriage.

Will frowned. "Yeah, what was that all about?"

Candy gave him a jaded look. "Like you don't know? He's definitely got the hots for her," she said in her most woman-of-the-world voice.

"No way. They hardly know each other." Will didn't want to think about something like that, especially not with his dad. He changed the topic of conversation. "I really like your bike. Is it new?"

"No, I got it for my graduation from middle school last year. You should ask for one this year. It really helps to get around. You're not stuck waiting for someone to drive you places. Like my mom—she's never around."

They reached the coffee stand and got in line. "That's a good idea. Maybe I will ask for a bike." Will broke off another piece of the dog biscuit. "Sit, Buddy." He held up the treat and gave it to Buddy when the dog obeyed.

Candy watched Buddy crunch the cookie. Bits of the baked treat scattered everywhere, but Buddy vacuumed them up. "I don't know if I'd let him do that," she said.

"What? Eat the crumbs?"

"No, let him eat a biscuit shaped like a dog. It's not a good message to send Buddy." She smiled.

Will looked at Buddy, who was still searching for invisible crumbs on the ground. "That's why I broke it up. I didn't want him to get a complex."

Candy gave him a look.

He laughed. "I'm just kidding you. Even I knew you were being funny."

BRIGGS HAD FINISHED arranging all the flowerpots and signs by the time Will and Candy returned. He held out his hand to take the iced coffee. "Oh, great! Thanks, guys." It was a surprise to see his introverted son walking with a

self-possessed, independent-minded teenager—
a girl, no less.

Her purple hair and nose ring were pretty
cool, especially for a quiet place like Hopewell.
It took a gutsy kid to pull off the look. Will
hanging out with Candy was something wonderful. A friend. Unbelievable—and someone
seemingly so confident. Someone older. Someone who worked with Jessica.

A car pulled in behind the tent, and Briggs
slanted his head to get a better look. Myrna was
at the wheel of her SUV. Norman was in the
passenger seat, his crutches poking up between
the door and his shoulder. He was holding on to
the dashboard with one hand, and Briggs didn't
blame him. Myrna drove full-on, the way she
did everything. Someone should probably help
Norman out of the car as soon as possible. He
nominated Will.

Briggs looked for his son and saw that Will
and Candy were discussing something with
great earnestness, oblivious to everything else
while Buddy lapped up water from his bowl—
that Briggs, not Will, had filled. Not that Briggs
had minded.

"Will," he called out. "Aunt Myrna's arrived.
Could you help Dr. Trombo get out of the car?
It'll be a little tricky with the crutches and the

tight space. I'll hold on to Buddy meanwhile. Thanks," he added before his son had any chance to make an excuse.

Briggs watched as Will muttered something to Candy before he reluctantly ambled off. Was it Briggs's imagination, or were Will's shoulders not as hunched as usual?

He turned to Candy. "I'm glad that Will has you for a friend."

She shrugged. "He's a good guy." She sounded wise beyond her years.

"It's not always easy for Will to make friends. We haven't been here that long, and middle school is especially hard when you don't know anyone."

Candy studied Briggs through narrowed eyes. "Yeah, middle school sucks, but Will seems to be doing okay. He even told me all about the science project he's working on and how Jessica's helping him out." She waited, giving him an extra critical look.

"Great to hear. He hasn't shared too many details about the project with me. Says he wants to do it all by himself and doesn't want anyone thinking his schoolteacher father had any input."

Candy looked in the direction of Myrna's parked car. "I get that. Too many parents do their kids' homework, you know. Especially the moms. They're super competitive."

Briggs bit back a laugh. "Tell me about it. But sometimes parents find it hard to hold back from being overprotective."

Candy grunted. "C'mon. It's all about themselves, not their kids." She seemed to speak from experience. There was a pause. "Will told me about his mom."

The change in the conversation took Briggs by surprise. "What's that?"

"Will told me that he didn't have a mom, that she left you guys when he was a baby. He said you were really young when it happened. Like, still in high school."

"Something like that." Briggs was in shock. He and Will never talked about his mom. "He told you all that?"

"Don't worry. I won't say anything to anyone else. I think he just needed someone to talk to."

She did seem to have the wisdom of a much older person after all. But as the others joined them, the conversation ended. (Luckily.) Instead, Briggs watched as Myrna trailed behind Norman, reminding him to be careful of the uneven ground.

"I know, I know," Norman responded. Still, he kept his tone civil. "I thought we might head to the picnic table and pick up some cookies from Nada's stand on the way. I can still taste the rugelach from last week."

"For every cookie I insist you get a carrot," she informed him.

"Sounds like a deal." Norman hobbled along next to her. His acquiescence would have surprised Jessica. Speaking of…

Jessica bounded over to Briggs's flower stand. "Sorry I'm late," she said, breathing heavily. "I had a surgery to finish up, and it was easier to run over to the market than try to find a place to park."

"How's Daisy?" Candy and Will asked simultaneously. They crowded around her.

"How did it go?" Will added.

"Is she all right?" Candy looked concerned.

"She's on the mend as we speak." Jessica gave them the details, treating the two like colleagues. She used professional terms, mentioning the steps in the surgery and the recovery. The youngsters nodded their heads in shared seriousness.

Briggs couldn't help smiling. He felt something repeatedly thwack his shoe, and he looked down to see Buddy's tail thumping enthusiastically at the sight of Jessica. "I know the feeling, boy," he said softly.

Jessica glanced over and offered a discreet wave.

Briggs nodded. People were starting to mill around his stall, and he turned his attention to them. He fetched the bouquets he knew would appeal to his regulars and joined in the by-now familiar banter. He also helped newcomers decide which pre-fashioned bouquets worked best or made new ones from loose stems. And he was just finishing wrapping up a bouquet when he felt a tap on his shoulder.

"I'm going to check in with Pops and Myrna. Then I'll return. Can I get you anything?"

He grinned at the familiar sound of Jessica's soft voice. "I'm okay, thanks." He handed off the bouquet to the middle-aged woman who wore a loose beret, a calico jumper and Birkenstocks. She brought to mind the image of Mama Bear from the Berenstain Bear children's books. Will had insisted Briggs read him one of those books every night before bed. Years later he'd found out the authors had also lived in Bucks County. (It was meant to be.)

"Next?" he asked and peeked over to see Jessica stepping away.

She waved. "See you later."

"Hold up," he shouted above the din. The mob of customers were chatting among themselves as they bent over buckets of flowers on the ground and the table. The organized chaos was invigorating if a little overwhelming. "I'll do it," he said out loud.

She squinted in confusion.

He waved his arms. "The flowers? For the wedding? It'd be my pleasure."

Jessica clapped before turning to join Myrna and her father tottering on his crutches.

Candy and Will were standing by the back of the tent, out of the way of all the activity. Buddy let Candy rub his back and ears, especially because she had just fed him a part of a cheese stick.

She nudged Will with her elbow. "See, what did I tell you?"

Finally, Myrna, Norman and Jessica returned to the flower stall. Myrna's reusable shopping bags were brimming with early season vegetables: zucchini, eggplant, peppers and even the first cherry tomatoes. "I've got enough to make a glorious ratatouille," she announced, raising her bags for all to see.

"And Pops okayed us getting some mixed salad greens." Jessica indicated her more meager haul in a paper bag provided by the farm stand.

Norman pointed to the large rectangular bakery box in Jessica's other hand. "It was a fair trade-off since you agreed I could get a Linzer torte—"

"Don't forget the oatmeal cookies," Myrna added.

"Those are for Will and his friend," Norman insisted. "Hey, kids. C'mon over. Here're some cookies for you."

Buddy was panting at Will's feet—exhausted from all the stimulation—but he trailed slowly behind as Will and Candy sauntered over.

"Here you go," Norman offered, leaning on his crutches as he held up a paper bag. The teens had no problem digging in.

"Don't spoil your lunch, now," Myrna warned.

"Nonsense. They're growing kids," Norman objected.

Myrna gave him a look.

Jessica and Briggs shared one of their own.

"Maybe not all half dozen at once." Jessica played mediator.

Myrna and Norman offered knowing shakes of the head, a clear comment regarding the "younger folk" thinking they knew best. Briggs and Jessica raised their chins in a silent rebuttal. Candy and Will wisely munched away. Buddy waited patiently for the crumbs.

"I tell you what." Norman interrupted the silent discourse. "Why doesn't everyone join us for a barbecue at our place tonight? We've got a picnic table, and Jess can work the grill at least."

"Thanks, Pops." Jessica didn't bother to hide the irony.

"Aw, I'll do my part, too," he protested. "I saw that Libby Family Farms has a meat stand, and their stuff is great. I'll treat for sausages and hamburgers."

"I'm sure we can find chicken sausages and lean hamburgers." Jessica valiantly pressed her healthy-eating campaign.

"I know, I'll bring my ratatouille," Myrna said with the proper amount of spirit.

"What about me? What'll I bring?" Will gave the last bit of oatmeal cookie to Buddy, who wolfed it down without bothering to chew.

"You bring Buddy," they all chimed in. Will blushed and looked at his sneakers.

Myrna turned to Candy. "And you must come, too, dear."

"I'll have to ask my mother, but that would be sick." Candy pulled out her phone.

Jessica leaned toward Briggs, who was finishing up with a customer. "She's ringing Alice. Maybe we should invite her, too?" she asked.

He smiled at the customer before growling under his breath, "That is such a nonstarter. Don't even go there in jest."

With a wide grin on her face, Jessica turned back to the others. "I'll go pick up the meat, but then I've got to check on a patient. Pops, I'm happy to drive you home after I'm done. Or maybe Myrna can, if it's not too much trouble, that is?" She offered a tentative smile—an indication of a truce or maybe a self-acknowledgment that she, too, could be polite.

"No trouble at all," Myrna replied.

"I've got my marching orders, then," Norman agreed.

Briggs quickly handled another sale. It was a good day—a very good day, indeed. "You all forgot about me," he said in a mock-wounded tone. "What should I bring?"

"You've been working all day. You get to take it easy," Jessica replied.

"Why, just bring your charming self," Myrna suggested with a wry smile.

Norman was more direct. "You get to bring the beer."

CHAPTER FOURTEEN

BRIGGS BROUGHT TWO six packs. He also brought flowers.

"They're beautiful!" Jessica exclaimed when he swept them from behind his back.

"But there's more," he announced, and he soon returned with a large Dutch oven with ratatouille.

"You can put it on the stove." Jessica twisted her hair into a ponytail and flipped it over her shoulder before she turned the burner to low. She opened a cabinet door and pointed to the top shelf. "And could you reach that colorful vase up there? I think your cream-and-blue flowers will look great in it—an oasis of calm in this 'carnival of color.' That's what I call my mother's decorating style."

Briggs looked around the kitchen. "'Carnival' is right." Each wall had been painted a different hue. Purple collided with blue. Orange chafed against green. The trim showcased hot-pink polka dots. It was over the top, but it worked—somehow.

Jessica placed the bouquet on the counter and filled the pitcher-shaped vase with water. "I love these flat white ones. What are they called? I think you used similar ones, only pink, in the bouquet you made Pops."

"That's right. You remembered." Briggs looked pleased. "They're ranunculus, my favorite of the tender bulbs this time of year. I start them indoors because our winter's too cold. And the blue ones are bachelor buttons. Those are from seed, and I germinate different batches in sequence. That way I'll have blooms for a longer period of time." He winced. "Too much information, sorry."

"No, it's great. Great to learn and great to see your passion." She held out the vase. "You can put these on the table outside. They'll make the whole occasion look festive."

He placed his hands beneath hers. Their fingers brushed. They stared. She raised her head. He did, too. Silence followed.

The kitchen screen door banged. "Oh, terrific. You already put the pot on the stove. The veggies are cooked, but it wouldn't hurt to keep them warm." Myrna stopped a few paces into the kitchen when she saw them holding the vase. "Oh."

Jessica backed away. "Briggs was just about

to take the flowers to the table for me. And could you also see how my father's doing with the barbecue?" she asked him. "I checked that the propane tank was full, but you never know. I'm sure it's been a while since it was fired up."

"No problem." He nodded and made a swift exit.

Myrna watched Briggs leave before redirecting her attention to Jessica. "It was sweet of him to think of bringing flowers, wasn't it, especially after working at the market and all."

Jessica opened the fridge and buried her head inside. "I'm just rounding up the condiments—mustard, relish and ketchup. I bought them today because the ones I found in the fridge were so past their expiration date they could have been designated historic artifacts."

Myrna laughed. "When I don't use my reading glasses I can run into the same problem." She indicated the packages on the counter. "Oh, I see you bought some buns. I was going to call, but I figured you'd have it under control."

Jessica nodded. "I picked them up with the condiments. Plus ice cream. I figured you can never have enough ice cream where kids are concerned."

Myrna smiled. "You have good instincts with kids as well as animals it seems." She walked over to the round kitchen table. "Looks like you've already got a tray ready with the plates and utensils. Why don't I take them outside?" She lifted the large melamine platter.

Jessica was still fussing around the refrigerator. "Oh, that would be great." She pulled out the paper-wrapped bundle. "I think we've got enough meat here for a carnivore convention. I couldn't make up my mind, so I got all three types of sausages." She dipped into the fridge again. "And the hamburgers are somewhere in here, too."

"Jessica?"

"Ah, here they are. Behind the green bean casserole from Mr. Mason. It was very sweet of him, but I have a hard time dealing with all that cream of mushroom soup." Jessica backed out. "Oops, sorry."

She hadn't realized that Myrna had walked up behind her, and the tray clipped her in the back. Jessica eased her way to the counter before turning to smile. "Is there anything else I can get you?"

Myrna hesitated. "I know I mentioned it before, but I wanted to say again how much I admire the way you've come back to help out with your father—taking over the workload and taking care of him."

Jessica shrugged. "I'm his daughter. I was happy I could help out."

"Naturally, but it still can't be easy. You have your life and your job after all in Chicago. Just to drop everything like that is very generous. I know your father appreciates it."

Jessica pursed her lips. "I'm sure he does." She waited. It didn't take long.

"You realize, don't you, that I'm just trying to help out in whatever way I can. Norman is a friend. And I'm certainly not looking to replace your mother." Myrna paused. When Jessica didn't respond, she went on, "It's just that I can offer to do or say things that perhaps your father finds difficult coming from you. As I see it, parents like to think that they're the ones who should take care of their children, not the other way around."

"Yes, so I've read." Jessica suddenly felt compelled to sponge away nonexistent crumbs in the stainless-steel sink. That took no time at all. Having no more excuses, she rotated back to face Myrna. "Look, I'm sorry if I've given off the wrong vibes. I don't think you're trying to take over from my mom." She was being truthful, right? Maybe. "And I appreciate all you've done to help Pops. It's just…just that

I don't want him to get any ideas, you know, unfounded expectations because he's…he's…"

"Lonely? We all experience loneliness—even me, surrounded by more testosterone than I can sometimes deal with." She shifted the edge of the tray against her hip. "I don't want to make a big deal out of this. I just felt it was necessary to clear the air. I like to be straight with people. Your father and I are both adults, and we're both benefiting from the companionship. It's nothing more than that." She stood there.

Jessica inhaled deeply. "I appreciate your candor. And I know you're not babes in the woods. So—" she paused "—I should trust that you know what you're doing." She held up her hands. "Anyway, it's not like I'm such an expert on people relationships. Now, animals, that's another matter."

Myrna chuckled. "I have no doubt. And don't sell yourself short on the people part. I have eyes." She glanced at the tray. "Speaking of which, it's time I get this out of here and check on the menfolk. Make sure they've actually got the fire going. They're more likely to be having beers and munching on chips." She walked across the kitchen and was about to open the door when Will, Candy and Buddy came barging in.

"How's Daisy?"

"Was she okay to go home?"

"Does she have to stay overnight?" they asked as one. Buddy sat next to Jessica's sneakered foot, inching a little bit closer with each thump of his tail on the linoleum-tile floor. He made a show of sniffing in the direction of one of her pants pockets.

Jessica crossed her arms and leaned back against the sink. "Hold on. First things first." She reached into her pocket and pulled out a treat. "Because you were so polite, Buddy, you go first." She fed him the liver snack, and being Buddy, the dog sat for another in the cutest fashion ever. The dots above his eyes waggled up and down, a silent request of *Please, pretty please*.

Jessica caved. "Okay, okay, I'm a sucker." She fed him one more. "But that's enough for now."

She eyed Candy and Will. They seemed to have become inseparable in a short time, and it appeared to be good for both of them. Wendy had told her that Candy had begun working at her father's practice as part of the high school's outreach program. And from Jessica's limited exposure, the girl seemed bright and a hard worker. As for her relationship with her mom?

Jessica had limited knowledge based on the dog-training classes, but from what she could gather, Alice was a single mom who had the uneasy task of running her own business and raising her daughter at the same time. True, she'd made the unfortunate decision to name her daughter Candy (Had it really seemed cute at the time?) and was desperately looking to find a man—witness her apparently futile attempt with Briggs.

As for Will? The combination of Buddy's presence and Candy's insouciance seemed to have given him a sense of self-confidence that she hadn't seen before. And their relationship seemed strictly on the pal level and a strong one at that.

Justifiably or not, Jessica took a modest amount of satisfaction from the notion that she had played a part in the two young people finding the gift of friendship. That she was lukewarm—she'd progressed from entirely cold—when it came to Pops and Myrna forming a bond was a topic for further exploration. And one she eagerly pushed to the nether reaches of her brain.

"No worries as far as Daisy is concerned," she reassured Will and Candy, and she told them that Daisy had gone home at the end of the day. "No one likes the idea of their pet staying overnight in a cage, so I was happy to oblige, with the proviso that Daisy be kept in a warm restricted area and definitely no running or going up and down stairs. I'll call first thing tomorrow to check up on her. In fact, if the owners are cool with it, I'll recommend that the two of you come visit her tomorrow. Check on her in person and report back to me."

Will and Candy looked at each other. They pressed their foreheads close together and talked rapidly, planning. Buddy, sensing their excitement, stood up and did a little dance.

Jessica couldn't help it. She had to laugh. Then she bent down and pulled out a large platter from a bottom drawer. "All right, everyone, could you pile the packages of meat on this and carry everything outside? I'm just going to check that the veggies from Aunt Myrna are properly heated. Then when I've dished up the potato salad, I'll join you." She refrained from shooing them out the door, not wanting to find out who would be more embarrassed— them or her.

The ratatouille looked in good shape, so she focused on finding a bowl for the potato salad. The one on the kitchen counter looked to be the right size, and she started emptying the apples, bananas and oranges she'd bought Pops. That the bowl was still piled high attested to the futility of her gesture. Oh, well.

When she got to the bottom, she grinned at the ceramic bowl's lively painted design of red apples against a yellow-and-blue-striped background. A flowing cursive script asked, *Have you had your apple a day?* The bowl had been her mom's (of course it had been her mom's)—a purchase at her school's annual craft fair. It had served as the family's fruit bowl ever since it'd made an appearance next to the sink. Had she been unconsciously replicating her mother's role when she replenished the stock of fruit? Gosh, she hoped not. Jessica didn't want to be her mother. She didn't want *anyone* to be her mother. She wanted her mother to be here, which wasn't possible. She heaved a sigh and reached for the potato salad.

THAT THEY'D EATEN more than their fair share was an understatement. Pops sat at one end on a folding chair, better able to stretch out his leg. Myrna faced him from the other end. Meanwhile Candy and Will sat on one bench, and Briggs and Jessica on the other. Buddy was curled up underneath.

The conversation had been easy: talk about the start of the baseball season, questions about

Laura and Phil's wedding and town gossip. Apparently the new brew pub was going to be named Mason's in honor of the former owner.

("Isn't that so fitting."

"As long as it doesn't smell like motor oil.")

Also, the fact that Betsy Pulaski-O'Malley's baby had been born with curly red hair was not entirely a shock even though many babies were born bald. Then, there was the welcome news that Mayor Park was going to run for reelection in the fall.

"Sheba should be on his campaign poster," Candy suggested.

"Maybe we'll finally get a dog park?" Will said hopefully.

With those topics dealt with, Pops returned to more pressing issues. "If no one else is going to have any more of the torte, I might as well have another little piece. It's a shame to let it go to waste." He held up his empty plate.

Jessica decided not to nag him about watching his weight. He seemed so happy—the first time in so long. She didn't even care when Myrna gave him a generous slice. Instead, she looked contentedly across at Will and Candy. They were doing a good job of scraping the last of the ice cream from their bowls.

"Any more, you guys?" she asked.

Both said no, although they looked longingly at their empty dishes.

"What's that over there in the back of the yard, in the corner behind the bushes and stones and stuff? It looks like something's growing out of a tree." Will pointed to the back of the yard. Ice cream didn't seem to have diminished his curiosity.

"Those bushes and stones and stuff happen to be a Japanese garden. And the thing up in the tree? Why, that's the treehouse where Jessica and her friends spent a lot of time when they were little," Norman answered.

Will whistled. The noise roused Buddy from his sleeping position under the table. When there was no immediate sign of food, he hunkered back down. "It looks more like a castle built around a tree," the boy observed.

"That's Jessica's mom's doing," Norman explained. "Vivian didn't do anything in half measures when it came to design. She drew up the plans—a mixture of a Swiss chalet and a medieval fortress. See the crenellation atop the door opening?" Curlicue trim also surrounded the windows, and there was half-timbering painted lavender. "It's getting dark now, but if you go up closer, you'll see something written over the doorway. It says *Jessica's Place* in a Gothic script."

"But how do you get up?" the boy asked.

"You use a rope ladder," Jessica explained. "See, it's looped on a hook partway up the tree."

"Can we go up?" Candy asked.

Jessica looked at Pops. "Is it still in one piece?"

"No worries. When your brother was back the last trip, he spent all his time making the necessary repairs."

"He must have broken up with someone if he was doing carpentry. Drew used to save that kind of work for getting over failed relationships."

"Knowing your brother, you're probably right."

Jessica placed her hands on the table and swung her legs over the bench. "C'mon, everyone, let's take a look." She stood up. "Who's coming?"

Norman waved her off. "Count me out. I'm not moving." He indicated his crutches.

"I'll stay on dry land and keep your dad company. I might start to clean up in the meantime," Myrna said.

"Don't do it all," Jessica responded. "We won't take that long, I promise." She made her way across the sloping grass of the deep backyard.

Will started to follow her but stopped. "What about Buddy?"

"It's okay, son," Norman reassured him. "The gate's closed and the yard is fenced."

Briggs placed his hand on Will's shoulder. "Dr. Trombo's been taking care of dogs for a long time. I think he can handle Buddy for a few minutes."

Reassured, Will motioned Candy to follow, and Briggs brought up the rear. Their feet crunched on the garden's small white stones. Paths curved through clumps of bamboo and bonsaied pines.

"Back in the day, my mom used to rake the stones into these patterns. She called it her Zen garden." Jessica unhooked the ladder and let it swing down. "Who's first?"

"Let Will and Candy go first," Briggs suggested. "I can hold the ladder while they climb up."

Candy didn't need any coaxing, and she scrambled up quickly. The ladder swayed under her energetic climb even with Briggs holding on.

"You're next, Will." Briggs looked to his son.

The boy hesitated.

"I've got it," Briggs reassured him. He didn't say anything more, but Jessica saw how Briggs held his breath and then smiled with pride as

Will hauled himself up and into the treehouse. "He was great, wasn't he?" Briggs said as much to himself as Jessica.

"He was. Great. You're a good father," she said. "Now your turn."

"Are you sure you don't want me to hold the ladder steady for you? I bet it's been some time since you've made this climb."

She could tell he was joking. "Don't worry about me. I'm the one with the experience here."

"Right." He launched himself up the ladder, taking the rungs effortlessly, stopping only when Jessica waggled the ropes from below. He stared down.

She batted her eyelashes innocently. "Oh, sorry. My hand slipped."

"Serves me right," he laughed and continued climbing. "Leave room in there for me," he warned the kids before he disappeared through the doorway.

Jessica glanced back toward the table at Myrna and her father. Myrna waved politely. Maybe too politely? Without waiting another beat, she clambered up with practiced ease.

"THEY SEEM TO be getting on rather well—Briggs and your daughter," Myrna said quietly to Norman as she waved in the direction of the tree-house.

Norman was feeding Buddy some scraps of hamburger. "It's funny—this dog will take food directly from my hand, but he still flinches if I go to pet him." Buddy licked the remains of the food off his fingers. Then he shifted his attention to Myrna. "You were saying about Jessica and your nephew?"

"Yes, it looks as if they like each other's company."

"You think? Jessica's always been a nose-to-the-grindstone girl. I've never thought of her as having much of a personal life. Even her relationship with this fellow Roger is a bit of a mystery. Makes you wonder," he admitted.

"Well, at least for her time in Hopewell, I'm glad she's found some company her own age. Tell me, does she plan to stay for a while, then?"

Norman considered her question with a hint of a smile. "Do I sense a certain parental concern on your part regarding Briggs? As far as I know, Jessica still intends to go back to Chicago, though I'm a little iffy on exactly when."

"I know she's doesn't want to leave you in the lurch regarding your practice, not to mention managing on your own."

"I'm getting better, that's for sure. But I gotta

tell you, the longer I remain home, the less I feel the urge to go back to work. It's been coming on for a while, I suppose, but I didn't want to admit it. Now with Jess here, it's easier just to let her take over."

Myrna stopped stacking dirty plates. "Have you talked to her about that?"

Norman sniffed. "No. That's my bad. I was putting it off, saying I wasn't ready when she asked. But in a way, I was surprised she hasn't pressed me. I mean, it's been more than a couple weeks already. How long can her partners hold out for her to come back? She told me that someone is filling in for her now—a relative of the primary partner. And that makes me concerned. She might be jeopardizing her job because she doesn't want me to worry."

"And you mentioned there's a man, too? Roger, did you say?"

"Yup, that's what she says. But the weird thing is they never seem to talk, always missing each other's calls. Frankly, I don't know what's going on there. When she first got here, it seemed like she couldn't wait to get home. Now it's like she's in no hurry."

Myrna put her hand on Norman's arm. "It sounds like you have some serious talking to do."

"You're right."

"You should know, too, that Jessica is wary of me being around you. I think she thinks I'm somehow competition."

Norman sat up straight. "What are you talking about? She's my daughter. That's completely different."

"It's not about me competing with her. It's with her mother. Vivian."

Norman looked away abruptly. "I don't know where she gets that idea. You and I are just friends. And of course, Vivian was a big part of my life. We were married for thirty-five years, after all. She was my partner in every sense of the word." He scraped the side of his head with his fingers. "She's still a big part. Why, she's everywhere I look." He waved his hand around the yard and toward the house. "I still find myself wanting to share a bit of the news I've seen on the TV or tell her we need toothpaste."

"That's only natural," Myrna said. "Besides, she hasn't been gone that long."

Norman turned to face her. "Two years now. We thought we had the cancer beat the first time, but then that cruel beast came back. She tried so hard—we all did, but it was too much in the end."

"It must have been very difficult for you."

He bent his head and nodded. "It was. The

truth is I was so broken up, I didn't have the energy to worry about what effect it was having on anyone else, especially our kids. I'm not sure I do to this day." He raised his head. "My failing."

Myrna leaned closer. "It happens. We just have to try to do the best we can. And that's all anyone can ask for. Goodness knows, nobody's perfect—least of all me. That's why I tell myself that it's best to stay in the present."

"What if you can't? What if you can't get over the past?"

Myrna pulled back. "Sounds to me like you're talking about two different things—grief and guilt. Trust me, I know both, and I'm still dealing with them. But I try to look forward, to stay involved, to keep my loved ones happy. When I do that, *I'm* happy. As for figuring it all out? Tell me when you've got it licked. In the meantime, I just continue muddling my way through life." Myrna gathered the silverware atop the pile of dinner plates. "And tidying up after dinner is high on my list. It's my orderly nature. Besides it's getting dark. It's time we put the outside light on."

"The switch is just inside the kitchen door on the right." Norman indicated with a finger. "And, Myrna, thanks. I'm sorry I'm so pathetic."

She sniffed. "No, you're not. You're a little lost at the moment, maybe. But that's what makes you so sweet. It makes you human."

Buddy yawned loudly and stretched his legs to crawl from under the table. He shook himself and glanced around, his back legs skipping at the same time.

"Will?" Myrna called out. "Buddy's up and looking for a walk. Maybe you and Candy could leave the other young'uns up in the treehouse for a spell and come take him for a jaunt?"

Will stuck his head out the treehouse doorway. "Aw, we were just plotting how to take over the world."

"That can wait. Time and tide wait for no man."

"What's that supposed to mean?"

"Dog owners need to act pronto when it comes to their pet's bathroom breaks—or suffer the consequences."

Norman chuckled. "Better hustle, Will. Your aunt Myrna runs a tight ship. I'll have to watch out myself."

Myrna gave him a sly glance. "You better believe it."

CHAPTER FIFTEEN

BRIGGS WAS SILENTLY congratulating himself for not checking on Will and Candy—Will especially, Candy looked more than capable—as they descended the treehouse ladder. And when there were no obvious sounds of bones breaking, he felt safe enough to lean against the wall opposite the doorway. He tilted his head up and gazed through the opening in the roof. The limbs of the tall sycamore fanned outward affording a view of the open sky.

"He made it down without a hitch. You don't need to worry," Jessica reported.

"I figured." He watched the sky turning darker with the setting sun.

She peered out the doorway. "Jeez, I wasn't expecting Myrna to put on the outside light. I'd forgotten how bright that thing is. Kinda puts a damper on the mood."

Was Jessica making an implied criticism? Briggs didn't understand women sometimes—most of the time, for that matter. Not that he had much time to spend on thinking about women, let alone more intimate interaction. He'd always assumed his solitary existence was purely a matter of logistics, but he was beginning to wonder. He'd had a few less-than-serious dalliances over the years, especially in his younger days, but recently? It seemed like too much work, which was a sad commentary on his emotional state. But looking at the future...especially the near future...?

Briggs turned his attention to Jessica. "You were right. I was worried about Will climbing down."

"You're his parent. It's only natural. It shows you care."

"What about you? Were you always this caring? And don't say you aren't because it's obvious in everything you do."

"I think you give me too much credit. Mostly I care about furry things. Maybe the occasional family member." Jessica rubbed her finger along one of the floorboards in thought. She yanked it up. "Rats, a splinter."

"Here, let me see." He scooted closer.

"It's nothing." She scratched at the pad of her finger with her thumbnail.

"C'mon, give it over. As you said, I care." He took her hand in his and reached around in his back pocket. He pulled out his phone and hit the flashlight app. "Hold this. It's a two-person job." He passed the phone to her. "That's it. A little higher. Good." He bent his head within inches of her index finger. Her skin smelled faintly of hand lotion mixed with sausage juice—a not altogether unpleasant aroma. He wanted to both kiss it and lick it. Instead, he pressed his thumb where the end of the splinter seemed to be lodged. He gently touched the opening in her skin.

"Will I live, Doctor?" she joked. Their foreheads were close together.

"I haven't lost a patient yet. Voilà!" He raised his dark eyebrows and held up the offending splinter.

Jessica peered at her finger and admired his handiwork. Her hand remained in his. "Good as new," she proclaimed.

Briggs didn't want to let go of her hand, but he did—finally.

Jessica squirmed around on her bottom to rest against the wall and handed back his phone.

He turned off the flashlight and joined her. "So, this is where you used to hang out as a kid?"

She nodded. "Me, Laura and Phil. Practically every day after school when we didn't have sports or music lessons or something organized. We'd talk about what'd happened during the day, complain about what our parents were making us do, plans for the weekend. Stuff like that. We'd usually go through a bag of cookies in the process."

"Chocolate chip?"

"Sometimes. I remember that Laura really liked Fig Newtons. Phil not so much. Still, he was pretty easygoing—until we got to high school. That's when I kicked him out. As revenge."

"I'm sorry he was mean."

She shook her head. "I'm getting over it— thank goodness. The truth is by the time I got to high school, I really didn't want to share the treehouse. That was when my mom was first diagnosed with breast cancer, and I needed someplace all my own. I'd come up here and make these absurd bargains that in return for making sure she lived, I would get all As in school or not fight with Drew ever again."

"And did that work out?"

"For a while." She smiled thoughtfully. "What about you? Did you make any promises?"

If only she knew. "There's a lot about high school that's a blur," he confessed. "After my parents were killed in the car crash on I-95, I just kind of shut down. Myrna came to live with me as my guardian, and she did her best, but I was pretty mad at the world. I didn't want anyone telling me what to do or how to act. I was determined to prove how grown-up I was, that I didn't need somebody looking out for me." The sky turned a dramatic orangey yellow as the sun gradually dipped below the horizon.

"I'm sure she understood. She must have because you guys are still together. And you've got Will. So, in the end, things worked out."

"Yeah, Will. Not exactly planned, but somehow, I muddled through. With Myrna's help, of course. I couldn't have done it without her advice and guidance. I totally depended on her." Should he say something more? Explain? Probably, but Briggs wasn't ready. Not yet. There were still things that needed settling.

They sat shoulder to shoulder, looking up at the sky, occasionally making comments.

"I meant it when I said I'd do the flowers for Laura and Phil's wedding."

"I know. And knowing you and your passion, you're probably already working out what to use and where, what kind of bouquets…"

"You're right. I'm obsessing, I admit it."
She chuckled. So did he.
The sun set at last. A velvety darkness filled

the sky and caressed the branches and leaves. The lack of light made the tree limbs seem more massive, almost primeval. The stars had to fight their way through it all, random sparks of hope and mystery.

They sat in silence. Jessica's shoulder rested lightly against Briggs's.

Finally, he asked, "Just now, were you thinking of your childhood in the treehouse before adolescence came crashing down?"

"No." She continued to gaze upward through the hole.

"Of your mom?"

She shook her head.

"What, then?"

She turned. The outline of her face was silhouetted against the night sky. "The stars. I was thinking about the stars. What about you? Your flowers?"

He waited a beat. Then two. "I was thinking about the stars, too." *And you*, but that part he didn't say.

LATER THAT NIGHT at the farmhouse, Will barely managed to drag himself up to his bedroom. Buddy was so exhausted that Briggs had to carry him up the stairs, and the bone-weary pup was snoring before his head touched the extra pillow at the foot of Will's bed. By morning, Briggs knew the dog would be sure to have migrated under the covers next to Will, his furry torso curved against the boy's. Briggs never ceased to enjoy the sight of his son cradling the dog's head. Will's expression would be one of pure bliss, as would Buddy's.

With those family members having been tucked in for the night, Briggs made his way into the living room, his socks moving silently on the floorboards. He had gotten the old pumpkin-pine timbers refinished before they'd moved in, but the wood still bore a fair share of scrapes and dents, a testament to the years of use. It was one of the things that Briggs liked so much about the place—a visible history of the families who had lived and worked and played there. He hoped to continue that legacy.

"You want something?" Myrna didn't look up from her e-reader. Another one of her favorite mysteries, he figured. She was snuggled on the end of the overstuffed couch. The lamp on the side table produced a halo of light around her salt-and-pepper head of hair.

Briggs had never given much thought as to how old his aunt was, but tonight he realized she was no longer middle-aged. She was fit and trim and even though she was playful about her exact birthdate, she had to be in her sixties. There was no denying the crow's feet around her eyes and the thickening of her jawline. She was also wearing a pair of reading glasses that Briggs didn't remember from before.

He sank into the leather armchair at the corner of the fireplace. He loved to make a roaring fire, but not tonight. It was too warm. And he had other things on his mind. "That was a nice evening. I enjoyed myself."

"Yes, it was. I thought everyone had a good time."

"Candy seems like a nice girl. I'm glad that Will has found a friend."

"An older woman, too. Always a good thing. And they both have an interest in animals."

He studied the andirons. He'd swept out the ashes after the last fire, and they stood there as if waiting for their next assignment.

Myrna lowered the e-reader to her lap and raised her gaze. "Well, out with it. What is it you really want to talk about?"

Briggs swallowed. "Back at the farmers' market earlier in the day, when we were all around the stall?"

"Yes?"

"There were a few moments when it was just Candy and me together. That's when she let me know that Will had told her that he didn't have a mother."

"Did he now? I suppose it was going to come up sometime. Though I must confess, I wasn't prepared for it quite yet."

"You know the whole town talks about it, don't you?"

"Let them talk. It's nobody's business. Anyhow, talk or not, you know my opinion on the matter. And, as you may remember, we all agreed at the time that for Will's sake, it was best to keep her name a secret while he was still young."

"I remember. But sometimes circumstances change, especially as needs change. I just want to do what's really best for Will."

"What's really best for Will? You and I have been doing what's best for Will since before he was born. That's more than you can say for her. You are Will's father. She renounced all rights."

"I realize that."

"Besides, what more can you do for Will that you and I haven't already done or are doing? Will's therapist explained to him it wasn't a question of his mom rejecting him. That she knew, just as you and I did at the time, that she was ill-equipped to be a mother. We're all the family he needs."

"I don't know about that. I agree it all seemed

clear back then. But now? What if he has questions? Wants specific answers?"

"Then we'll deal with them one at a time if and when they come up. In the meanwhile, Will is healthier and happier than he's ever been. Don't rock the boat."

She lifted up her screen. "If that's all, I'm just at the good part."

Briggs thought about her words but didn't have an immediate answer. "Okay," he said reluctantly. "I'm going to call it a night."

But that didn't end things.

CHAPTER SIXTEEN

THE NEXT TWO weeks seemed to go by quickly for Jessica. Pops was getting better and moving around more easily with Myrna's help, she reluctantly admitted. But since he still claimed he didn't feel up to dealing with patients at the office, Jessica was manning the fort full-time. She'd spoken again with the founding partner of her office back in Chicago about this time-sink.

"I'm aware you're caught in a bind," Dr. Verner said. "And I don't want you to feel that we are pressuring you in any way. Obviously the sooner you let us know your return date, the simpler it is for the rest of the members of the team. But I have to tell you my niece is working out beautifully. Turns out Chicago and the practice are a good fit. So, we're fully covered on all fronts."

His news was both reassuring and disturbing. "I'm glad to hear that you haven't been inconvenienced too much. Like I said, it's just hard to gauge the situation, and I'm still hoping that it won't take much longer."

But did she really still hope that? Practicing veterinary medicine in a small town wasn't the boring exercise that she had anticipated. Just the other day, Jessica had realized how delighted she was to be able to treat a newly adopted rescue dog—an absolutely adorable mixed breed that looked like a combination of a wirehaired terrier and a dust mop. The family had recently moved to Hopewell with two-year-old twins and another on the way. "What's another little accident on the rug?" the mother had said with that surprising, cheerful weariness.

And getting a chance to interact with Will twice a week was such a treat. She watched how he was gaining confidence and how passionate he was about his science project. At the moment, he was writing up his report and feeling the usual pangs of anxiety that came with tackling such a large project.

"Think of one idea at a time," Jessica advised. "And instead of starting with an introduction, why don't you just think dog by dog? Once you've summarized the findings on each dog, step back and see what conclusions you can reach. When you know them, you'll be ready to write your introduction. And the background research you've done will make more sense as well."

Will had pulled out his laptop, and while she was seeing patients in the late afternoon slots, he managed with progressively less teeth gnashing to describe his findings.

Then there was the joy of leading the dog-obedience classes. The dogs were progressing at varying rates—just like their people. But overall, they were starting to master multiple commands: *sit*, *fast* and *slow*, *stand*, *down*, *stay sitting* and the all-important and most difficult *come fore*. She was fast running out of liver treats, but it was worth it. And it was wonderful to see how the owners were bonding with each other. Denise, Earl the boxer's owner, was an enthusiastic provider of Chex Mix. Mayor Park brought dumplings one evening. Even Robby managed beef jerky. And Jessica found herself becoming less critical of Alice, Peanut Butter and Jelly's owner and Candy's mom.

She came to understand that Alice was maybe overly keen to be in a relationship. Jessica had heard her questioning Robby to see if there were any bachelors in his plumbing business, and he'd conveniently sidestepped the issue by having to take an "emergency" phone call.

And then, of course, there was Briggs. Despite claiming Buddy was Will's dog, he regularly attended class. He seemed more relaxed and smiled a lot. His mood rubbed off on Will, who held his head up more. Even Buddy braved a tail wag every once in a while when he thought no one was looking.

"You and Buddy have mastered *stay* quite nicely," she'd congratulated Briggs during last week's session. She stood to the side with her arms crossed and her stance locked. She looked like a soccer coach inspecting the action of her players from the sidelines.

"You chose a good moment to notice. I'd say we manage one out of four times." He shrugged good-naturedly. There was something appealing about his genuine self-deprecation.

"More than most of your students remember after one lesson, I bet," she remarked.

"True. But then they don't have the incentive of liver treats."

"Perhaps something to discuss at your next teachers' meeting?"

He shook his head. The smile he sent her made her heart skip. "You don't want to know what we discuss at teachers' meetings."

"Hey, Dad, what *do* you discuss at those meetings?" Will came over, his mouth half-full of Chex Mix.

"Oh, Will," Alice called him over. "How about you help with Peanut Butter while I work with Jelly? I need one-on-one coverage today on this *sit*, *stay* and *come* drill." She sent a helpful nod Jessica's way.

Jessica definitely was reevaluating Candy's mom.

But this evening, Briggs came into the clinic with a problem. He had on paint-spattered jeans, a ratty Temple University sweatshirt and a worried look on his face.

He'd never looked better to Jessica.

"Sorry, but I've got an emergency with the sprinkler system in my greenhouse. I can't stay for class, but I'll be back in time to pick up Will. I'll text him if I'm running late."

"Briggs, did the pumps I dropped off help at all?" Robby asked. Schnitzel, his mini schnauzer, strained on her leash to smell Buddy. Buddy backed off before tentatively inching forward and braving nose-to-nose contact.

"Thanks, Robby, especially for coming through on such short notice and after hours. I've already got one going, but I need to work on the other. I'll probably have to reconfigure some pipes, but I think a major crisis will have been averted."

Jessica caught him before he headed out. "If it helps at all, I can bring Will and Buddy home."

"You're sure?" Briggs had his hand on the door.

"No problem. It's hardly out of my way."

He saluted her offer and took off.

Jessica saw him again ninety minutes later when she pushed open the door to the barn. There was the mop bucket filled with water, and water-soaked towels were rolled up in the corners and around the legs of benches. But otherwise, the concrete looked to be simply damp.

"Is it safe to come in?" she called out. She closed the door behind her and rested her rear end on the rough wood panels. She spotted Briggs sprawled on an ancient swivel chair, his head back and his eyes closed.

He opened them at the sound of her voice. "It's you."

She stepped closer and held a bottle of beer in each hand. "Myrna said you could probably use one. She said I looked like it, too."

He sat up and held up a nearly empty bottle. "I'm one ahead of you." He ran a hand through his wet hair. The water had turned its tawny color a darker shade. His sweatshirt was wet on the shoulders and down the front in a V.

"From the looks of things, you could use another." She handed over one of the beers and took a swig from the other. "Did you manage to fix it all?"

He finished off his first beer with one gulp and placed the empty on the table. Then he hooked his work boot around a castor and pulled a lab stool from under the table. "Have a seat." He offered a weary grin. "And to answer your question, yes, I managed to salvage things before this downpour damaged too much of the indoor crop. The sprinkler system had set itself off for some unknown reason. I don't mind telling you, I was really worried about ruining the flowers for Laura and Phil's wedding. He wouldn't have been too pleased."

Jessica settled onto the stool. "I think it's more Laura you would've had to answer to."

He tipped the new bottle in her direction before taking a sip.

"How's it going anyway? With the flowers for the wedding?"

He sighed. "Well, I think I've got a good idea what type of flowers I need. There'll be bouquets for you and Laura. A corsage for her mother. Boutonnieres for me, Phil, her dad and her brother. Flowers for the tables and the area where they'll stand for the ceremony. Laura said she didn't want anything along the aisle for the procession. So that's one less thing to think about." His lips curved into a small grin. "Though I've got a surprise for when they recess. And no, I'm not going to divulge what that is because you and I both know that if she has any idea that you know a secret, she won't give up until you confess."

"Thank you for that." Jessica reached over and clinked her bottle against his.

"How are you anyway?" he asked.

"Other than carrying the whole load at the office, plus managing my dad? Your aunt's doing a fair share with helping out with Pops, by the way, which relieves the burden on that score. Then there's Laura's stuff. The invitations are out already—thank you, thank you, Alice. I will never harbor bad thoughts about you again."

"You harbored bad thoughts about Alice? How come? I found her initial interest in me rather flattering. I'm starting to feel rejected now that she no longer bats her false eyelashes at me." He batted his natural ones.

Jessica found a clod of dirt on the floor and threw it at him. He ducked. "Every woman's entitled to her own sense of personal style and direction—provided she doesn't try to foist it on her daughter. Candy is unique for her age and background. I wouldn't want to see her lose any part of who she is. Her individuality stands out."

Briggs agreed. "Self-image is a fragile thing among teens, especially, but Alice and Candy will just have to figure that out as they go along. Like Will and me, sort of." He sipped from his bottle before resuming. "But anyway, back to the wedding. So it's under control?"

"If you're asking whether we've finished scouring the local thrift shops to look for a dress for the bride and that Laura, Nonna and Nada have settled on menus for the reception and the dinner, the answer is yes and no, in reverse order, that is. The food is all set, the dress less so. I'm trying to talk Laura out of a red cocktail number with sequins and feathers, and a décolletage neckline, but you know these creative types."

"Not really, but I'm thinking that maybe I've missed something."

Jessica ignored his comment. She held up her empty hand and ticked off items. "Then there's the music. I never realized how easily bruised the egos of a men's choir are if you say Leonard Cohen is not your favorite choice for music."

"My, you are brave, but a woman after my

own heart." He gave her a gallant bow. The swivel chair rocked precariously.

"Careful there. Your ship looks like it's listing to starboard."

"Nothing that two feet firmly planted on the ground can't fix." He took another swig. "So, you conquered the choir."

"With the help of Mrs. Horowitz. Speaking of ships, if ever anyone needs a captain in a storm, she's the one. Even organized getting her piano to the wedding site." She stopped. "That reminds me, I need to email the mayor to remind him he should get together with Laura and Phil to talk about their vows. I also should get in touch with Wendy's husband, Carl— Wendy's the office manager at my dad's clinic. Carl's an absolute dream at logistics, but I need to update him on the current head count so that he can finalize the number of chairs and tables and figure out the table arrangements on the grass behind the gallery. He said he could get a paper carpet for the procession area, too, but I need to measure the space. Oh, and the lighting. Do you think strings of little white Christmas lights are too much of a cliché?"

"I say you can never have too many Christmas tree lights," Briggs uttered with utter solemnity.

"Stop teasing me. It doesn't help." She was smiling, but put her hands on her hips, anyway. "Whatever, you get the gist. I'm sure I'm forgetting something, and the only way I'll stop obsessing about it is if I go home immediately and find solace in my spreadsheets." She stood and placed her half-empty bottle on the worktable.

"What's life without spreadsheets?" Briggs stood as well. He placed his empty bottle next to hers. "You're not much of a drinker, I see."

"All things in moderation. That's my motto." She fished her keys out of the side pocket of her zip jacket.

"Well, it's good to know you're keeping everything under control. And in your copious spare time you're also…?" Jessica could tell he didn't really expect an answer.

Still, she took his comment seriously. That was what half a bottle of beer and one slice of pizza as your total calorie intake did to your sense of judgment. She grimaced. "Let's just say I'm spending time up in the treehouse these days."

"Looking at the stars?"

"That and thinking about my life. Before this all happened—my dad's fall, coming home, Laura's wedding—" she paused "—and you. But don't get too full of yourself. I mean interacting with you and Will and Buddy—"

"And Myrna?"

"Mustn't forget Myrna." She looked away.

"You can't, you know—forget Myrna."

"I know, for all sorts of reasons. Anyway, up until all that, and probably more, I thought I had my nice, comfortable life all figured out. It wasn't exciting, but it was…well, it was satisfying in its own mundane way."

"And now?"

"Now? I don't know. My whole life, all I ever wanted was for things to be calm, orderly, manageable. I could deal with change but only if it occurred in a safe manner."

"And you're finding that's no longer possible?"

"That and perhaps that it's no longer entirely desirable."

"Oh, wow. Stop the presses. Dr. Jessica Trombo has just admitted that she's willing to take risks." He blocked out the headline with his hand in the air.

"Oh, please, you're one to talk, buried up here in your little barn with your garden and your tight little family."

"Excuse me, I became a single father at the age of eighteen. You think that wasn't a risk?" What Briggs didn't mention was the risk he was considering taking in regard to his relationship with Will. He was still trying to figure out what was best for his son, no matter what Myrna said.

"All right, I stand corrected. That *was* a big risk. I'm just saying that it's all new to me, and I'm not sure how to deal with it."

"Are you saying you're not sure what you want?"

"No, that's the weird thing. For once I actually know—no, feel—what I want. And that's what scares me. I'm not sure I'm ready for it."

"Do you want to tell me what that is?"

She managed an enigmatic smile. "No, because if I told you, I might have to kill you. And that would ruin the whole thing."

"Not to mention bringing down the wrath of Laura."

She laughed silently. "Speaking of which, I really need to go do my duty. And I probably need to check on whether Pops has eaten a whole pint of mocha-chip ice cream since he's been by himself all evening."

"Don't you think it's time he made those decisions for himself?"

"That's all part of the equation, isn't it?"

SHE WAS ONE to talk, Jessica thought. There she was, standing at the sink with a tablespoon stuck in a container of maple walnut. Her cell phone sounded, and she glanced at her phone lying on the counter. Roger's name lit up the screen. She pressed the green button and put it on speaker-phone.

"Roger." She dug her spoon into the ice cream. "How's it going?" She sucked on a nut.

"Just getting ready to attend the annual accounting convention in Traverse City. You remember Traverse City?"

"Of course. Traverse City, Michigan. Everything cherries. I still have the dish towel with cherries on it that you bought me one year." In fact, Traverse City was a lovely town. She didn't mean to act snippy, but, really, how many dishtowels could a girl have, especially when the amount of cooking she did was limited? Jessica let a spoonful of ice cream slide into her mouth. She was never the type who bit into ice cream. Just the thought made her shiver.

"That's right. I'd forgotten that. But then you have a great memory."

Jessica swallowed. "Thank you."

There was a pause. "Listen."

Uh-oh. Jessica thought it was never a good sign when someone started a sentence with "Listen."

"I just want to let you know that I'll be pretty

tied up when I'm there. So don't be concerned if you have a hard time reaching me."

Jessica didn't feel she'd be concerned. But she found she was mulling over the image of him being tied up…well, maybe not him exactly. She shook her head. It must have been the beer on the empty stomach.

"Have a good time, then," she offered. She stuck her spoon into the ice cream again.

"I'll try. But it's really for work, you know. Anyway, I'll be in touch as soon as I can. Have a good night for now."

"Yes, you, too."

He hung up before she had a chance to say a perfunctory goodbye. And come to think of it, he'd never asked how she was doing. She frowned and took an extra-large mouthful.

NORMAN SAT IN the TV room and pretended not to hear the phone conversation between Jessica and Roger. The call ended, and a minute or so later the door to the freezer slammed shut. He picked up the newspaper.

Jessica glided into the room in her bare feet. "You can stop making a show of reading."

He let the paper drop onto his lap. She had him dead to rights. After all, it was open to the business section, and he never read the business news.

"Late day at the office, hon?" he asked. Norman knew Jessica's workday was well and truly done because her shoulder-length hair hung loose and she'd changed from a blue polo shirt to a T-shirt advertising something called Fat Rice, which he thought might be a restaurant—either that or a video game. The message of the graphics confused him.

She pushed her mother's throw pillows to the end of the couch and stretched out prone. Jessica, Norman realized for the first time, was not a throw-pillow person.

"You know the story," she related. "A full day of patients. Then I picked up a small pizza from Conte's while I did paperwork. The leftovers are in the fridge, by the way. After that there was the dog-training session."

"How's that coming?" He had the leg rest up on the recliner to support his cast. The darn thing was really starting to itch. Next week he had an appointment with the orthopedist. He couldn't wait to hear when the half cast was coming off. They had said six weeks at the hospital, but he was hoping to persuade the doctor to put him in a walking boot instead of this cumbersome fiberglass job. Showers were a nightmare, as Jessica knew only too well. His combination of swear words was, no doubt, enlightening at times.

"They're making progress. Some more than others, as to be expected. But all in all, it's a nice group. Even Sheba's mellowed, especially since we've all learned the complete verses to this song from *Encanto* called 'We Don't Talk About Bruno.' It's pretty good. If you ever got a streaming service, we could watch it together."

"You've gone beyond me. You know my incompetence when it comes to technology. If it hadn't been for Drew giving me that smartphone for Christmas, I never would have gotten one of those contraptions."

"And thank goodness he did. If you hadn't had it on you, you could have lain for hours in pain after your fall from the ladder. I still can't believe that." She rolled her eyes.

Norman ignored her unveiled reproach. "The class must have run late, though. I checked my watch when you got in, and I noticed it was after nine."

Jessica stared out the window. The curtains behind the couch were still open, and in the darkness of night the stars sparkled above the treetops. "I drove Will and Buddy home afterward. Briggs was busy fixing a broken irrigation system in the greenhouse."

"Well, that's nice that you offered. And it's only fair given the way Myrna's pitched in and helped me so much."

"Myrna's wonderful, all right." Jessica didn't sound totally convinced.

Norman didn't want to go there. He was a simple man with simple needs—well, maybe he wasn't quite so simple. Whatever—he preferred not to wade into complicated matters, especially where women were concerned. Still, it was time to discuss certain things. Myrna had pushed him a while back, and he had finally admitted to himself that she was right.

"I've been meaning to talk to you," he said. Not a particularly original opening, but it would have to do. "About work."

"Work? What work?"

"Work here. In Hopewell. At the practice. I know I've been putting off going back, something I'm sure you figured out, too. But I've got my reasons."

"Right." She looked him square on. That was one thing about Jessica. There was no monkeying around.

"I'm getting better. I know that. But my heart's not really in it. Oh, I want to go in and see Wendy,

Joseph, even say hello to a few patients. But I'm not up to running the whole show anymore."

Jessica swung her legs off the couch and sat up. "What do you mean? Are you telling me you're planning on selling the business? But it's a fixture of the community. The townspeople have depended on it—and you—for years. And you can't possibly want to put Wendy and Joseph out of a job."

He inhaled. "I don't want anyone to lose their jobs. What I was hoping for was that... How can I say this?"

"Just say it, Pops. It's been a long day." She didn't need him dithering.

"I was hoping you'd take over the practice." He made a face. "There. I've said it, okay?" His tone was defiant.

"You can't ask me that!" For Jessica, it seemed a bridge too far. "First, I come home to take care of you after your accident. By the way, you're welcome for your unsaid thank-you."

He nodded. "I know, I know. I should have said something. I'm sorry. I am truly thankful."

She relaxed her shoulders. "Never mind—you were in shock, in pain. I get it. But I gotta say, I put my life on hold, ran back to Hopewell to take care of you, let you push me into running your practice—unpaid, mind you, which is neither here nor there, but still—and *now* you just expect me to take over?"

"Not expect, hope. I *hope* you'll want to take over the practice. I just thought you seem to be fitting in so nicely with everyone, and I'm getting better—"

"Thanks to Myrna's help."

"Yes, thanks to Myrna's help in addition to yours. I don't understand what your problem is with her. She's a nice lady who's good company. And you know, it's not like I'm looking to replace your mother."

Jessica sighed. "No, I don't know that for sure, Pops. In fact, I don't seem to know a lot of things for sure these days."

Norman let the leg rest drop to the ground. He stood up and hopped over to the couch.

"Watch it there," she cautioned. "I'm pretty sure I can't pick you up if you fall on your keester."

Holding one arm of the couch, Norman lowered himself next to her, letting gravity do the work for the last bit. "I'm sorry. I'm not trying to make your life difficult, even if it seems like that's what I'm doing. What I'm merely suggesting—and I may be wrong here—is that you don't seem all that anxious to go back to your work in Chicago. And I know this is none of my business, but from what I can glean from your few conversations with this fellow Roger—"

Jessica blinked in slow motion.

"Forgive me, but it's not like I've been purposely eavesdropping. The walls in this house aren't that thick, so it's easy to overhear. Regardless, you don't appear to be missing him all that much."

"There's missing and there's *missing*, Pops."

"Don't I know it. All I'm trying to say is I want you to be happy. Because I love you." When was the last time he'd said that? "And you seem to be happy back here running the office and being with friends—old and new. Obviously, it would suit me to a tee if you took over the practice. But I also thought it would be good for you, that it would be something you'd like. I'd help out, of course, but you'd be strictly in charge."

He put a hand on her shoulder. When was the last time he'd touched her? Norman knew he wasn't demonstrative, a toucher, but still. "Jess, I know something about being back here bugs you, and I hope it's not me. I know I'm not the easiest person to get along with, nor the most sensitive sometimes."

"Sometimes?"

"Give the old man a break, okay?"

She reluctantly nodded. "Okay. That was a low blow."

"Thank you, because this is one of my few not-entirely insensitive moments. These past few days, I can see how something's troubling you. And you know how I know?"

She shook her head.

"Because you've been spending a lot of time up in your treehouse, and I'm not just talking about the other night when we had the barbeque. Though that was a pleasant time, I admit." He grinned at the memory before he got back to the point. "You were always a self-contained kid growing up. But when something was bothering you, when you needed to work things out, you used to seek sanctuary up in that treehouse."

Jessica rested the back of her head against the couch. "You're right. I *am* spending time there. Before returning to Hopewell, I thought I had my life all nicely organized with no bumps in the road." She turned to look at him. His face wasn't far away.

"But then a big bump came along, didn't it?" He could smell a slight whiff of beer on her breath. That made him smile. Jess didn't usually drink unless it was with friends.

She scrunched up her lips. "Yup. But that

one bump has set off other little bumps. And I'm not quite sure how to deal with them." She waited.

He shrugged. "What's that line from the old movie? About fastening seat belts on account of a bumpy night? I'd say that just about sums up life. So, think about what I said. That's all I ask."

"I will. I promise."

He patted her knee. "Thanks. I appreciate it. Meanwhile, you'll be pleased to hear that I'm done with my philosophizing for the night. It's bedtime for me. So, I'll just try and wiggle over to get my crutches without landing on my keester, as you so delicately put it. It's the least I can do to try to minimize the bumps."

Jessica bounced up. "I'll get them." She retrieved the crutches and positioned them as Norman eased himself up.

"Thanks, Jess. You always were at the ready. But you don't need to help out all the time, you know. I might complain—okay, I do complain—but sometimes it's better to let me muddle through on my own." He placed the crutches under his arms. "Boy, will I be happy when I can get rid of these things." He started to hobble off in the direction of the guest bedroom but stopped. "Could you turn off the lights, then?"

"I thought you said I should let you muddle through things on your own?" There was a teasing to her voice. That was a good sign.

"I did. But I didn't mean starting tonight."

CHAPTER SEVENTEEN

THE FOLLOWING WEEK Jessica and Will could be found clutching each other's arms. Immediately followed by screaming and jumping up and down. Poor Buddy. His dots spiked precipitously, and his brow crumpled in absolute horror. He scurried to safety under the examining table and pressed himself against the wall. Only his trailing leash stuck out and betrayed his hiding place.

When the bedlam finally died down, Jessica stepped back and exhaled. "Will, that is *so-o* great! I *can't* believe you won the science award. I mean, I *can* believe you won the science award. Your paper was absolutely amazing. I'm just glad the teachers were smart enough to recognize your contribution."

Will, his fingertips pressed against the sides of his face, was still taking it all in. "I know. I'm...I'm so happy. I even texted my dad during the day, although I'm not supposed to text during school hours except in cases of fire or blood."

"I'm sure he was overjoyed with the news, even more than I am." Jessica felt the need to lean against the credenza. The examining room felt much too small.

"He was." Will waited. "There's one not-so-great thing, though. Winning the prize means I'm supposed to give a speech at graduation." He looked at Jessica. If he had had spots over his eyes, they would have been anxiously jiggling along with Buddy's.

Speaking of which, where was the dog? "Buddy? Buddy? Where'd you go, boy?" Jessica peered around the room. It wasn't easy for a thirty-five-pound dog to go missing in a ten-by-ten room. Then she spotted the leash.

She squatted down and duck-walked under the table. "Here, Buddy. We're so sorry. You're such a good dog. We didn't mean to scare you." She rolled a treat toward him. Buddy scrabbled forward and scarfed it down. "That's so brave. Will, why don't you grab his leash? Don't pull him, though. I don't want to scare him any more than we've already done."

With gentle coaxing, Buddy reappeared, mollified if not completely convinced that all the commotion wasn't going to resume.

Jessica watched Will crouch down to cuddle the dog's face and give him a kiss on the nose.

"Buddy may be a scaredy-cat, but he knows how to survive," she remarked. "At the first sign of trouble, he immediately protects himself. Let that be a lesson." One of many, she thought.

But now that one crisis was solved, she turned to Will. "You were saying something about giving a speech?"

Will gave Buddy another kiss before he stood. "Yeah. I'm supposed to give a speech about my project in front of all the people at the middle school graduation. You know me… I'm not…not exactly great at talking to one person I don't know, let alone…alone a whole bunch of strangers." He stopped and gave her a pleading look. "Could you call the school and tell them I can't do it?"

Jessica ran her hand down the length of her ponytail as she considered her response. Her mother, a gifted educator, would have said that this was a "teachable" moment. The question was whether Jessica the right teacher for the moment. She could only try.

"I understand that giving a speech can be scary. I know 'cause I have trouble speaking in front of people, too. Give me animals, and I'm fine. People? Not so much. I mean, I was petrified before our first dog-training class."

"You were? You didn't look it."

"Thanks—it was a good act. But you know, the more I got into it, the easier it became. I may not be a natural like your dad probably is in front of a classroom, but at least I stopped being terrified."

Still, it wasn't good enough to talk about her own hang-ups. Jessica needed to address Will's and help him allay *his* fears. "Now, as to your prize… The way I look at it, winning is an honor, a privilege. But it's also an opportunity to share your learning with others. And make your fellow graduates and their families feel proud of what students at your school can accomplish when they put their minds to it."

Jessica tried desperately to recall the pep talks the coach of her middle school field-hockey team used to give before matches. But her coach's primary job had been as the school's speech therapist, and all Jessica could remember was that Ms. Kay had had clear diction. (Jessica had also never been sure if Ms. Kay was her first or last name.) Which meant Jessica was going to have to wing it. "When's graduation?"

"In only ten days." Will scratched his ear. It was already red.

She nodded with encouragement. "Okay. You have enough time. Trust me, it's going to take work, no doubt about it, but I know you can do it. And do a good job to boot." She pulled out several drawers in the credenza until she found a pad of paper. She handed it to him. "Do you have a pen?"

He pulled one out of his backpack.

"Good. You're going to use it. Let's start by writing the answers to a few questions. What was your project? What were your results? Why did you pick the topic, and what did you learn? C'mon, write away."

While he was scribbling, she asked, "How long are you supposed to talk for anyway?"

"Ten minutes," he answered.

She began pacing back and forth. "Good to know. Once you've answered those questions, you'll have the basis for your talk. Then what you'll do is practice, practice, practice—just like a musician before a concert. And don't worry—I'll be there with you. And I know your dad will be happy to help, too."

"No, not my dad. I don't want people thinking he did it all since he's a teacher. And I want to prove to him that I can do it, too."

Jessica nodded. "I get what you're saying. And he'll be so proud of you, for sure, because you'll practice so much that you'll basically know your talk by heart. You won't have to read every single word as you speak. And you can even practice giving it in front of someone else—Candy, for instance. That way you'll get used to an audience."

Will looked up from writing. "But what if I still can't do it? What if I freeze and make a fool of myself in front of everybody?"

"I promise you that won't happen. Everyone who's attending will be there because it's a happy occasion, and they'll be rooting for you. They're not about to judge anyone, especially you. And you know what, we'll make sure to have Buddy with you. After all, you're the expert on animal/human communication, and he's your dog, really and truly *your* dog. He'll tell you what to do."

Will took a large gulp of air. "Okay. I'll try. But you promise you'll help?"

"I'm like Buddy. I'm here for you all the way. And I don't even require treats. That's how good a friend I am." At the mention of treats, Buddy scampered forward and stared at her coat pocket. "See, Buddy's already going to work."

THE DAY OF the Hopewell Middle School graduation was gloriously sunny. That was the good news. This being Hopewell in June, the humidity level registered close to 100 percent. So, while it was lovely to have the ceremony outdoors on the front lawn of the school, the lone red maple tree provided barely enough shade to cover the back row of the student orchestra. (For once, the tubas were rewarded.) Still, the members soldiered on under the guidance of the music teacher/conductor with a valiant if scratchy rendition of Elgar's "Pomp and Circumstance." That the middle school *had* an orchestra was a remarkable feat in and of itself.

Will had sent Jessica a printed invitation with a note that she could bring a plus-one. Briggs was already attending with Aunt Myrna, so she'd decided to ask her father. Now that he was in a walking boot, his life was so much easier.

"I'd be delighted," he'd said. "And Myrna's going to be there as well. She already told me about the little do they were having afterward at the house. I presume you're invited, too?"

Briggs had mentioned it in passing, not offering a specific invitation, but Jessica was pretty sure that would come. And by now she wasn't surprised that Myrna had extended an invitation to Pops. She found she didn't even grind her teeth.

As planned, the four of them sat together in one row—Jessica on the left, then Briggs, Myrna

and Pops on the center aisle. They were surrounded by excited parents, grandparents and
younger siblings glued to their phones. Before
Jessica had taken her seat, she caught a glimpse
of Candy lurking in the back.

Since most of Jessica's clothes were still back
in Chicago, she'd hit up a fancy women's cloth-
ing shop in upscale Lambertville and bought
a black-and-white polka-dot sundress with a
matching cotton cardigan. She used the sweater
to sit on so her dress wouldn't completely stick
to the plastic folding chair. Unfortunately, that
didn't stop a line of perspiration from trickling
down the middle of her back.

Jessica glanced at Briggs. The father of the
graduate looked dapper in his light blue long-
sleeved Oxford-cloth shirt and khakis. But even
he wasn't immune to the heat and humidity or
the stress of watching his only child graduate.
Beads of sweat dotted his forehead. He looked
down and discreetly wiped them away with the
back of one hand.

Jessica leaned lightly against him. "You must
be very excited," she said.

Briggs swiped at another drop of perspiration. The sign of vulnerability only made him
more attractive. "Will insisted on cycling here

on his own on the new bike he got for graduation. I just hope he made it," he answered.

"He made it." She didn't mention that she'd driven another passenger besides Pops to the ceremony. Soon enough.

"Did you know that Will's supposed to give a speech?" Briggs asked.

"Yes, he mentioned something about it." It had been their little secret—all the work she and Will had put in.

Briggs frowned. "He wouldn't let me help at all. Said he wanted to do it on his own." He looked to the heavens. "I don't care what he says or how good it is. I just don't want him to stress out."

"He'll be great. Trust me." Soon enough.

And then the ceremony started. Mrs. Horowitz played "Gaudeamus igitur" on an upright piano. (The orchestra was almost depleted since too many members were marching in the graduating class.) Her forceful performance provided an efficient beat to the somewhat erratic procession of graduates, and her floral-print chiffon dress added a certain flourish as well. When everyone was seated, the principal rose to do his thing.

Jessica was sure the ceremony was all very moving, and she could see how proud the parents were as their graduating sons and daughters joined in singing "Tomorrow" from *Annie* and "We Are the World." And the speech given in French by the winner of the French award—a diminutive girl in a mini tailored skirt and matching jacket, with Doc Martens—was impressive. But all this passed in a blur while Jessica focused on Will as she tried to send him courage vibes.

Once or twice, she peeked at Briggs, but despite the stoic set of his jaw (he did have a very nice profile, she decided once again), his neck muscles were straining with tension.

"He'll be great," she whispered at one point.

"Whatever happens, it'll be over," he murmured back with a pained smile.

And then the principal called Will to the microphone. He stepped down from the top riser, his hunched shoulders partially filling out his new blue blazer. Myrna held her hands together in prayer. She smiled in anticipation.

When he got to the mic, Will made a tentative wave with his left hand to the back of the seated crowd. Everyone turned and—except for Jessica—got a delightful surprise.

Buddy, sporting a bow of the blue-and-gold school colors, made his way to the front under the guidance of Candy. Shoulders back, purple hair swaying, Candy held the leash tautly as she delivered Buddy to the dais. The audience clapped and laughed. Buddy turned to face them, ears pricked, spots at high alert.

Will quickly took charge. He accepted the leash, made the hand signals for *sit* and *stay*, followed by a reward. Buddy responded like a pro—a nervous pro, but a trained one, nonetheless.

Jessica clenched a fist on her lap. Briggs covered her hand in his. "Breathe," she whispered.

"You, too," he responded.

After the crowd noise died down, Will unfolded the pages of his speech. "Thank you, Principal Conyers, and thank you to the teachers who awarded me the science prize. My project was the study…the study of nonverbal communication in…in humans and animals."

At first his voice was tentative as he explained the various forms of nonverbal communication that he'd found in the dogs he'd studied. These included good behavior—such as holding up a paw when a dog wanted food—to bad behavior—chewing a shoe when anxious because the owner left the dog alone.

The papers shook in Will's hands. He raised his eyes and spotted Jessica. She nodded. He swallowed and went back to the typed copy.

He explained his methodology of observing the behavior of different pets and their owners in Hopewell and how he'd discovered certain trends. Not only had the animals learned to communicate their needs in a special way but the humans had also learned to comprehend these signals, and they'd started to use nonverbal cues more, too.

"As I discovered, dogs and people communicate with each other in expected and unexpected ways, but I also learned something about myself and what attracted me to this topic in the first place." He let his gaze roam over the crowd, showing how he was addressing everyone. "I chose this topic because, as you may have noticed, I'm not great at verbal communication. Sometimes…sometimes I give up trying to talk to my classmates, or I quit trying to make friends because I'm convinced that it's just not worth it, that it'll be too much work for them to listen to me."

He lowered the sheets of paper and smiled down at Buddy. "This is my dog. His name is Buddy," he said. Buddy sat frozen, his eyes fixed on Will, and for that he got a reward—two treats. Will looked up at the crowd again. "Buddy also lacks confidence because he was abandoned. He would rather hide from strangers even though he really wants to make friends. Together, Buddy and I are slowly learning to communicate in verbal and nonverbal ways, and not just to each other. And what's really exciting is that we've both learned that communicating—in all sorts of ways—is the first step to building trust. And when you can build trust, you can get to know other people *and* other dogs. That means other people are able to help you when you need it, and you can reach out and help them, too. There's a saying—'A dog is man's best friend.' I think Buddy's more than that. With apologies to the great teachers at Hopewell Middle School, he's my best teacher."

Will lowered the copy of his talk and smiled wide. "I thank you, and Buddy thanks you, too." He bowed from his neck, raised his eyebrows and waited.

For a second or two, there was stunned silence. Then everyone started clapping. Behind him, some of his classmates stomped their feet in approval. A few high-pitched whistles pierced the air.

That was too much noisy approbation for Buddy. The startled dog jumped up and jerked his head back and forth. His tail curled defensively between his back legs. Will gave a quick tug on the leash and made the *sit* signal. Despite his evident fear, Buddy responded, and as a reward, Will took more treats from his blazer pocket.

While Buddy gobbled them, Will patted the dog's ears and stretched to reach the microphone. "Thanks, everybody, for your support, but maybe hold off on the loud noises and whistling. Like I said, we're a work in progress." He waved and walked Buddy (who was looking for crumbs) to the side of the stage where Candy was waiting. She gave Will a thumbs-up (black nail polish emphasizing the gesture) and helped Buddy off the stage.

The laughter and clapping died down, and Jessica leaned forward to see the reaction of Myrna and Pops. Myrna was crying, and between some serious head nodding and forthright clapping, Norman pulled out a handkerchief. "The kid did great, Myrna." He passed her the handkerchief. "I consider him a worthy colleague. You should be very proud."

She blindly reached for the hanky. "He was wonderful, wasn't he? And he's mine. All mine and Briggs's."

Jessica looked at the man on her right. "I just noticed that Myrna's crying," she said.

"I know. Don't say anything, though." Briggs

wiped a corner of an eye. "I am, too." He gazed at her.

Myrna and Briggs weren't the only ones crying. Jessica was blubbering like a fool, and her nose was running like crazy.

"Sorry I don't carry a handkerchief like your dad," Briggs apologized.

Jessica waved him off. "No big deal. That's what the back of my hand is for." This was no time to stand on ceremony.

Briggs studied her with a goofy smile. "Did you help Will with the speech?"

Jessica finished wiping her nose and sniffed. "Yup, a little. But it was really all Will and Buddy's doing. They helped each other. I merely provided support."

He took both her hands in his.

"Oh, don't. I'm gross." She tried to pull away, but he wouldn't let her. He held on to her gently. "You've never looked lovelier." He leaned forward and rested his forehead on hers. "You'll come afterward to the house?" he asked.

"I'd love to." She held her breath.

He angled his head.

She angled hers the other way. Her lips parted.

"I can't thank you enough," he said, the last words as his mouth inched closer to hers.

"Jessica? Jessica? Is that you?"

CHAPTER EIGHTEEN

"JESSICA? OVER HERE."

Jessica pulled back from Briggs and looked to the outside aisle. "Oh, my gosh, Roger? What are you doing here? I thought you were at an accounting convention."

"That was a couple of weeks ago," Roger replied. "I decided I needed to speak with you. We seem to have lost contact." He made a statement in a green polo shirt with a logo for the Onwentsia Golf Club printed on the pocket.

"Shhh," several parents warned them.

Jessica looked around. The principal was handing out diplomas in alphabetical order and was up to the *D*s. Audience members were holding up phones and randomly popping up to take pictures of their graduating loved ones.

"We really need to talk," Roger insisted.

There was another chorus of "Would you mind?"

Roger looked around, not sure what to do.

Briggs slanted Jessica a confused look. "Do you want me to give him my seat?"

"Absolutely not," she whispered.

"I'm fine standing." Roger was prepared to sacrifice.

The woman seated on the left of Jessica politely tapped her on the shoulder. "I have to get up to take a better shot of my daughter anyway. Perhaps the gentleman?" She nodded in Roger's direction. She had barely risen when Roger sidestepped his way into the row, tripping over the open-toed shoe of the woman sitting directly on the aisle, who happened to be Gloria "I Never Miss a Graduation If I Can Help It" Pulaski.

Thank you, Jessica mouthed to everyone and tried not to feel completely mortified as Roger slid into the seat next to her. "How did you find me anyway?" she murmured under her breath.

Roger leaned sideways. He smelled of expensive aftershave and Altoids peppermints. "I stopped by the house first, and no one was home, but this very nice man was walking an enormous dog—"

"A bullmastiff named Sheba?"

"I really didn't pay much attention to the dog. But the man told me you were probably at the graduation ceremony and gave me directions

to the middle school. He also gave me this."
Roger showed Jessica a *Park for Mayor* button.

On her right side, Briggs cleared his throat.
He held his hand over his mouth. "We're getting to the *L*s, if you want to see Will."

"Yes, of course. Thanks." The whole situation
was getting very confusing. "Roger, could we
wait to talk until after the ceremony's over? I
really don't think this is the right time or place."
She sounded like a schoolmarm, but she needed
to establish some order in her mind, if nowhere
else.

Roger nodded, chastened, and leaned back
in the chair. Which is when Myrna stood to
take photos of Will with her camera and wave
the white hanky that Norman had loaned her.
And the rest of the boy's fan club—his dad,
Jessica and Norman—rose to cheer his accomplishment.

Finally, after the last diploma had been given
out, Mrs. Horowitz and her chiffon dress re-
inhabited the piano stool. And to a rousing
version of Schubert's "Marche Militaire," the
graduating students—with nary an attempt to
follow the tempo of the music—shuffled and
chattered their way off the bleachers.

The audience clapped and rose and soon dis-
persed to find their offspring, who were far

more interested in gathering with their friends than their families. In short, it was the typical chaos and enthusiasm one associated with a grand passage in life.

Jessica stood along with everyone else, retrieved her by-now wrinkled sweater from the seat of her chair and rolled up her program. She felt slightly lost as to what to do next and smiled a smile that wasn't at all happy.

She turned to Briggs. Myrna and her father were already sliding to exit via the center aisle. "So, I guess…" Her voice trailed off. She could feel Roger looming. Jessica wasn't short, but he was tall and broad shouldered like a basketball player. Well, he had subbed off the bench for the varsity basketball team for University of Illinois—no small accomplishment. Not at all what you'd expect from an accountant. In fact, standing here now, she realized he was taller than Briggs, who topped her by a good four inches.

"Oh, Roger, this is Briggs." She started to make the introductions. "Briggs's son is a member of the graduating class. And, Briggs, this is Roger. Roger is…is a friend from Chicago." Jessica craned her neck to see over the milling crowd. "I'd introduce you to Myrna, Briggs's aunt, and my dad, Norman, but they're already making their way to the front to find Will and Buddy. Buddy's the dog."

Briggs stuck out a hand and offered a brief shake. "Nice to meet you. Unfortunately you chose a hot and humid day to come to Hopewell."

"I'm lucky. Heat doesn't seem to bother me." It was true. Roger appeared to be pore-less.

Briggs turned to Jessica. "I'm going to get going now once I round up Myrna. Will has his bike, so he'll probably cycle home, but I'll need to take Buddy with me. I can also take your father so you two can do…whatever."

"Oh, that would be great," Jessica replied with a little too much enthusiasm. "It's been a big outing for Pops. He's probably in some discomfort, even though he'd never admit it. Maybe Myrna and he could wait at the sidewalk while you bring the car around?"

"Good idea. And don't forget about later at our house. By the way, Roger, you're invited as well. We're having a little family celebration, you see. Very low-key."

"That's very kind. But I'm not sure with my flights. Thank you anyway." Roger had been brought up the right way.

"I'll definitely try to be there," Jessica said. She was hoping Briggs realized she was sincere.

Briggs clasped his hands together. "Good. I'll

be in touch about the time. And nice meeting you, Roger." He gave a farewell nod and maneuvered through the crowd to locate the others.

Jessica pointed to the opposite direction. "Shall we go, then?" she asked Roger. "I'm guessing you drove, so it's probably best if you follow me. Did you want to go somewhere? Do something?"

"I think just talk. There's no need to go anywhere special."

"Then why don't we just head home?" She started walking toward the large parking lot. Roger took one step for every two of hers. Jessica remembered when she used to find this pattern amusing. Now she found herself trying to lengthen her stride. She had to look down to keep from tripping on the uneven lawn.

"Briggs seems very nice. Is he someone from work?"

"His son's dog is one of my patients." She didn't add more. They proceeded to chat about mutual friends and the accounting conference that Roger had attended until they reached the parking lot.

Jessica drove home with Roger following, and she waited for him next to the flower bed. The irises that were first blooming when she'd returned to Hopewell had already withered. Roger pulled up in a freshly washed BMW. He'd obviously opted for a more expensive rental package.

"Why don't we go inside? I've got some iced tea in the fridge," she suggested.

"That sounds perfect." Roger pocketed the key fob and briefly looked at his phone. Then he glanced around. "Quite an interesting house your father has. I like that it still has all the historic details." He pointed toward the fenced backyard. "What's that in the middle of the Japanese garden?"

Roger prided himself on his sense of design. You'd never catch him with pink flamingos in his yard, not that Roger had a yard since he lived in a condo in a gleaming high rise overlooking the Chicago River. It was quite stupendous, if a little soulless.

She looked to where he was pointing. "Oh, that's a treehouse. Pretty wild, huh? We could go up there. I find it a great place to talk, if you want?"

He shook his head. "No, thanks. I'm not exactly built for a treehouse. With my long legs, I might get stuck."

Jessica nodded. "Let's go inside, then. We can sit in the living room. It's got air-conditioning."

They walked through the side kitchen door,

and after Jessica poured two glasses of iced tea (two cubes of ice, no sugar for Roger; lots of ice and one desperately needed sugar for her), they moved to the front of the house. She offered him the velvet-covered Chippendale-style couch. The chartreuse upholstery clashed with his emerald-green golf shirt. She chose the wooden rocking chair with the cheetah-print pillow for herself. (A spotted dress for a spotted pillow, she realized.) Roger waited for her to sit first and distributed two coasters on which to put their glasses. (He really was well mannered.)

They were just seated when the sound of a car pulling into the bottom of the driveway broke through their awkward silence.

"That must be Pops. Let me help him since it's uphill. The walking boot is better than the crutches, but I want to make sure he's okay." She hopped up before Roger could unbend his knees.

She assisted Pops via the kitchen and made sure he was comfortable in the TV room with the trusty channel changer in hand. After bringing him two ibuprofens and a cup of water, she hurried back to the living room.

"Sorry about that," she said. "I just needed to see him settled post-outing. I'll introduce you after we talk and he's had a chance to recuperate."

"Of course. I think it's best we get started."

Jessica picked up her iced tea. The sides of the glass were slippery with condensation, and she decided two hands were a prudent idea. "First off, I want to thank you for taking the time to fly all the way here. I wasn't expecting it, but it was very thoughtful of you."

"I try, especially since our line of communication has disintegrated over the past weeks. That being the case, I thought it was best to come in person."

He was so sensible. Jessica clenched her teeth. "Roger," she began. (It was better than starting with "Listen.") "You're a wonderful, thoughtful guy. And I really hope that come what may, we will always remain friends." She lifted her glass and took a sip before carefully placing it on the coaster. "That said, since I've been in Hopewell—away from Chicago—I've had time to think. And I've come to realize that we can never be more than that—friends, I mean."

As Jessica spoke, the sounds of the local television news penetrated the walls.

"This isn't an easy decision on my part," she continued. "I've enjoyed your company so much, and, really, there's not one thing I can put my finger on that makes me feel this way."

"I know what you mean." He placed his hands on his knees. His drink went untouched. "While you were away, I actually found that I was perfectly comfortable with the prospect of not having you around."

"This breaking news just in from one of our affiliated stations. Tamara Giovanessi, the local evening news anchor in Phoenix, has been put on leave after questions arose regarding an award-winning series that she had produced concerning forced adoptions involving teenage mothers..." Jessica tried to ignore the television. "That's it, Roger! I also can live without you. And I say that even though I'm convinced that you will make someone a wonderful partner. Just not me."

The bottom line was, she wasn't prepared to simply be a trusted companion, a loyal stalwart. She wanted to be more, so much more.

"Giovanessi is accused of fabricating charges that allege corrupt practices by specific adoption agencies. Her credibility has been further damaged when it came to light that she herself was a teenage mother who allegedly abandoned her newborn."

Roger picked up his glass and sipped a moderate amount. "This really is very good to hear."

"Thank you," she replied. They were so civilized. No tears, no screaming.

"Until the investigation is complete, co-anchors will cover for Giovanessi's absence. We intend to keep you updated with the facts of this story as we obtain them."

"I'm glad we're on the same page, then—in terms of keeping our relationship as just friends," he went on, "because, as long as we're being candid with each other—"

"As good friends should be," Jessica emphasized.

He nodded forcefully. "Absolutely."

Outside, it sounded like another car had pulled into the bottom of the drive, but Jessica ignored it. Probably someone just turning around.

"Because I actually came to tell you that I seem to have become involved with someone else."

"Seem?" Strange—she wasn't even jealous. Just surprised. She hadn't been gone that many weeks. Roger didn't move that fast in her experience.

"More than 'seem.' She's someone I met at the

golf club. We happened to share back-to-back tee times, and somehow it went from there."

"Somehow?"

"Yes, somehow. It just overtook us."

Jessica put her hand to her mouth. She found she was quite giddy. "Oh, wow. How dramatic, romantic, even."

"Hmm, quite. And you remember that conference I went to?"

Jessica nodded. "In Traverse City. How could I forget?"

"Well, she was there. She's an accountant, too. And what I'm trying to say is that Ophelia—Ophelia's her name by the way."

"Very literary."

"Yes, her father is a professor of Elizabethan literature at Northwestern. He's written several notable books."

"How interesting."

"Yes, it is. So, Ophelia…or rather she and I… That is, at the conference one thing led to another and…and…"

Jessica held up her hands. "Say no more. I get the picture. And I must say I am delighted for you. I wish you all the best."

"Whew." Roger exhaled. For a moment, it actually looked as though he might have been sweating, but that was merely a shadow cast by the drapes as the sun streamed through the window.

"Yes, whew," Jessica agreed. She stood and approached him. "And may I add that I'm just glad that 'all's well that ends well.'" It was a cheap reference to Shakespeare, but Jessica couldn't help herself. "Let's hug it out—as a celebration of your new love and our friendship—and then I'll introduce you to Pops."

Roger stood. "I'd like that. In fact, this has all gone so well, I'll probably be able to make an earlier flight out."

"Perfect." She finally allowed herself to laugh. And she meant it. Truly.

"Perfect," he agreed and laughed along with her.

And in the laughter and the embrace they didn't notice the face looking through the front window.

Briggs knew he should have called before showing up at the Trombo house, but he really needed to talk to Jessica. This guy Roger who'd showed up suddenly? He had to be the person she was involved with back in Chicago. And that was all good. (Actually, it wasn't.) Jessica was a terrific woman and deserved to be happy and find someone who contributed to her happiness. And while Roger appeared to be a friendly, personable sort, he just wasn't the one for her. Briggs was convinced. He just was. Jessica deserved someone who she could kick back with at the end of the day, beer in hand. She and this special someone would be able to relax together, joke about the stupid things that had happened at work and make merciless fun of people who deserved it. And that "special someone" was none other than Briggs.

That's right. Briggs hadn't been looking to complicate his life any more than it already was. There simply weren't enough hours in the day to do justice to his job, his flowers, and most of all, his family. But for Jessica, there was always room in his heart. And he wanted her to know that, regardless of whatever was going on with Roger.

For once, she shouldn't have to take care of everyone else. No, the plain truth was she deserved someone doing things for her. Someone who'd bring *her* flowers, and not cliché long-stemmed roses ordered online and delivered by some random delivery person, one stop amid many.

So, gathering his courage, Briggs decided to show up unannounced so that he couldn't and wouldn't be turned away. He was ready. He was willing. He was on the porch of the Trombo house.

And then before he rang the doorbell, Briggs happened to look through the front window into the living room. That's when he saw them—Jessica and that Roger guy. Embracing. He even heard them. Laughing. And then they held hands, and with arms swinging, they walked out the doorway to somewhere else in the house.

So much for not failing. Briggs didn't think he was a coward, but the evidence was before his eyes. What he was was a realist. He was too late. It just wasn't meant to be. He'd go back home. Later on, he would take the time to nurse his hurt feelings in private. But if Jessica and Roger came to the house tonight, he wouldn't let on that his heart was broken. Instead, he would smile and eat cake along with everyone else and celebrate Will's triumph. How well his son had performed was no small feat, and Briggs wanted to make sure that Will knew how proud he was of him.

Which reminded him—he needed to send photos from the graduation to someone. He turned and headed off the porch. He hadn't failed, he told himself. He had everything that anyone could ask for. He stood next to his

Volvo, but before he opened the door he looked back. Not at the house, but at the back garden, at the treehouse. He thought back to that night. He didn't have the moon and the stars. But then, who did?

JESSICA SAID GOODBYE to Roger. They promised to keep in touch, but beyond Christmas cards and probably baby announcements (Jessica could see Roger as the father of 2.5 perfect children, all with long legs), she figured the likelihood of further contact was unlikely.

She retrieved her shoulder bag from the kitchen and pulled out her cell phone. No messages. Strange. Briggs had promised to call about the party tonight. She wanted to know if they should bring something, although, knowing how efficient Myrna was, everything would already be taken care of.

She dialed Briggs's number. It immediately went to voice mail. Maybe he was tied up with something else, in the barn perhaps?

What was she thinking? Pops would know what time they should be there. Myrna had invited him. She headed to the study, where the sound coming from the television indicated the news had given way to some game show that had been running practically since a man landed on the moon.

"Hey, Pops," she called out as she entered the den. "What time—" She stopped speaking when she realized he'd fallen asleep in his recliner. He was snoring gently with his mouth open. A thin line of spittle leaked from one corner. Jessica smiled, reached for the remote and turned off the set before a contestant could ask for a vowel. She pulled the patchwork afghan blanket off the arm of the sofa and draped it around his body. Then she stepped back.

Pops looked old but not as drawn as in weeks past. That was a good thing. A very good thing.

Then she climbed the stairs to her room. She planned to scroll through her phone and maybe let her eyes shut for a few moments. But a few moments stretched far longer. And as the sun set, the Trombo household gently snored through the cake cutting up the hill.

CHAPTER NINETEEN

THE NEXT DAY was Sunday. Briggs woke early and headed to the barn. Thank goodness the sprinkler problem was a thing of the past, and his usual place of sanctuary was restored. Alas, peace was not to be found. The bad news began when he discovered a portion of the fencing around the flower beds had somehow broken, and deer had eaten a large portion of the Emperor tulips. Then, when replanting a tender shoot in a potting tray, he snapped it in two. To make matters worse, he tripped over a bag of peat moss that wasn't tucked all the way under the table.

Briggs didn't bother to hold back. He swore a blue streak and kicked the bag with his work boot. Not content with a single outburst, he decided on another swift kick. Just his luck, he missed and sideswiped it, managing to jam his toes into a metal leg of the table. With the shot of pain came more colorful language.

The barn door slid to the side. "Briggs! I can

hear you practically halfway to the house. Could you keep it down? It's not exactly a good example to be setting for your son."

"Please—Will is still sleeping off his big day." Briggs tried to calm himself. "And, yes, I know, there's also Buddy to consider. But I think he's sleeping off his big day, too."

Myrna wisely didn't respond. Instead, she handed him a mug of coffee and pulled out a stool. She sat and sipped on her own, quietly surveying the full greenhouse and the bunches of flowers drying overhead. There seemed to be more than ever. "You've got a lot going on out here."

Briggs took a large slug of coffee. "Thanks, I needed that. And you're right. With Laura and Phil's wedding coming up, on top of the usual market sales, I'm up to my eyeballs. At least the market was cancelled yesterday due to the middle school graduation. As it is, though, it's all I can do to stay ahead of the game. Robby Bellona of all people goes on the top of my Christmas-card list for coming through with the sprinkler system."

Myrna listened. "Glad to hear that. I hate to see you running yourself ragged, though. At least classes at the high school come to an end this week."

"Followed by end-of-year teachers' meetings, classroom cleaning and who knows what else. But yeah, it helps that things are winding down. On the other hand, Will's going to be home for the summer. I know he's enrolled in tennis camp, but that's too far for him to bike. So, it'll mean chauffeuring duty."

"I'll help out there," Myrna piped up. "And I was thinking of talking to Jessica about maybe arranging some kind of part-time internship at the veterinary clinic. I know he'd love it."

Briggs finished off his coffee with a gulp, stood and plunked the empty mug on the workbench. "Sure, whatever. Though I'm not sure she'll be around much longer." He realigned the row of mason jars that were already in marching order.

"Actually, I came over to tell you that I got a call this morning from Norman. I was surprised when he and Jessica didn't come last night to the party for Will, but apparently he fell asleep as soon as he got home and didn't wake up until earlier this morning. Jessica didn't have the heart to disturb him. I assured him we'd saved them some cake."

Briggs flipped through a seed catalog, suddenly engrossed with the selection of melon varieties.

"Briggs?"

"Mmm?" He seemed mesmerized by the Crenshaw offerings.

"Briggs!" Myrna was more forceful. "Look at me when I'm talking to you, please."

He rotated swiftly and then plunged his hands into his jeans pockets. "Okay, sorry."

"Sorry's fine. But there's something else. What's really bothering you? And don't tell me some story about the flowers. I've lived with you too long not to recognize when you're upset. So, spill the beans, or there'll be none of my famous pot roast tonight."

"Pulling out the big guns, are you?" He chuckled.

"That's better." She waited. "Briggs. Don't suffer alone. Tell me what's going on. I can't keep tippy-toeing around, trying to avoid upsetting you any more than you already are."

Briggs leaned back against the table. "I messed up."

"Messed up? How?"

He dropped his head. "I fell for Jessica. What a mistake. I should have known to be content with what I've got. You and I and Will, we've got a good life, don't we? Why should I think I deserve more?"

Myrna reached out and rested a hand on his. "How can it be a mistake to find love?"

Briggs pulled his hand away. "Excuse me, we both know the answer to that—at least what I perceived to be love at the time."

"Will's a gift, not a mistake. Raising him was hard. But it was absolutely, positively the best thing that has ever happened to you and me." She pursed her lips. "But I don't understand what's gone wrong with Jessica. You two seemed to be getting on so well."

"'Seemed' is the operative word. Her friend or whatever from Chicago came in yesterday, unannounced. I'm not sure if you saw him at the graduation."

"Norman mentioned something this morning to the effect, but it looks like that's all over—not that Norman ever thought it ever was really 'on.'"

Briggs was confused. "But I saw them embracing when I stopped by the house. I'm not making this up. I was there, all ready to pour my heart out when I happened to look through the front window. That's when I saw them—laughing and hugging each other. It was pretty obvious what was going on. The message was loud and clear. So, I left. And that's that."

Myrna shook her head. "Oh, brother. You got the message—the wrong message! They were agreeing that it was all over. He was saying goodbye. In fact, Norman told me that this fellow Robert, Roger—whatever his name is—has already moved on. Seems to have found the love of his life—and, trust me, it's not Jessica. Apparently she's fine with the whole thing. Norman's even been talking to her about staying on in Hopewell, having her take over the practice, with Norman still involved on a part-time basis."

Briggs stood there with his mouth open, taking in what his aunt had just told him. "You mean...you mean..."

Myrna crossed her arms. "That you're a fool to give up so easily? You better believe it. So now, what do you plan to do about it? Go on pretending to study that fancy catalog? I don't even like melon!"

"You're right. I'll do something. But first I need to tell you about something else I did yesterday."

"Whatever it is, it can wait. Go, go, scram." She shooed him away. "And take these mugs to the kitchen. I taught you to clean up after your messes—in all senses of the word."

WHEN JESSICA HAD fallen asleep the previous night atop her bedspread, she'd still been dressed in her new polka-dot sundress. Giant wrinkles were crisscrossed in the fabric, and she thought it was unlikely that they'd ever come out. But wrinkles were the least of her problems. For reasons she couldn't fathom, she might very well have found and lost true love all in the span of twenty-four hours. She wasn't talking about Roger, either. He hadn't been the one.

Jessica sought some quiet time in the one place where she'd always found consolation. The treehouse. Before the sun had even come up, she made her way to the big tree. She was still dressed in her wrinkled dress but had thrown on a hoody she'd found in her brother's closet. It was two sizes too big and had a mysterious stain in the left breast area with the faint smell of ketchup. But hey, who was there to notice?

She rested against the wall opposite the doorway with her knees bent and her arms encircling her legs. As she rocked gently, she stared out the opening in the roof. She thought of the evening she'd sat there with Will and Candy and Briggs. And then alone with Briggs. It had been a moment of such peace, such contentment.

She'd tried to call Briggs a couple of times, but on each occasion, it had gone to voice mail. Logically, Jessica told herself he was busy with graduation stuff. Completely understandable. But another part of her was not so rational. She couldn't help sensing that he was purposely avoiding her. Had Roger's presence somehow spooked him? It had spooked her when he'd first showed up. And that Roger had found happiness with another woman so quickly was a little strange, but who was she to judge? Her feelings for Briggs had evolved quickly, too, and she'd been sure he'd felt the same way.

Only now when she needed to talk to Briggs, get some important things off her chest, he'd suddenly gone AWOL. This thing they had or were about to have, was it over before it had even begun? Should she admit that she'd been wrong about Briggs and her getting together? The old Jessica would have said yes. The new one said no. No! She wasn't willing to walk away without taking a stand.

Determined, Jessica shimmied over on her butt and turned around to descend the rope ladder. As a kid, she'd always let go before reaching the bottom rungs to jump to the ground. A silly act of bravado. She did it now—

And landed against a lean body. Strong arms encircled her. She didn't panic. "You," she said.

"You," he said.

They gazed at each other until Briggs broke

the silence. "I've been a fool. As my aunt Myrna had no trouble informing me."

"I'm getting to like your aunt Myrna more and more."

"I'm glad."

"Me, too." She breathed in the smell of soap, coffee and loamy soil. "We need to talk. *I* need to talk."

"As do I."

She tilted her chin upward. "You game?"

"Always." He held the rope ladder. "You first."

Jessica winked. "I like your style."

They immediately took the same positions they'd sat in that special evening of the barbecue.

"Before you say anything, I really want to speak," she announced.

He took her hand. "I said you go first, and I meant it."

Jessica didn't hold back. "When I found out I had to come back to Hopewell to help Pops, I was pretty mad about the whole prospect. I didn't have good memories of Hopewell at all. My parents had encouraged both Drew and me to seek our own paths, and I'd done that without looking back, which wasn't all that hard at the time. I'd blamed it on that nonsense in high school and what I considered to be Phil's betrayal of our friendship. I was more than happy to leave and find comfort in the world of animals—which I completely love, by the way."

"I figured that." Briggs rubbed his thumb against the palm of her hand. It was both tingling and reassuring—a potent mix.

"If you keep doing that, I'll never get this out."

"Sorry. Go on." He didn't stop.

"Anyway, I let those unpleasant experiences color my whole attitude about Hopewell and the people here. But I now know that my issues in high school weren't solely due to the bullying. My real anxiety was all about my mom being diagnosed with cancer. I was afraid that she was going to die, and that fear and being in Hopewell somehow became totally intertwined."

"High school is a really tough time to come to grips with losing a parent. I know full well."

"That's right, you do. So, to make a long story short, while it's true that I was pursuing my dream, at the same time, I was also running away from things I couldn't deal with. I was trying to play it safe and avoid taking any risks. Which also helps to explain my relationship with Roger. Safe and unthreatening. But that's all over now."

"Yeah, about that… I gotta confess that I showed up unannounced at the house yesterday. Bad timing. I got there to see you two hugging and laughing, and I…well, I immediately jumped to conclusions. The wrong ones, I discovered. Myrna set me straight on that this morning in no uncertain terms."

"I said I was warming up to her." Jessica placed her free hand on Briggs's lips when he looked like he was about to say something more. "Wait. I need to finish getting this out."

He planted a soft kiss on her fingers.

She sucked in a breath. She only had so much willpower. "In coming back to Hopewell and in reconnecting with family and friends and old memories, I've finally grasped what life is all about—loving and learning to appreciate the joys of those you love and who love you in return. And to do so without trepidation."

That was a lot to admit, but Jessica wasn't done.

She drank in every angle of Briggs's face, noticing each handsome feature and imperfection. (His dimple was a little off center, and a bottom tooth was slightly chipped.) He was all the more perfect because he was imperfect. "And now that I've accepted all that, or at least I think so, I'm ready to take a chance," she continued. "To take a chance on leaving Chicago, coming back to Hopewell and running Pops's practice. Making our father-daughter relationship work in ways we never did before. Being open to getting involved in a community and all the weird and messy personalities. And incredibly, unbelievably, I'm ready to admit that for the first time in my life I have feelings for someone, strong feelings—love, actually. I'm in love with you, Briggs Longfellow. And I may be totally embarrassing myself in blabbing away like I'm doing, but I have to take the risk. 'Cause you're worth it, and for that matter, so am I. I don't know what it all means, or where it's all going. But whatever it is, I think loving you is more than worth the risk." She stopped abruptly. And waited. Oh, no, had she blown it? She didn't think so, but…

"That's a mouthful, Jessica Trombo. When you decide to bare your soul, you don't hold back."

"Is that a bad thing?"

"Not at all. It's quite something. Really brave. I wish I was that brave."

"What do you mean? You're the one who raised a wonderful son as a single parent. Who pulled up stakes to come here and make a better life for his family. Who agreed to supply the flowers for Laura's wedding."

He laughed. "Don't go there. I don't want to talk about Laura. I want to focus on you. Because you're brave and talented and funny and sensitive. And you love animals." With each quality he brushed a feathery kiss on her forehead, cheekbones and chin.

Jessica closed her eyes and breathed it all in. "What about beautiful?" she teased.

"That goes without saying. And it's incredible and unbelievable that all of this, all of you is in love with me. Because that's who I've been falling in love with—all of you. And I agree. Let's see where we go from here." He placed the last kiss on her lips. And when the kiss ended, he murmured into her ear, "One thing you should know, though."

"You have a wife hidden in the attic?" She laughed at her reference to *Jane Eyre*.

"Not quite. I just want you to realize that I'm far from perfect. And not nearly as brave as you when it comes to revealing what's deep inside—what I'm only beginning to grasp myself."

He'd get there. She was sure. Maybe he wasn't quite there—yet. That was what love was for.

CHAPTER TWENTY

PHIL TURNED INTO the long gravel drive of La-
Valle Stables. Carefully pruned dogwoods and
cherry trees displayed their joyful pink blossoms on either side of the entryway. Phil, on
the contrary, felt far from joyful or in the pink.
He was downright queasy, and his distress had
nothing to do with the meatball hoagie he had
chowed down an hour earlier.

With the high school classes finally over and
the summer-school program still weeks away,
he should have been reveling in anticipation of
his wedding, scheduled for the coming weekend. Instead, he was dreading his unannounced
visit to his father.

He parked his Subaru wagon (the honorary
badge of a long-time resident of Hopewell) next
to the historic white farmhouse. Phil dearly
wanted to back out and give the whole encounter a miss, but that was not going to happen.
Now more than ever—with the wedding and
impending fatherhood—he felt an obligation

to act like an adult. An adult secure in his life decisions.

He turned off the engine and got out, taking in the serene scene. The equestrian center catered strictly to elite riders competing on the professional circuit. Horses munched on grass and swished their tails to bat away annoying flies in the various paddocks. The three barns, as always, were painted a pristine gray and surrounded by flower beds filled with tulips, miraculously uneaten by deer (none were allowed at LaValle Stables). Elegantly dressed riders on magnificent horses were using the outdoor dressage and jumping rings.

Henri LaValle usually conducted lessons in the indoor arena, and Phil headed that way. Even before he entered the building, Phil could hear his father's heavy French accent as he doled out criticism. After all these years of living in Pennsylvania, Henri had yet to lose his accent. If anything, it had gotten stronger.

Phil stopped at the open door. Sure enough, his father stood at the side of the large ring, sternly instructing a young woman that the hind legs of the beautiful thoroughbred weren't fully engaged. Phil slipped inside. His footsteps were muffled due to the sand covering the floor, but not subtle enough to evade the discerning ears of Henri LaValle. Nothing evaded Henri LaValle in the ring.

Despite seeing his son, Henri continued teaching until the end of the lesson, a full fifteen minutes later. Then there was the usual chitchat between the instructor and pupil to show they shared a personal rapport and not just a professional bond—a complete farce, of course. But that was Henri LaValle.

And after he had kept his son waiting as long as possible, Henri stared at Phil with a condescending look. He beckoned him forward.

Phil gave a curt nod. "Father."

"Philippe. To what do I owe the pleasure?" Henri walked to a cupboard by the entry and stashed the dressage whip he'd been carrying.

Phil forced a smile. "I wanted to let you know that Laura Reggio and I are getting married on Saturday. Naturally, we wanted to invite you to the ceremony."

"Naturally?" Henri walked outside the building, finally stopping next to a fenced-in field. A placid horse, busy eating the new grass, was unperturbed by a nearby frisky pony.

"It's a family event, and we'd love to have you there. It will be at the gallery in Hopewell and in the backyard," Phil went on.

"Backyard?" He made it sound like they'd

be taking over the town dump. "And who will be there?"

It was twenty-questions time. "Our friends, Laura's family from out of town, people from Hopewell we've known forever. Jessica Trombo is back, even. You remember her? Dr. Trombo's daughter?"

Henri rested his hands on a wooden rail and stared out over the gently sloping grasslands and forested hills beyond—*his* grasslands, *his* hills. The local horse trail ran through the woods, and it was a big draw for the boarders. "Yes, Dr. Norman Trombo. A small-animal veterinarian. I never took my dogs to him. And of course, he wasn't for horses, not that I would have used him."

Phil didn't bother to ask why. His father's snobbism was legendary. "No matter—we'd love to have you come."

Henri turned slowly and faced his son. "I think not. The Reggio family is not for me. And certainly, I would have expected more from a son of mine—in more ways than one, not simply his choice of a marriage partner."

Nothing had changed. "I'm sorry to hear that."

Phil was ready to give his goodbyes, but he didn't, not yet. Long ago he'd made the break from his father, but that break had come after a chest-thumping, screaming display of immature bravado, far from a demonstration of rational decision-making. So, he stood his ground.

"Papa," he said, using his childhood term for his father. (Some things never changed.) "I'm sorry that's your decision. Laura and I are very much in love. I'm proud that she will have me as her husband and that we will be welcoming a baby in the near future."

He could have said something about his mother, Henri's wife, skipping out on the family when Phil had been young. That would have been unnecessarily immature, and he didn't really blame her for leaving his father. As for leaving him? There was always some baggage to carry, wasn't there?

"Papa," he repeated, "I am proud of my decisions to be a teacher, to do something worthwhile for the community—the whole community, not just those who can afford to join country clubs or ride expensive horses. There was a time when you called the shots, and I let you. But not anymore. I'm all grown up. I'm in control of my life, and it feels good—excellent, in fact." And it did. Really good. "All I can add is that I'm sorry it won't include you. So, good day."

As he walked away without a look back, Phil knew it was a good day—for him. He was a lucky man.

LAURA SAT AT the Trombos' kitchen table and peered at the spreadsheet on Jessica's laptop. She nursed a peppermint tea to help ease her nausea. "I don't know why I'm feeling like this. It usually happens in the morning, not in the evening."

Jessica was drinking a glass of white wine. Now that they were in the final stretch of wedding planning, she found it a must. "Speaking as a doctor, it's all normal. You've got wedding stress in addition to being pregnant, not to mention the fact that your parents and brothers have already flown in."

Laura groaned. "I love them dearly, but thank goodness they're staying at the Carriage Inn. Can you imagine all of us living under one roof?"

Frankly, Jessica could, the memories still fresh of the Reggio household with its never-ending dramas. Yet despite the many squabbles concerning boyfriends, chores, money and fender benders, family loyalties always won out.

Jessica eyed the checklist of last-minute items. "Carl's setting up the tent, table and chairs on

Friday. He'll put out the linens, glasses and silverware on Saturday morning. He and the movers are putting Mrs. Horowitz's piano on the spot she requested. Mr. Portobello has already delivered the wine to the gallery and left it in the office per my instructions." (Jessica so appreciated that he had also sent her a case of Verdicchio as a present.) "And Serafina, Pops's cleaning lady, will give the place a final going-over. She insisted on making sure it was up to her standards. Joseph will have the choir there at two p.m. on the dot—plenty of time before the ceremony at four o'clock. Denise—the salon owner and Earl the boxer's 'parent'—will do hair and makeup at noon. Mayor Park said he'd arrive at three, so if you have any last-minute changes—and I don't mean backing out of the ceremony—speak to him then. And Nonna and Nada Bellona are coordinating all the food and servers. They've promised me that everything's set."

"Their word is gold. No worries there." Laura sipped her tea.

"Mr. Mason asked if he could drive you to the ceremony in his vintage Studebaker, by the way."

"But I live right over the gallery. Where's he gonna drive me?"

"Humor him. Let him take you around the

block." Jessica ran her finger down the screen. "Let's see, that just leaves the flowers. Briggs tells me he has everything under control. Early Saturday morning, he'll bring the floral arrangements for the individual tables, the two buffet tables and the area where the bride and groom will take their vows—"

Laura sighed and looked beatific.

Jessica was all business. "He'll also distribute the boutonnieres and bouquets. He still refuses to let me in on 'the Surprise,' but whatever it is, he promises it will be special."

Laura clapped. "I love surprises."

"I don't. But there you have it." She closed the lid of the computer and faced Laura. And frowned. "What? What's with all that eyebrow waggling and knowing smile?"

Her friend leaned forward. "Don't play dumb. I may have been caught up in all this wedding and baby stuff, not to mention having to be the good daughter to my folks—"

"Are you saying you've been self-centered?"

"Well, yes, but deservedly so."

"Agreed."

"But I haven't been so out of it that I didn't hear about the whole middle-school-graduation situation—the one involving a certain tall handsome stranger? And don't pretend it didn't happen. Word gets around. So? Spill the beans."

For once, Jessica had no problem admitting her feelings. Laura was the closest thing she had to a best friend. And friends—true friends—deserved the truth.

She sat back and folded her arms. "The mysterious stranger you referred to was Roger from Chicago, my ex, uh, I'm not technically sure what he was. We dated. Sometimes. Whatever, he showed up unannounced."

"Ex?" Laura cut to the chase.

"Most definitely. He's moved on. As have I." She wet her lips.

Laura rubbed her hands together. "Ooh, the good stuff. I no longer feel nauseous. Tell me more."

A sip of wine was in order. "Well—" another sip "—after some soul-searching, I've made a bunch of decisions. First—"

"Oh, goody. There's more than one."

"Yes, there is. So, if you'll let me proceed."

"Proceed, proceed. Don't let me hold you back." Laura placed her hand on her chest.

"I'm trying." Jessica's frustration was only partly in jest. "First, Pops has asked me to take over his practice, and I'm pretty sure I'll do it."

"Wow!" Laura exclaimed. "You'll be moving back to Hopewell."

"Eventually. There're still bugs to be worked out, like how much he's going to be involved and how soon this would actually happen. And I still haven't talked to my colleagues back in Chicago. I certainly don't want to just up and leave them. Though, from the sound of things, they may already have a replacement in place."

"Not that anyone could replace you," Laura reminded her.

"Kind of you to say so but let me finish. You see, when I was considering coming back to live and work in Hopewell, I decided to do so because it wasn't so much about moving *back* as it was about moving *forward*. Does that make sense?"

"Completely. Time to move on." Laura made a rolling motion with her hand.

"Right, and for the pièce de résistance… drum roll, please." Jessica gave the signal, and Laura responded by tapping her teaspoon. "The big reveal is that Briggs and I have admitted our feelings for each other."

Laura jumped up and did a dance around the room. "I knew it, I knew it. I said as much to Phil, but he swore that Briggs never mentioned anything to him. But then, you know guys. They're hopeless when it comes to divulging personal stuff." She stopped to catch her breath. "So, when's the date?"

"Please, no talk of weddings—at least not mine and Briggs's—as of yet. We're still finding our way. It's been only a short time, a matter of weeks," she reminded her friend.

"Here we go with the old Ms. Cautious routine. I thought you decided to throw that out the window."

"Excuse me, uprooting my very existence is not exactly being cautious. But it does feel right. And I'm so excited. I'm...I'm..."

"Face it, Jess." Laura leaned in like the all-knowing friend she was. "You're in *lo-ove*. And just think, you'll never be at a loss for flowers. What more could a girl want?" She beamed triumphantly before suddenly clutching her stomach and making an ominous gulp. She started to turn a bilious shade of green not unlike the couch in the living room.

Jessica rushed to get a bowl should the need arise for more drastic measures.

As to Laura's pronouncement about an endless supply of flowers making a basis for a perfect relationship? Jessica could have rattled off a few more important considerations, but she knew that her friend was already composing

Jessica's vows in between dry heaving over the bowl. And come to think of it, having someone regularly bring you flowers wasn't a bad basis for a relationship after all.

CHAPTER TWENTY-ONE

THE SUN SHONE, the birds sang and the angels wept. And that was before Laura and Phil had exchanged their vows.

"I'm going to cry," Laura declared.

"That's allowed. You look so beautiful." Laura's mom and Jessica cooed after they helped Laura into her dress, making sure her hair and false eyelashes remained in place.

Then they escorted the bride downstairs from her apartment and out to the driveway. Mr. Mason was standing beside his shiny gold-toned Studebaker. He waved and bowed deeply when Laura approached.

Jessica excused herself and took this opportunity to do one final sweep. Inside the gallery, she saw Briggs offering to affix the pale rose bud and fern boutonniere to the lapel of Phil's blue suit jacket. Briggs, Laura's father and her brother had already pinned theirs. Since the situation appeared under control, she hurried out back to check on the scene there. On one of the wooden folding chairs (no sticking to plastic seats!), she noticed Betsy Pulaski-O'Malley rocking her sleeping baby. After three children, she had the routine down pat. Her mother, Gloria—at Briggs's behest—was busy handing out small paper bags to the other guests with the instructions that they were only to be opened and distributed during the recessional. Norman and Myrna had found seats to the side so that he could stretch his leg out. Robby Bellona was holding his wife Nada's shawl on his lap while she and Laura's *nonna* discussed how to serve hors d'oeuvres during the cocktail hour before the dinner. Mrs. Horowitz, adorned in yet another chiffon dress (jewel toned for the occasion), was warming up the crowd by playing "The Shadow of Your Smile." Meanwhile, Joseph, pitch pipe in hand, was prepping the choir. Luckily, yesterday, Wendy had been corralled into being the photographer. Given her successful history of taking portraits of the veterinary patients, it was a no-brainer. And she was tickled pink to be part of the festivities. Finally, Carl, the ever-efficient Carl, was doing last-minute checks on the tent poles.

Oh, and Will was by the fence trying to teach Buddy how to catch a small plush ball. The dog seemed much better at throwing it up in the air than catching it.

Jessica heard a car pull in the driveway, and she knew it had to be Mr. Mason's distinctive set of wheels. The time had come for the formal parts of the festivities to get underway. Joseph and fellow choir members performed "Over the Rainbow" as Phil processed with his best man, Briggs; next came Jessica, escorted by Laura's brother. Laura was last, making a grand entrance with her mother and father flanking her on either side. Her smile was gigantic, her skin aglow (Denise's work only added to Laura's natural radiance) and her eyes watery with happy tears.

Laura passed her bouquet of purple peonies to Jessica. Her immediate duties of bridesmaid fulfilled, Jessica stole a glance at Briggs. He looked so handsome in his tailored blue suit and striped tie. He caught her eye at the same time. The look he sent her was in no way sweet and innocent. All the money she'd spent on the pale lavender tulle dress with the matching slip had been worth it.

Mayor Park delivered a personal, amusing and, much to everyone's relief, brief welcome. Laura's brother read a Maya Angelou poem. Briggs read the closing passage from the book

The Boys in the Boat. The choir sang "My Funny Valentine," and then came Laura and Phil's personal vows: in-jokes and joyful references to their love for each other and shared happiness at becoming life partners and parents. After which Mayor Park totally earned everyone's vote in the next election by declaring them husband and wife.

At which point Mrs. Horowitz and the choir brought the house down with a rousing rendition of "Alexander's Ragtime Band" as Laura and Briggs began to recess down the aisle. And the drama was further capped off when all the guests opened their paper bags and got to throw handfuls of dried delphinium flowers over the happy couple. Laura caught some of the larkspur-blue petals on her palm and gleefully blew some back to the guests. The mood was giddy. The colors riotous, the sensation magical. Briggs's surprise was a total success!

By the time the newlyweds returned with the rest of the wedding party after the group photos were completed and the license signed, the cocktail hour was fully underway.

"You look amazing," Briggs murmured into Jessica's ear. They were standing next to the bar away from the seats. His fingers brushed hers.

"I'm just going to check on Myrna and Will. Make sure they're doing okay."

Jessica watched him slip through the crowd. And she knew without question that she loved him completely—and not just because he made her knees go to jelly and her heart do a rapid two-step. Only when Gloria Pulaski tapped her shoulder to ask about her dress did Jessica come back to Earth.

Which was when she heard a woman cry out.

Everyone heard a woman cry out. The friendly chatter suddenly gave way to dead silence.

Jessica looked in the direction of the scream, somewhere by the far side of the seats. Had something happened to Pops? She pushed her way through the guests and sidestepped a waiter carrying a tray of pigs in a blanket.

Pops was standing, leaning on his walking boot. Otherwise he seemed fine. Not so the rest of the little group. Myrna had her arms at her sides, her hands curled into fists. Briggs was alternately staring at her and a small woman with black curly hair. Tears streamed down her face. Will was looking fearfully from one adult to the other. Buddy strained on his leash, trying desperately to escape. The boy seemed not to notice. Feeling the need to help, Jessica grabbed the leash.

"I don't understand," Will cried out. His tears were coming fast and furious. "Who are you?"

"Who invited her? She...she has no right to be here," Myrna stammered.

Briggs came alongside Myrna before glancing at Will. "I did. I mean, not to the wedding, obviously. We'd been emailing when I heard about problems at her work, and I realized she needed some place to get away. I think I did say where we'd be. But I meant for us to meet after to sort things out. It was a spur-of-the-moment thing, really, her arriving in town." He wet his lips and spoke softly. "This isn't at all how I wanted to do this, but, Will, this is your mother, Tamara Giovanessi. Tamara, this is your son, Will."

Will jerked his head from one person to the next and back again. He started crying harder. He began to hyperventilate.

And then he ran.

CHAPTER TWENTY-TWO

"WILL," BRIGGS CALLED OUT. "Will, come back, please!" He raced down the driveway toward the front of the building.

Jessica blinked as she watched the love of her life hightail out of their collective best friends' wedding. Her mouth dropped open. Buddy looked up and did the same. He started to whine. A first.

"Well, that's one way to put a damper on the mood," Robby announced, glass in one hand, Nada's shawl in the other.

Nada happened to be going by, carrying a tray of mini crab cakes when he said those words. She frowned and shook a finger at him in warning.

Ever a quick thinker, Mrs. Horowitz raced to the piano—thank goodness she was wearing her Easy Spirits and not heels on the uneven lawn. She began pounding out "Fascinating Rhythm." Sensing the moment, Joseph commandeered members of the choir who were not already into the appetizers, and they surrounded the piano. The guests, still dumbfounded from the sudden drama, knew the best recourse was to hit the bar hard.

Jessica sought out Laura. She saw her friend reach up to hide her face. The long sleeve of her antique white lace dress slipped to her elbow. Phil circled her shoulders and pulled her close to his chest.

"Laura, Phil, I'm so sorry. It's just a little misunderstanding that I'm sure will be cleared up in no time," Jessica announced without the faintest idea if any of what she said was true. The truth didn't matter. This was Laura and Phil's day. They deserved the best, and she intended to make sure that happened.

She looked around, snitched a fancy-looking cocktail from the nearest guest, who happened to be Mr. Mason, and raised it high.

She tapped it with her fingernails and projected her voice. "Hello, everyone. If I could have your attention for just one moment?" No one listened. In the end, she circled her fingers and whistled. That did the trick. She waited for the murmurings to hush. "I think it's the sworn duty of the bridesmaid to toast the bride and groom. They're my longest and dearest friends—so I don't dare say anything remotely

negative about them because they know too
much about me!" There was a smattering of
laughter. "What I really want to do instead is
wish them the best of the best. They've earned
it in more ways than one. May you both live
a long and happy life together and be forever
merry. So, let's everyone join in a toast. To love
and merriment," she saluted.

Buddy immediately sat at the sight of her
raised hand. Rounds of "Hear, hear!" and "To
love and merriment!" filled the backyard.

She passed the drink back to a stunned Mr.
Mason. "Thank you, sir." She nodded toward
Mrs. Horowitz and Joseph. "And keep up the
good work."

The buzz returned to the crowd, and she
slipped behind the bar to grab her evening bag.
But there were still two tasks to do before she
rushed out. First, and probably contrary to respected veterinary practices, she grabbed a
crab cake and offered it to Buddy who was sitting so, so patiently. He gobbled it down. "Good
dog," she complimented him. She needed him
raring to go.

Next, she located her father. "Could you take
care of Myrna until we get back? It could be a
while. And about the woman who showed up
unannounced? She seems to have fled, but if

she returns, could you see if she needs a ride somewhere—only not with Myrna?"

Norman straightened up, demonstrating a strength he hadn't shown her whole time back in Hopewell. "I'll make sure they both get to wherever if necessary." He shooed her on. "Skedaddle now, Jess. It looks like you've got your work cut out for you."

Jessica nodded and turned to Buddy. "We're off to help save Will. I'm counting on you, Buddy." She was completely earnest.

The dog took off at a clip. His tail shot out straight, and his ears streamed back. He stretched the lead to its maximum length. Jessica held on for the ride.

When they reached the front, Jessica searched the sidewalk in both directions. She spotted Briggs pacing on the other side of the road.

"Briggs! Briggs! Wait up!" she called out. They raced in his direction.

"He's disappeared. I don't know where he's gone off to. I'm just going crazy." Briggs raked his fingers through his hair. His tie was already loose, the furrows in his brow were deep.

Jessica put a hand on his heaving chest. "I know you're upset. It's only natural. But I'm pretty sure I know how to find him." She pulled out her phone from her tiny bag and called Candy.

CANDY MET THEM at the base of the treehouse in Jessica's backyard. She'd biked there at top speed and was breathing heavily. "I shouted to him that I was here," she told Briggs and Jessica, "but he told me not to come up." She looked scared, like the kid she was.

Briggs gently touched her shoulder. "You did the right thing, Candy. I can't thank you enough. I think it's best that I go up alone. If you want, you can stay down on the ground with Jessica and Buddy."

Candy nodded. Jessica offered an encouraging smile. Buddy sidled closer to Jessica and sniffed at her hip. "Not this time, Buddy. Soon, though. You've got another job to do before any more rewards." She motioned downward with her forearm, and Buddy lay obediently at her feet. But his eyes shifted to the treehouse as they all watched Briggs climb the ladder.

He reached the top quickly, but he hesitated before entering the doorway. "Will, it's me. I'd like to come in and talk." He was met with silence. "Is that okay?" He heard a muffled grunt and took that as a yes.

Will was seated, huddled in a corner. He was grasping his knees with all his might. His face was tearstained, and he rested his head down-

ward, a sign of emotional exhaustion and confusion.

As Briggs settled down next to him, the boy
raised his chin. "How'd…how'd you find me?"

Briggs hated to hear the hesitation in his
son's voice, but he plowed on. "Jessica thought
to call Candy."

"Ca-Candy told you?"

"She was worried about you. We all are."
Briggs sat in silence. He waited to see if his
son had more to say.

After what seemed an eternity, Will spoke
up. "Why…why didn't…didn't you tell me who
my mom was? I know you had all agreed to
keep her name a secret while I was still young.
But couldn't you have given me a hint?"

Briggs looked heavenward for guidance. There
were cobwebs in the corners of the wooden roof,
but through the opening, the sky blazed a bright
blue. "I know it can be hard to understand, but
hear me out. Like you already know, your mom
and I were just eighteen, seniors in high school,
when we found out she was pregnant. But I never
told you about this next part. At the time, her
family refused to help her, and she had just gotten a full scholarship to study journalism at the
University of Arizona.

"I was determined to keep the baby—you—

even though raising a kid wasn't in the cards for Tamara. Neither of us wanted to give you up for adoption to a stranger, you see. So, with Aunt Myrna's help, we reached out to a family lawyer who drew up a contract where I would become your sole guardian. We were both legally adults and old enough to do that. Then we all agreed that she would remain anonymous until you turned eighteen yourself. At which point, you could decide whether you wanted to make contact or not. It wasn't a question of her rejecting you, it was more that she had no other support and her life was headed in a different direction. We were only trying to do what we thought was in your best interest." Briggs looked at Will, who still wouldn't meet him eye to eye.

"But how come she showed up now? I didn't ask her to come. It's not like I need her after all this time." His voice was defiant and deflated all at once.

"Good question. I guess I'm the person you should be mad at, not her. So, let me try to explain." He chose his words carefully, articulating what was difficult even for him. "I know it hasn't always been easy for you, growing up in an unconventional family like ours. That's why when you were younger, we all went together as a family to therapy to try to help you understand that you've always had our love. Even so, other kids can be cruel for reasons that really have nothing to do with you. I worried that you were suffering because of the decisions *I* had made, not you."

DOWN BELOW, Jessica and Candy gave up standing and, by silent agreement, decided to sit on the grass. Jessica unhooked Buddy's lead, and the dog did some exploratory sniffing around the boundary of the fenced-in backyard. The corners of the house and several boxwoods along the side fence seemed to deserve particular attention, and when he'd done them justice, the dog wandered back and plopped down between them. Jessica and Candy both began petting him, a convenient and willing source of reassurance.

They sat in silence, listening to snippets of conversation from above. Buddy rolled over and let the sun warm his delicate belly fur. It had been sparse when Will had first found him lurking near the dumpsters at the middle school. "Stress will often do that to dogs," Jessica had explained. Sure enough, just a few weeks later, he was already developing a downy covering, and it was perfect for stroking. Buddy jerked a front leg toward the desired spot where he wanted them to concentrate their efforts.

"As to Tamara showing up when she did, I gotta confess it wasn't completely planned that way. After Candy revealed to me that you'd told her about your mom not being around for you—ever, I started to question whether we had the right to keep withholding your mom's identity." He didn't mention that Myrna had been adamant about keeping it secret. This was about Will, not his great-aunt's opinions.

"So, I decided to contact Tamara. I knew she'd stayed in Arizona, and after a little digging on the internet, I found out she was a news anchor at a local TV station in Phoenix.

"I figured it was only right to let her know how great you were doing, that you rescued this crazy dog, that you won the science prize and stuff—and how proud she'd be of you. I didn't get a response right away, but then sometime around your graduation, I heard about this big brouhaha at her station and that she was put on leave.

"To make a long story short," Briggs continued, "she got in touch after that because she was worried there might be some blowback that could affect you. I said that if she needed a place to hide from the spotlight, there was always Hopewell. I said she was welcome to come, and we could arrange some kind of reconciliation—but only if you wanted. I didn't know it would be today. I swear. I would never have wanted to surprise you like the way it happened."

Briggs's confession was met with silence.

"What do you think?" he asked. "Tamara's not in a good place right now, and she could use some support. But your happiness is what matters most. So, if you don't want to meet her, I understand, and I'm sure she will, too. But if you do want to meet her, she's in town. The bottom line is we're kind of feeling our way. But just like when we were young, she and I are trying to do the right thing by you. We loved you then, and we love you now. Whatever you're comfortable with is fine by us. It's your call."

Will played with the leather lace of his boat shoe. "How do you know she loves me? She doesn't even know me."

"She does. Trust me. She was just trying to do what we all thought was best when you were born. And she is really, really proud of how you've grown up."

Will abandoned the lace and looked up. "Are you guys gonna get married or something?"

Briggs shook his head. "Tamara and I don't even know each other anymore. But she'll always be your mom." His voice was quiet, barely above a whisper.

Speaking of quiet, he noticed that it had gone silent below. "Shall we go down, then?" Briggs asked. "Jessica and Candy are there. They're worried about you. And of course, Buddy's waiting for his best pal."

Will untangled his long legs. (Had he grown in the last few days? Briggs wondered.) He descended first while Briggs waited at the top for his son to find solid ground. Then he looped around and hustled along after.

At the sight of Will, Buddy went bananas, jumping all over *his* Will, doing a happy dance and yipping madly. Will knelt down and hugged him, *his* dog. "It's okay, Buddy. I'm here for you. I'll never leave you." It was impossible to miss the implications.

JESSICA AND CANDY had glued themselves to the tree, after having heard Will's final question. They strained to hear Briggs's response.

"Did you get it?" Jessica whispered.

At the same moment, Candy asked softly, "Did you hear what Mr. Longfellow said?"

They shrugged when neither had the answer.

Suddenly, Buddy was on his feet, and Jessica spotted legs dangling above. Will reached the ground and cuddled his dog.

"We're so relieved that you're all right, Will," Jessica declared. "Candy was wonderful to let me know where you were. I can't thank her enough. But after all that's happened, I bet you're both really hungry. Why don't we head back to the wedding and have some of Nonna and Nada's food? I'm sure it's amazing. And Buddy deserves his share, too, don't you think?"

Will looked at Jessica. "Thanks for coming after me. I think food is just what Buddy needs." He picked up Buddy's leash and attached it to the dog's collar. Then he spoke to Briggs: "After food, I'm ready to meet my mom."

Jessica nodded along with the others—not that she was totally reassured. One crisis was averted, but she couldn't help wondering: What *was* Briggs's answer to Will's question about him and his mom getting married?

MYRNA AND NORMAN stayed at the wedding while Briggs and Jessica went on the hunt for Will. Myrna was clearly shaken by the unexpected encounter with Tamara, who had quickly disappeared from the festivities, and she shied away from joining the crowd at the tables. Norman looked at her with concern. "Jess and Briggs will find him. Don't worry. Will couldn't have gotten that far on foot."

"I'm just afraid he'll do something reckless." She couldn't face Norman and instead gazed at the now empty chairs in front of the wedding altar.

"Nonsense. That boy would never abandon his dog. Trust me. One thing I know about is the bond between a boy and his dog—or a girl and her dog, in Jessica's case."

Myrna scrunched up her mouth and reluctantly faced Norman. "It's all my fault."

"Come now. There's no need to be so hard on yourself. You've done a wonderful job by that kid." He patted her knee.

She shook her head. "It's more complicated than you think. There're things you don't know."

"There's no need to tell me if you don't want to."

"No, I think it's time." She rubbed her hand up and down the white linen slacks she'd worn with a navy tunic. Earlier, before the whole ruckus occurred, Norman had teased her that she looked like a sailor. "I had always wanted children, you see. And later, when Briggs's parents were killed in the car crash, it was like someone had handed me this miraculous gift out of a tragedy. The then-teenage Briggs became my son. It was a challenge at first, but we managed. Then, just before his high school graduation Briggs told me that his girlfriend was pregnant.

"At first, I was shocked and angry that they hadn't been more careful. If they were old enough to have sex, then they should have been responsible enough to use contraception! Then things only got more complicated. Tamara's parents refused to give her any support. On top of which, she had made all these plans for her future.

"Still, they agreed to try being parents, but it wasn't long before Tamara realized she was on the wrong path. Meanwhile, Briggs asked if he could have the baby to raise by himself—well, with my help, of course. I was happy to do it. The opportunity to look after another child seemed like a gift. One I gratefully but perhaps jealously kept."

"So, you wanted to help Briggs raise Will... there's nothing wrong with that," Norman said softly.

But Myrna still felt bad. "The idea was that Briggs would take legal custody. Tamara would give up all rights. I consulted my attorney, and he drew up the agreement. And then, following my suggestion and Tamara's request, mind you, the three of us agreed that her identity would remain secret until Will turned eighteen. I thought I was doing right by Briggs, and Will, but maybe it was wrong to put such a barrier between mother and child?"

"I suppose. I wasn't there, so I can't evaluate the circumstances adequately," he said.

"But I was. Now I see I may have made a mistake," Myrna went on. "And now I worry that Briggs and Will will never forgive me."

"I'm sure that's not the case—at least not in the long run. But only time will tell."

THEY DIDN'T HAVE to wait long.

Will and Buddy raced into the yard. "Aunt Myrna, Aunt Myrna," the boy shouted. He and Buddy knelt in a tangle of legs and paws and leash. "I'm so sorry I ran away, but I was all mixed up."

"I was scared I would lose you." Myrna's words held a truth that went beyond a momentary loss.

Will rose and wrapped his arms around his aunt. "You'll never lose me, Aunt Myrna. No matter what. You're my family."

Myrna smiled. "I hope you remember that

as time goes by, Will." She winked at Norman who smiled back at her. Then she lifted her chin and spoke in her usual no-nonsense manner: "Now that you're back, it's time you had some food. It all looks positively wonderful. And if you get a chance, how about you pick out something for Dr. Trombo and me? The two of us have been having a quiet time to ourselves away from the crowd."

"We'll help out on that score," said Briggs. He, Jessica and Candy arrived right behind Will. "Will, you and Candy can go find something for yourselves—and I don't mean just the wedding cake. Though it does look really good. Leave Buddy with us while you're at it. It'll be easier."

He watched his son and his friend head toward the buffet tables. They were laden with a vast assortment of food: lasagna, poached salmon, risotto, grilled vegetables with feta cheese, salads and more.

He turned back to Myrna. "See, nothing calms the soul of a boy quite like food."

"So, is everything settled?" she asked.

"I'd say it's just starting, but that's a good place to be."

The four adults nodded in agreement.

Jessica waited a beat. "I'll get Myrna and

Pops some food, then. You can keep them company, Briggs." She turned to walk toward the buffet tables.

He put out a hand to stop her. "Are you okay? With all this, I mean?"

"I'm still processing. To tell you the truth, it's kind of a shock."

"To me, too."

Jessica looked down at where his hand touched her arm. "Why don't we talk about this later? Let me just get the dynamic duo their nourishment. They look like they could use it. After that I need to reassure Laura that everything's all right. Then I'll mingle with the crowd— bridesmaid's duties."

Briggs held on. "I can help."

Jessica shook her head. "No, you've got enough on your plate. What with Will, his mom, Myrna." She smiled at a passing guest.

He reluctantly released her. "I don't want you to go. And I don't just mean here at the wedding reception."

Jessica swallowed. "Right now, you need time to work things out with your family, especially Will. I don't think it's going to be easy, Briggs—truly, I don't. And I don't know what kind of solutions you'll settle on. And I don't think you can predict anything, either."

"But I love you. I don't want to lose you."

She closed her eyes and rubbed the skin where his hand had held hers. When she opened them, tears stained her lashes. "I get that your situation is really complicated. But at the same time, you never told me about any of this. It was a big step for me to admit my fears and learn to take risks and move on. But you held back. You weren't truthful—you hid some really important details about your past *and* your present plans. I get that it's hard. But I need to protect my heart. And I can't do that if you're not up front with me."

"I told you I wasn't as brave as you. Please, just give me a chance. Give *us* a chance," he pleaded. His eyes filled with tears as well.

Jessica willed herself to be strong. "Like I told you earlier, I've learned that sometimes you have to know when to let go of the thing you love."

She went off to find food. And maybe more.

CHAPTER TWENTY-THREE

JESSICA HAD MORE clothes to pack than she'd counted on. Had she made that many trips to the mall to stock up on socks, underwear and extra shirts and slacks, let alone a few fancier items?

She held up a cream-colored silk camisole. "What had possessed me anyway?" she asked.

Fortunately, it was Sunday, the day after the wedding, and Jessica didn't have to figure out how she was going to fit all this…this stuff she'd accumulated in between seeing patients at the office.

Pops's office, she corrected, at the same time telling herself she shouldn't feel guilty that her plans to take over were on temporary hold.

Speaking of Pops, he was at the bottom of the stairs calling up to her. She dropped the camisole on the bed and walked to the top of the stairway. "If you're looking for your slippers, Pops, they're under the kitchen table where you left them yesterday."

Norman looked up. "That's not why I called, but thanks for the tip. No, I was wondering if I could make you some tea. You've been going at it pretty hard."

Jessica shrugged. "Sure, why not." She skipped down the stairs and joined her father in the kitchen. "I've accumulated so many things since I got back that I might have to borrow an old suitcase from you. My carry-on simply isn't up to the job."

In companionable silence, she retrieved a tea bag from the pantry while he waited for the electric kettle to heat up. "Is lemon tea okay?" she asked.

The kettle knob flipped to Off. "Perfect." He poured the hot water into two mismatched mugs, and Jessica dunked the bag to the strength she knew suited her father and herself.

"I'll let you carry yours." Norman hobbled on the boot to the table and sat in "his" chair.

Jessica sat in "hers." She raised her tea. "Cheers." They clinked cups.

"I'm pretty sure the suitcases are on a shelf in the garage. You might try there first." Norman looked around the table. "There wouldn't be anything to go with the tea, would there?"

Jessica smiled. She grabbed a tin of cookies from the seat of another chair tucked into the table. "I've been hiding these. Nada Bellona gave them to me after the wedding party. Rugelach." She lifted the cover and passed the container.

Norman took one, then two. He bit into the first. "Raspberry—my favorite."

Jessica decided all her activity warranted an afternoon snack, and she took one, too. They munched and sipped their tea. She was grateful that Pops wasn't pushing her. But at the same time, she knew he deserved some clarification.

"You know, I'm coming back, don't you?" she said. "I promised I would. I've learned that running a small practice is more my style."

"I think you're right. And you might not want to admit it, but I bet you'll miss the owners as much as their pets here in Hopewell."

"Maybe." She drank some more. "As I said last night, I've got some things to work out, and it'd be better to do that at a distance—gain some perspective, if you know what I mean."

"I do. And it's only fair that you return to the practice in Chicago for a while. They were kind enough to cover for you all this time. And meanwhile, don't worry about me. In another week or two, this thing will come off." He indicated the boot. "And with Wendy and Joseph at the office, I'll have all the help I need there. Myrna said she'd lend a hand with the driving, and who knows? Now that you downloaded the Uber app to my phone, I can enter the world of ride hailing. Next I'll get into food delivery. The possibilities are endless."

"Promise me you won't overdo it, though, Pops. I really feel guilty about abandoning you."

"You're not. You put your life on hold for me, and now it's time to take care of yourself. I might not always show it, but I'm here for you, too, kiddo." He smiled at her. "Go for as long as you need to. And if in the end you decide that Hopewell and the practice aren't for you, I'll figure out something else. I know that I've never been the most demonstrative father, and I realize I've been kind of hiding out these past few years—not letting go of your mom. And it's not that I want to forget her, but I've finally come to accept that I need other people. And don't get on your high horse about me and Myrna. We're just a couple of people later in life who are finding comfort in friendship."

Jessica smiled and felt tears in her eyes. (That seemed to be happening a lot recently.) "Then go for it, Pops. And, you know what else? I don't say thanks enough, either. You're the greatest. Well, maybe not all the time— you're pretty cranky when it comes to taking showers with a garbage bag over your leg."

Norman chuckled and munched on his second cookie.

The front doorbell rang.

Jessica frowned. "Weird—were you expecting anybody?" Norman shook his head. She stood. "I'll see who it is."

She returned with Gloria Pulaski.

Gloria joined them for tea. "What's this I hear about you leaving us, Jessica? No offense to you, Norman, but Jessica has the magic touch when it comes to taking care of Betsy's cat, Alfie. I hate to think that you'll go away and forget him." She peeked in the tin of cookies and took one. "Mmm. I'd know Nada's rugelach anywhere."

"How could I forget Alfie?" Jessica eyed her father with raised eyebrows. "And not to worry, Mrs. Pulaski. I haven't made any definite plans."

"Jessica's smart enough to make her own decisions" was all Norman said. "Here, Gloria, have another." He pushed the cookie tin closer.

"I shouldn't, but maybe one for the road. I could only stop by for a sec because I have to babysit my two older grandkids. Betsy has to take the baby to the pediatrician. He's got the sniffles and is running a low-grade fever. But like I tell her, what can you expect with the older one in school and the middle one in child-care? It's an endless cycle of colds and runny noses."

Jessica thought she might wipe down the table with disinfectant as soon as Gloria left. She rose. "Well, thanks so much for stopping by. It's nice to be appreciated. Why don't I walk you out?" *Before Alfie makes a sudden appearance*, Jessica thought.

She held open the front door. "I'll see you then. And give my best to Betsy."

Gloria stopped on the porch. "You won't get more grateful patients and their owners in that big city of yours, you know."

"I'll be sure to remember that." Jessica nodded and waved goodbye.

She went to shut the door when a familiar figure came walking up the steps from the front sidewalk. "Mr. Mason!" she exclaimed.

He tipped the bill of his driving cap at the departing Gloria before removing it on the porch. He fidgeted with the brim.

"Can I invite you in, Mr. Mason?" Jessica asked.

"Oh, no, I wouldn't want to put you out."

"It's not a problem."

"No, you must be busy, packing and all."

Jessica tilted her head. "Packing?"

"Yes, talk after the wedding was that there was a good chance you'd be leaving. People kind of assumed with what happened…with Will's mother showing up and all. Word got around, you see." He rubbed the tip of his nose. "You know, I never thanked you for letting me chauffeur Laura around before the ceremony. I got a real kick out of it. So, thank you. I know it wasn't necessary—with her living in the building already. But it made it kind of special—for me, mostly."

"It was my pleasure. I know she had a lot of fun, and it was much more dramatic than just traipsing down the stairs. You're sure you can't come in?" she offered again.

"Oh, no—no, thanks. I'd best be going." He settled the cap on his head.

"I like your hat, Mr. Mason. It's very appropriate for the former owner of a garage."

He smiled, rather pleased. "I'm kind of fond of it myself." He placed one hand on the railing before stepping down to the path. "If it'd make a difference about your leaving, I'd be willing to let you put that Jungle Red polish on Bismol's beak, like you mentioned at our first visit to the clinic."

This time her smile was more than polite. "It's kind of you to offer, but she's beautiful

enough without all that froufrou." Jessica bade
farewell and headed back to the kitchen.

She plunked down onto the hard chair and
drank the last of her now cold tea. "That was Mr.
Mason. Do you think the whole town's going
to stop by to try to persuade me not to leave?"

Her dad raised his hands in a *who knows?*
gesture. "I'd guess mostly the ones with pets,
but you never can tell."

Jessica's phone buzzed. She shimmied it out
of her back pants pocket. "Laura's texted," she
announced. "Seems even she's in a beseech-
ing mood. Listen to this," she said to Norman.
"She writes, 'Jess, how can you leave me? You
did such a good job as my bridesmaid that I
need you to be godmother to our baby.'" Jessica looked up. "Can you believe it? The girl's
on her honeymoon in Hawaii..." She stopped
to check her watch. "Yup, they're there already,
and she's trying to make me feel guilty."

She texted back, I think you must have more
important things to think about now. Aloha
oe. Jessica pressed Send, then gathered up the
mugs and stood to take them to the dishwasher.

"I'm going to the garage to look for a suitcase," she announced. "If anyone else comes
wanting to talk me out of leaving, you're to tell
them... Frankly, I don't know what you're to

tell them. Think of something." She popped the lid on the cookie tin and stood with her hands on her hips.

"People just want to help. They're concerned about you. They love you."

"Sometimes you can have a little too much love."

"You can never have enough love."

She sniffed. "Don't get maudlin on me, Pops. This is hard enough as it is."

"I'm sorry. I promised I would be here to support you, and I am. How about I say that you've gone fishing?" Norman suggested.

"I like that." Jessica went out by the kitchen door. The screen banged shut behind her. She went through the gate in the backyard fence and opened the side door to the garage. She flicked on the light switch to reveal years of dust, an abandoned lawnmower, beach chairs and carpentry tools that her father wouldn't know how to use but were her brother Drew's babies.

She spotted a large drop cloth covering a bulge atop a bench and lifted it. Ta-da! A couple of hard-case suitcases dating back to the Nixon administration, but one would do in a pinch. She hoisted the twenty-four-inch Samsonite off the counter and carried it to the side door where the bright sunlight hit her in the face.

There, silhouetted against the light, was a petite person. Jessica squinted and shielded her eyes from the glare.

"I don't mean to bother you, but your father said I'd find you here."

Jessica stepped to the side so that she wouldn't have to look directly into the sun. She recognized the person.

Tamara Giovanessi.

CHATER TWENTY-FOUR

To say Jessica was stunned was a gross under-statement. Gobsmacked was more like it. Still, inspired by Mrs. Horowitz's *the show must go on* performance at the wedding (being dressed in chiffon would have provided a certain touch, but Jessica would make do), she drew herself up to her full height. "Can I invite you for tea?" Jessica asked, sounding braver than she felt.

"Oh, that's not necessary. I'm sure you're busy enough, what with packing and all. You wouldn't believe it, but when I stopped by the diner and asked for directions to your house, I must have had three or four people tell me how crushed they were that you're leaving."

"You know how small towns can be," Jessica deferred.

"Actually, I don't." Tamara glanced toward the picnic table. "Shall we sit there?" She didn't wait as she marched across in her high heels. Paired with designer jeans and a whisper-thin ribbed top, she looked ready for her close-up, which was probably the point.

Jessica, feeling a little outclassed, followed. She rested the suitcase on the ground. "So, how's Will?" It was a "gotcha" question, but she *was* genuinely concerned.

"You don't waste any time, do you? Will's another of your fans, by the way."

"I just helped him with a few things."

"That's not what I heard. He wanted to come himself, but I said it was probably best if we met each other first." She glanced around. "It's nice back here."

Jessica wasn't sure how much Tamara really noticed, but she had a feeling nothing got by her. "It's all my mother's doing. I'm a total incompetent when it comes to gardening."

"Ditto." She raised her chin. "Briggs told me about your mother having passed not that long ago."

What else did he tell her? Jessica wondered.

"I'm sorry for your loss, truly I am. But to answer your question about Will, I wasn't sure how he'd react to meeting me for the first time, and I'm sure it didn't help that I showed up without any warning. Anyway, his feelings are what you'd expect—all over the map. Anger—

at me, at Briggs some, too. Interestingly, not so much at Myrna, which frankly bugs me."

Interesting indeed.

"Then there's confusion, but I think Briggs has been pretty good at trying to explain that sometimes things are more complicated than you would hope, that we certainly never meant to hurt him. And speaking of confusion, I think the only one more wary of me is the dog."

"Poor Buddy. He's naturally timid. You just need to give him time—and treats."

"So I've been told."

For someone seemingly so direct, Tamara gave all the appearances of stalling.

"So, what brings you here?" Jessica asked. "Have you made any plans?"

Tamara laughed. "Plans? I typically thrive on plans, but at the moment, mine are pretty much up in the air. I don't know if you've heard, but I've been put on leave from my news station in Arizona. A jealous colleague decided to smear my reputation. They willingly spread these lies invented by some really unsavory types I'd exposed in a story about teens being coerced into putting up their babies for adoption."

"I'm sorry. I hadn't heard. I'm afraid with everything that's been happening around here, my news consumption hasn't been all that great."

Tamara nodded. "Probably just as well. My first reaction to this ridiculous problem was to fight it tooth and nail, but my agent convinced me it was probably better to lie low and let him handle it. Unfortunately, there was also the rumor that my story was somehow tied to my own carefully hidden pregnancy."

"Oh, that's terrible. You must have been devastated."

"For me. But then I realized how horrific it could be for Will, not to mention Briggs. He'd gotten in touch with me not that much earlier, thinking I'd want to know about how great Will had turned out. Who knows, maybe someone hacked into my email?

"In any case, I knew it was time to come and try to make amends." She paused. "Back then, my decision to give up my rights had seemed to be the best solution. I was young, had no money, no family support. And I had plans. Dreams, even."

"I'm sure it wasn't easy for you. You were just a teenager. And I'm sure it's hard to grapple with it now. It's a lot to deal with."

Jessica searched for the right words to get at what she really wanted to know. "So, even if you don't have any concrete plans, have you considered any options for your future? Any ideas? Commitments, maybe?"

Tamara splayed her fingers on the rough-hewn boards of the table. Her burgundy nail polish was immaculate. "Good questions. As for work, I guess I'll just see how it plays out. But the whole mess has kind of made me re-think what I want professionally. And as for the whole family thing—" she suddenly clenched her fists "—that's a work in progress. Briggs has offered to let me stay at the farm until my job issue's resolved. And I've decided to take him up on the offer for the time being, but I'll still look for other accommodation.

"While that's happening, I'm going to try to make things better with Will, follow his lead, do whatever he feels comfortable with. I'm not great about opening up, and I know zilch about kids, but I figure I owe it to him. He deserves to get to know his birth mother. And that just because she gave him up, doesn't mean she can't love him."

Jessica felt her heart constrict. "And what about you and Briggs? Do you have plans on getting back together?" There, she'd said it.

Tamara shook her head forcefully. "Absolutely not. We're not the same people we were when we were young and never will be." She stopped. A knowing smile spread across her face. "He loves you, you know. Briggs. He told me as much. And I gotta tell you. It made me a little jealous—and I'm not the jealous type. Sure, Briggs and I were a serious item, but in that adolescent, selfish, experimental way. No, the kind of love he feels for you? I should be so lucky."

Jessica wasn't sure how to respond.

Tamara leaned closer. Jessica could sense she'd be great at interviewing people. "Listen—" a surprising tip-off as to just how nervous Tamara was "—we all make choices, not always the right ones, mind you. My life was pretty miserable there for a while. And I regret putting Briggs through all the heartaches back then and in the years that followed. But, truthfully, back when we were teens, he wasn't the thoughtful, complex man I can see he's become. Not to mention this whole flower thing. Wild, huh?" Her attempt at humor only emphasized her vulnerability.

Jessica told herself to breathe. "Tamara, I admire your candor. And if I'm being truthful, I have to admit I'm relieved to hear you think Briggs loves me. Though maybe 'relieved' isn't exactly the right word, but then you're the wordsmith, not me."

Tamara spanked the table with her palms and stood. Somehow her stilettos didn't sink into the grass. Amazing. "I've got one more thing to say because I always like to get in the last word." She laughed at herself. "By his own admission, Briggs had gotten pretty hardened after our involvement—which was all our faults, maybe mine the most. But *you* got through to him. You really did. Don't let that go. Truly—you'd be a fool to let the opportunity pass you by."

AROUND FIVE O'CLOCK in the afternoon, Norman dialed Myrna's number from the privacy of the guest bedroom's bathroom. Just to make sure Jessica couldn't overhear, he ran the water in the sink and flushed the toilet. He'd seen enough spy movies to know what to do. "We've got a crisis."

"You mean us? And is that the toilet?"

"No, not us, and forget the toilet. The important thing is Tamara was here, talking to Jessica. And I did some discreet eavesdropping."

"That woman! I know I'm supposed to be understanding, but I still find it impossible to embrace her with open arms. Ach!"

"That's a totally different problem, Myrna. It'll take time—time *and* work on both your parts. Right now, we don't have time, and we need a group effort to fix something else entirely. I'm talking about Jessica and Briggs. Our children. We're going to interfere in a way that no children, especially adult children, ever want their parents to do. Are you with me?"

"Of course I am. Since when have I ever shied away from interfering in other people's business?"

"Good, because this is what I'm planning."

JESSICA PACED UP and down her mother's zen garden. She was seeking peace, enlightenment. All she felt was discomfort as the tiny stones bit into the bottoms of her flip-flops.

Tamara had left—leaving her more confused than ever.

Briggs loved her—so it seemed—but his family life was in turmoil. And she loved him—no "seems" about it. She had taken a risk and admitted her deepest feelings to him. But he had hidden his. If he loved her, wouldn't he have trusted her enough to confide in her? And if he didn't trust her, could she really ever trust him?

"Jessica," Pops called out from the kitchen door. "I need your help. I've got an emergency. Come quickly."

Fearing the worst (Did fears never go away?), she sprinted across the lawn. "What's the matter? Have you fallen again?"

Norman was standing at the kitchen table wrestling with the cookie tin. "I can't get this darn thing open." He held it out.

Jessica gave her father a withering look. "You call this an emergency?"

"It is when you need a rugelach." He offered a sheepish grin.

She grabbed the container and wrestled off the lid. "Here. Are you satisfied?" She looked around the kitchen. "You know, instead of eating cookies, why don't I just make us an early dinner? Something nutritious."

Norman shook his head while he chewed and swallowed. "Nothing nutritious. This conversation definitely calls for sugar and fat."

"Pops, I'm really not up for another heart-to-heart." She hunched her shoulders.

"Then here. Have one yourself." He held up the cookies.

Jessica sighed and took a cookie. "What do you need to talk about?" She sat at the table.

He joined her. "I listened in to your conversation with Tamara."

"You listened in?" Jessica was indignant.

"You better believe it. And while I don't know

a lot about what she was saying, one thing struck a note. Briggs loves you. So, kiddo, what are you going to do about it?"

"What do you mean? What am *I* going to do about it?"

"Exactly that. Do you just intend to go back to hiding in your room?"

"Excuse me, I was packing. I have obligations back in Chicago, or did you forget?"

"About certain things I forget. Not that. But speaking of obligations, your main obligation is to yourself. Tell me, do you really want to move back to Chicago?"

Jessica wet her lips. "What is this, your version of Truth or Dare?"

"This is Truth *and* Dare. Do you really want to go back to Chicago? Truth."

"No."

"Do you want to run your own small practice?"

"Yes." There was no hesitation.

"Do you love Briggs?"

She inhaled. "Yes, but it's more than tricky—what with Tamara showing up and with making sure Will's okay. And the fact that Briggs never was up front about the whole thing with me. And…and I just don't know how to handle it all. I'm not good at these people complications.

Animal problems I can handle. People ones not so much. They scare me. I tell myself I want to take risks, but then stuff happens, and I panic." She grimaced at the sound of her own words.

"So, hear me out," her father responded. "You say you're not a people expert. How many of us are? My suggestion then is to think about what you'd say to a pet owner. For example, what advice would you give Will if he told you that Buddy was afraid to walk next to garbage cans, which I'm sure that poor dog probably was in the beginning?"

"Pops, that's an entirely different situation. Briggs isn't scared."

Her father waved his arms in the air. "Of course he is. All people are basically scared, trust me. It's just that some of us don't like to show it." Norman took another cookie and nodded in thought. "Just consider Briggs's situation for a moment. He meets the most remarkable woman he's ever gonna meet in his life—you, my dear. He gets to know you over the weeks that follow and finds you're even better than first impressions."

"His first impressions over the phone were not great, let me tell you."

"Don't interrupt. I'm on a roll," Norman warned her. "So, Briggs finds himself in awe, which means he's completely out of his depth—this, added to the fact that after his youthful romance fizzled he'd avoided all serious entanglements. Ultimately, of course, he was overjoyed to be a father, but it's been a tough row to hoe, compounded by the fact that he still feels guilty about the whole thing. Are you following me?"

Jessica frowned. "I think so. I'm not used to you talking so much."

Norman ignored her crack and made like he was stirring a witch's brew. "So, gripped by this maelstrom of emotions, Briggs realizes he's fallen in love. The woman of his desires—I'm still talking about you—has taken the risk and opened up to him, but can he? Especially when he's dealing with his son's growing interest and conflict about his mother, all of which is brought to a head when the same woman—who herself is facing a possible career-ending crisis of her own—suddenly shows up. What's Briggs to do when he's trying his best to take care of the people around him? Hide? Run? No, in this case, he draws on his caring instincts and decides to come to everyone's aid. Why? Because it's in his nature." Norman wiped his forehead. "And we're still not at the end of the story."

Jessica found herself taking another rugelach without worrying about the nutritional aspects. She considered her father's words. "Tell me, Pops. When did you get so insightful?"

"I haven't. I just used my professional expertise—the same one you have. Veterinary science. I decided to consider the problem from a dog's perspective. A dog instinctively performs the duty that he feels is expected of him. Then he hopes for his reward. And if his owner is smart, he gives him one."

Jessica tipped her chair on its back legs. "But what's his reward—I mean Briggs's? I don't think he's into liver treats."

"You never know. Stranger things have happened." Norman raised an eyebrow and studied his daughter. "Think, Jessica. What's Briggs's reward? What is it he wants most in the world?"

Jessica let her chair plunk forward. "Pops, you're a genius."

He smiled. "No, I just tried to think like a dog. They're so much wiser than we humans are."

CHAPTER TWENTY-FIVE

"BRIGGS, BRIGGS, can you come here? Quickly."
Myrna stood in the driveway and called to her
nephew. He was on his knees, working in the
flower beds, but he looked up when he heard
her. He stood and rushed over.

He removed a dirty glove and wiped his
brow. "What's up? What's going on?"

"I just got a call from Norman. There's some
kind of emergency at his house. He needs someone to come over and help out right away."

"Now?" He slapped his glove against his
thigh and looked down at his jeans. "I'm totally muddy. Besides, wouldn't it be better for
you to go over?"

"No, he specifically asked for you. He obviously doesn't think I can handle it, which
frankly I find a little insulting. But there you
have it. From the way he sounded, it seemed
important." She gave him a pleading look.

Briggs sighed. "Okay. But you owe me."

"Of course, of course. And look, I even brought

your car keys and wallet. No need to come back in the house." She held them out.

"Don't you think I should clean up a bit first?"

She eyed his muddy clothes, ruffled hair and smudged forehead. She pursed her lips and smiled. "No, no. I think you look just fine the way you are."

WHEN BRIGGS DROVE up the driveway, Norman was waiting for him on the front porch. "It's around back. Quick. It really needs your attention. Just go on ahead—I'll join you in a minute."

"Whatever you say." Briggs shook his head. Norman was acting a little weird. He pocketed his keys and headed to the backyard. He opened the gate. And there was Jessica.

She was standing in front of the treehouse. She had on a pair of cut-off jeans and a shrunken Cornell T-shirt. The hem was unraveling, and the logo was faded. Still, she'd never looked better.

"You," he said, trying not to show just how desperate he felt.

"You," she replied. She held out an arm.

Briggs stepped closer. Jessica was holding what might generously be called a bouquet of flowers. "For me?"

She nodded. "I'm sorry they're only dande-lions from Pops's lawn. I can't pretend to have your green thumb."

"They're beautiful." He took them and smiled at the drooping yellow blossoms. He raised his gaze. "This was the emergency that couldn't wait?"

"Well, even to an unintentional flower-killer such as me, it looks like they're in serious need of TLC."

"Maybe some water?"

"Good idea. Why didn't I think of that?" She rubbed her mouth. "The point is they're for you. All the time, you're the one doing the nurtur-ing, bringing beauty into other people's lives. I thought that maybe it was time you got a little beauty yourself." She pointed to the flowers. "I wanted to bring flowers for the teacher—you."

He smiled. "Thank you. That's a lovely ges-ture."

But instead of being pleased with his reac-tion, Jessica looked impatient. "This is not just about making lovely gestures. It's an overture. Don't you get it?" She started shaking her head and hands at the same time.

He squinted. Maybe he did, maybe he didn't. He could only hope. "You'll have to spell it out, I'm afraid."

"Okay." Jessica licked her lips, preparing to go on.

But Briggs was hung up on her lips— *eminently kissable* was his conclusion. He wasn't sure how long he could keep this up.

"Okay," she repeated. She stared directly into his eyes. "It's like this. Over these past weeks, I've learned a lot. How to embrace the joy of the moment and not dwell on the slights of the past. I've been willing to take risks. I told you I loved you. I'm still in love with you. And I know...I know that things are pretty complicated now with Will and Tamara. But you should know—all that doesn't deter me. It frightens me, I admit it, but not enough to make me give up on the best thing that's ever come my way—loving you. So, despite all the rumors, I'm staying in Hopewell, and I'm going to take over my father's practice. That way, if you're willing to take a risk along with me, we can see what happens—if you're interested, of course." She sucked in her lips. "So?"

"So-o." He acted as if he needed to think about it.

Jessica stamped her foot. No kidding. She really did. "Stop it. I know you want it, too. Pops just gave me this whole lecture using a little dog psychology to understand why."

Briggs stepped forward. There was no holding back his smile. "Hey, who am I to argue with a dog expert?" Still holding the dandelions, he placed both hands on her shoulders. "Of course I'm interested. I'm more than interested. I love you. I'm just sorry that I wasn't more up front about all these complications. That wasn't very smart."

She beamed at his face. "You're right. You should have been more open. But let's move on. We'll work on them—and us—together. We just need time."

"And I just need you to trust me."

"I do." Jessica nodded, her eyes bright.

"I'm counting on it. And I'll try not to disappoint you even when the problems seem to mount. But most of all, we'll take our time—*our* time to create a life of love together. And it starts now."

Briggs didn't waste a beat. He took her in his arms, and they shared a long, long kiss that went from lust to reassurance to the promise of all that and more. The flowers, forgotten in the embrace, fluttered to the ground, forming a cheerful carpet.

When they broke their kiss, he looked down. "Oh, no. I dropped them."

Jessica kissed him gently on the chin. "That's

okay. There're lots more where they came from." She brought her hands behind his neck and went on tiptoe. But just as she was about to lean in, there came the thunder of shouting and the pounding of feet.

"Is she staying, Dad? Did you get her to stay?" Will asked, out of breath after running from the car. He dropped Buddy's leash, and the dog bounded in their direction, hopping around them, dancing excitedly.

"She's staying." Briggs grinned. He reluctantly released his hold except to reach out and grasp Jessica's hand.

They heard some huffing and puffing. Myrna was trailing behind carrying two large pizza boxes. "Young man, some day you need to learn to shut the car door," she scolded Will. He didn't take any notice and joined Buddy in dancing. Myrna looked at the happy couple and appeared rather pleased. "I hope we're not too late?"

"No, the timing's perfect," Briggs said.

"Thank goodness. I was worried. I had told Norman on the phone that I'd bring dinner. But then I decided not to cook after all. I was just too excited."

"You and Pops?" Jessica asked. "You planned this?"

"Let's just say we helped things along."

On cue, Norman maneuvered out the kitchen door. "I was wondering when you were going to get here, Myrna. You missed quite a show."

"Po-ops," Jessica moaned. "You were spying on us."

"Criticize me all you want. I wouldn't have missed it for the world." He turned to Myrna. "What kept you?"

"Will and I stopped at the pizza parlor on the way here, and we had to wait for our order. Two large—one pepperoni, one half sausage and half peppers and mushrooms. The last combo is for those watching their cholesterol." She rested the flat boxes in the middle of the picnic table. The aroma of cheese and tomato sauce wafted in the gentle breeze.

"There're beers in the fridge and red wine in the pantry," Norman declared. "I've already got plates and napkins on the kitchen counter."

"Excellent! I'll collect everything and set up outside," Myrna directed. "We can leave the lovebirds alone for a few more moments before we question them closely. Will, you come and help, too."

"In a sec." He lifted the lids on the boxes and inspected the pizzas. "Me and Buddy aren't worried about cholesterol." He peeled off a slice of pepperoni and tossed it into the air. Buddy jumped and caught it. Then the dog sat, wagged furiously and cocked his head in the demurest of poses.

"Buddy and I," corrected Myrna as she held open the screen door. Will came reluctantly with Buddy following him. She gave the dog a pat on the head. "Good dog. You finally learned how to catch." The door banged shut behind them.

Jessica entwined her fingers more deeply in Briggs's. "You know that I'll have to go back to Chicago at some point. And don't get all worried," she said when he started to sputter. "I've got to wrap things up with work, end the lease on my apartment, move out all my stuff. It's a lot."

"Take all the time you need—but not too long." He twirled her around to face him. They stood arm in arm…when a lanky, narrow-hipped fellow with a slow gait and an easy smile ambled into the backyard like he owned it. The sun glinted off his dark blond hair and gave him a beatific glow. Though his grin was anything but angelic.

Briggs raised his eyebrows at the sight of the approaching stranger. He turned back to Jessica, keeping his grip firmly on her. "Tell me I shouldn't be jealous." His tone was more playful than worried.

"No need. Just prepare to meet another member of my family—my prodigal brother, Drew, has decided to return to the fold. He always did have annoying timing..."

* * * * *

Stay tuned for the second book in the Return to Hopewell series, featuring Drew Trombo and Tamara Giovanessi!